Tough As Fine Silk
Escape from Beijing

A novel by

UTA CHRISTENSEN

Strategic Book Publishing and Rights Co.

Strategic Book Publishing and Rights Co.
12620 FM 1960, Suite A4-507
Houston, TX 77065
www.sbpra.com

ISBN: 978-1-61897-088-6

Interior book design: Judy Maenle

For Ken, Hedi, Marc, Andrea, Athena,
Shu Mei and Chia Chi

Also by Uta Christensen

Fiction

BED OF ROSES, BED OF THORNS
CAUGHT MIDSTREAM

Nonfiction

Her Father's Memoir
ZUM LEBEN ZU WENIG,
ZUM STERBEN ZU VIEL
The Story of Five Years in
Russian POW Hard Labor Camps
Published in Germany

Acknowledgements

I would like to thank my husband, Ken, for his unflagging support, encouragement, feedback and insightful commentaries. I also thank my sister, Hedi Roethel, for her enthusiasm about my writing, her reading of my manuscript, her valuable suggestions and steady encouragements. I feel indebted and grateful to my keen-eyed editor, Geoff Aggeler, for his in-depth editing, his support and encouragement. I love his wit, sense of humor and his inspiring and lengthy email communications. Thanks and appreciation to Josie Cowden, my dear friend and copy editor of the final version of the manuscript. My thanks and gratitude also go to Kalib, artist and photographer, for designing and creating the book's front cover.

This is a work of fiction. Any resemblances of my characters to persons living or dead are purely coincidental. Any names, persons, places, and incidents are either the product of the author's imagination or are used fictitiously.

Table of Contents

Escape Route

Beijing to Guangzhou

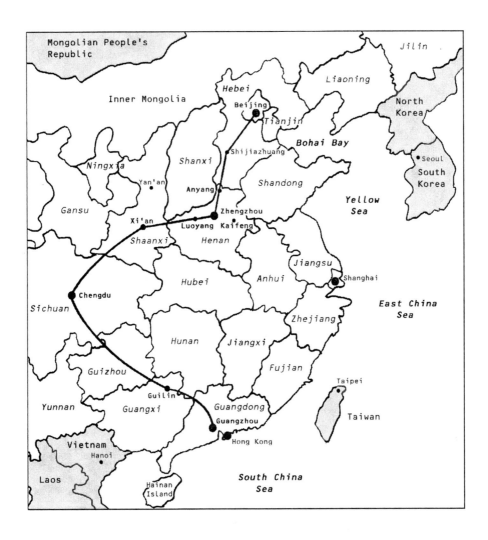

1

The Accident

It happened so fast in the early morning hour, so violently—with so much buckling metal at his back—that Michael lost consciousness at the moment his treasured car turned over onto the driver's side. On its side, the car took one full spin and skidded across the boulevard, scrunching and scraping over the asphalt, until it hit the curb on the other side of the boulevard, where it finally came to rest in eerie stillness. That's when Michael came to. At first he didn't know where he was. *That was a bad dream*, he thought, *similar to the scary ones I've had lately.* But within seconds he realized that he was strapped in the driver's seat of his overturned car. Suddenly a flash of remembrance lightened up his brain—he recalled seeing a black SUV racing toward him from a side street on his right as he was just passing through the intersection. He had jammed the accelerator hard to the floor, but a split second later he felt the crashing impact, heard a deafening noise, and became engulfed in darkness as he blacked out. When he regained consciousness, it crossed his mind that he might be badly injured, but he didn't feel any pain when he wiggled his toes and feet, just numbness. As he looked through the windshield he saw faces staring at him through the glass that wasn't even cracked. Concerned, perhaps, or just curious, they gaped at him, and their mouths and lips moved animatedly but silently as in a pantomime. Michael thought they might be discussing his demise. He couldn't hear them because all his windows were closed. Suddenly, he heard a tapping on the window above him, which was not his sunroof but the upturned window on the passenger side. He looked up and saw a hand making a rotational cranking motion. He understood. Someone wanted him to open that window. Since his car had no window cranks, he moved his right hand to the key in the ignition. He turned it gingerly without starting the motor and pressed the passenger window's button on his door's armrest. He was glad his arm and hand could function without pain, and, as he kept pressing the small button with his middle finger, the passenger window above him opened all the way. He turned his head and looked at his driver's seat window. It reflected his face. The black asphalt on which the window rested made it a mirror. At that moment he realized that he was still strapped in his seatbelt. With his left hand he felt for the seatbelt buckle and managed to undo the belt. He felt cool air rushing in through the open window above him. As he looked up he saw the same faces staring at him. All of his movements were slow and tentative, inhibited by a sense of unreality. It was difficult even to think.

"Ní méishi ba?" ("Are you all right?") He heard a man's voice speaking to him loudly in Mandarin Chinese.

"Shi de, wô méishi." ("Yes, I think so,") Michael answered in Chinese. Before coming to China he had studied Mandarin at the university, and after a year working in Beijing he became fluent.

"Let us help you get out. You're a lucky man."

"Thank you. But I don't know yet how lucky I am. My arms and hands seem to function all right but some other parts of my body may be injured. If you help me to get out, please be careful. Better yet, call the police and let them help me. They must be trained for that."

"I think you're still in danger," the stranger prompted him. "I smell gasoline. Turn your ignition key off. I think your gas tank is punctured or a gas line has been ruptured. The car might still explode. Let us help you, quickly. My friend and I will be careful. Don't be foolish. You must have been traumatized and can't think clearly. I think you are still in great danger," he said anxiously.

"OK. Please try to pull me out then. But do it slowly, please. I need to judge how my back and my legs feel."

The young Chinese man who had spoken to Michael, like a Good Samaritan, hopped onto the overturned car with his legs straddling the open window while Michael stretched out one arm toward him. He immediately grabbed Michael's hand and shouted, "Give me your other hand, too." When both hands were firmly clasped in his, the man pulled ever so slowly. Unable to budge Michael's body, he stopped and released Michael's right hand.

"Try to use your right arm to help push yourself out of the seat, but first try pushing your seat back as far as you can. That extra space will help in freeing your legs. Getting your legs out will be the hard part. Let me know if you feel pain," the man directed Michael.

"OK. I will." Michael felt a bit foolish, needing to be instructed like that. He should have thought of pushing the seat back right away. *What's wrong with me?*

A couple of minutes later, he was greatly relieved when he stood on the window of the driver's side that was pressed against the asphalt and his head protruded out the passenger window. His body seemed fine, only his legs were trembling a little.

"Use the arm rests between the seats as a step so that your body will be halfway out of the window. Can you do that? Are you sure you don't feel any pain?"

"No, I'm fine."

After performing the last movement, Michael was nearly free. With the help of the second young man, who had also jumped onto the car, they dragged Michael out so far that he was now sitting on the edge of the passenger window with his legs still dangling inside the car.

"Thanks so much for helping me. I don't think I could have gotten out by myself. But I can make it from here."

The two young men jumped off onto the sidewalk, and Michael, swinging his legs out of the open window, slid across the passenger door onto the sidewalk. A large crowd of onlookers had gathered while the rescue was in progress. One of the young rescuers asked Michael, "How did this accident happen? Where is the car that hit you? Didn't it stop after the crash?"

"I don't know how or why it happened. I only know it happened so fast and unexpectedly that it knocked me out. It was a hit-and-run. The driver of the vehicle escaped. I did see the car coming at me at high speed. I tried to get out of the way but couldn't do it fast enough. He must have hit my car at the rear wheel. If it had been further forward, I might be worse off."

"We're so sorry," the two young rescuers said with one voice. "Let us call the police."

"Yes, go ahead. I'll wait here and talk to them, but I doubt that they'll be able to track down the car that hit me. It's long gone. But I want to thank you again for helping me, and please let me give you something for your efforts and the time you've lost. You must have been on your way to work."

"No, no, we don't want anything. We are just glad you are alive and well."

But Michael had already taken out of his wallet two 50-dollar bills and handed one each to the young Chinese. They looked surprised when they saw the gleaming greenbacks and smiled as they took them. It was a lot of cash for them.

* * *

Michael stayed with the car until the police arrived—two of them in an official-looking car. During the time of waiting, the crowd of curious onlookers slowly dispersed. Seeing the overturned wreck, one of the policemen radioed for a tow truck right away while the driver stepped out and came over to Michael.

"How did this happen, sir, and where is the car that hit you?" he wanted to know.

Michael described the accident in the same words he had used when he told it to his rescuers. Only now, as he spoke, he recalled one more detail. "Oh, by the way, even though it was just a regular SUV, I noticed some heavy steel bars across the front grid, similar to the bars American highway patrol cars carry. They definitely shielded the front of the car, and it seemed to me the driver was deliberately trying to hit me. I'm sorry, but I blacked out when my car turned over. I've no idea which way the SUV went after it hit me. Please understand everything happened so fast and so violently. There's very little I remember."

The policeman shook his head slightly, then said calmly, "Don't worry. We'll do the best we can to find out who hit you. Please give me your driver's license and the car registration. Do you really think it was deliberate? Do you have any enemies? Does someone mean you harm?"

"Not that I know of, but I think it was deliberate." As Michael answered, he opened his wallet, took out the requested documents and handed them to the policeman. "I've no idea which way the SUV went after it hit me. I've lived in Beijing for a little over a year," he explained, "And I work for World-wide Electronics Systems, an American-Chinese joint venture company, as an electronics engineer. I prefer driving to work very early, before the heavy traffic starts. It's not the cars that bother me—there aren't that many—but the hordes of bicycles and motor scooters I'd rather avoid." He went on giving more information about himself than the officer probably wanted to hear. "I'm just not used to them. The people riding them look so vulnerable, and I'm afraid I'll hit and harm one of them. You know, I'd never want to hit or harm anyone." Then he caught himself, wondering, *Does he really care what I worry about?*

"OK, I understand. But let's get on," the officer prompted. "Is that the correct address on your driver's license? I also need phone numbers, private and work numbers. I assume you have insurance. We'll contact you soon."

"Yes, the address is correct." Reaching into his shirt pocket, Michael pulled out a business card. "Here are my phone numbers, business and private. It's best to call me at my work number. And, yes, I have insurance."

The policeman took Michael's business card as the tow truck arrived. He immediately went over to the truck driver, gave him details about the accident and asked him where he would tow the car. He then walked back to Michael.

"Listen, your car will be towed to this repair shop." He hastily wrote out the name and address. "It's situated in a side street just west of Tiananmen Square. You'll ride there in the tow truck. The shop owner will tell you what can be done with your car, whether it's repairable." At that moment the second policeman, who had stayed in the car, got out and tapped the one dealing with Michael on the shoulder. He informed him that there was another urgent call involving a car accident they needed to investigate. "OK, I'll be finished in a sec," his partner responded.

The policeman turned his attention to Michael again, while the other officer strode back to his car. "I'm sorry, but we need to attend to another accident. The truck driver will take you to the repair shop, and they'll call a taxi for you. Hope your car can be repaired. I'll call you soon at work. Is that OK?"

"Yes, sure. Thanks for your help, officer."

As the policemen drove away, he wondered if they would be able to discover the identity of the SUV driver or why this accident had happened. He doubted it, unless both cars wound up in the same repair shop and paint samples matched, which seemed unlikely. Assuming that the SUV driver had hit him deliberately, he would probably be staying out of sight.

* * *

Michael stood by as his car was righted and winched up onto the truck. He could see that the damage was heavy—the right rear side was crushed with the wheel bent and twisted, and the entire driver's side heavily dented and scratched. Gasoline was still dripping slowly from somewhere under it. He felt sick to his stomach looking at his beloved car, a black BMW 325i, not brand new, but buying it had consumed most of his savings. It made him very sad, but then he thought, *I could have lost my life. It's a miracle I survived and I'm OK.*

The news wasn't good at the repair shop. The owner spoke English, but not perfectly. "Not good news," he said. "I'm sorry, young man, I cannot repair. Your car is totaled. We will have to sell to junk yard. Worth very little. I will write it up right now. Then you go and contact insurance company."

Michael couldn't answer right away. Even though he had feared it might be a total loss, hearing that it was indeed shocked him. The extent of his loss was hard to grasp.

"I'm sorry," the man said. "But not my fault." He was still penning his notes regarding the car's condition.

"I know, I know. Thank you. Could you call a taxi for me, please, when you're done writing? And do you have a business card? I need it for my insurance company. They will contact you."

"Sure." He fished a crinkled card out of his pants pocket and handed it as well as his notes to Michael, who thanked him for them.

While Michael was waiting for the taxi, he thought about what his next move should be. *Go to work or go to Juan? She will still be asleep. She is accustomed to sleeping late because she used to work till late into the night. Now she needs to get up earlier because she has a new job in a book store and works day hours, but she still has a hard time rising early. What if Juan doesn't appreciate my waking her up?* But he couldn't think of going to work. His mind was too distracted and confused. He wanted more than anything else to talk to someone he was close to. Juan, his sweetheart, would be that person. He really couldn't think of anyone else. He didn't have any close friends or confidants yet. He socialized with some co-workers, but he didn't want to expose his private life, and wanted to avoid gossip. He felt for his mobile phone in his jacket pocket and called the receptionist at work to tell her of his terrible accident and ask her to let his boss know that he could not come in that day but would try to be at work the following morning. He also mentioned that he would see a doctor as soon as possible to make sure there wasn't some hidden injury like a whiplash that could give him trouble if not attended to immediately.

The receptionist, Brenda, a girl from Southern California, was sympathetic and concerned. "Sure, Michael, I understand. That sounds like an awful accident. I'll let Bob know right away. Be sure you take care of yourself. We'll see you tomorrow morning or hear from you."

Meanwhile, the taxi arrived. He jumped into the back seat and gave the driver Juan's address. She lived in the Hutong district. With a sense of relief, Michael sank into the upholstery and relaxed for the first time since he had felt that terrific impact about two hours before. He was a lucky man to be unhurt, and, as he reflected upon his good fortune in still having a sound body, his thoughts turned to the woman who gave him so much pleasure with her body. He had nearly been killed less than two hours earlier, but he had been spared, and now he was going to be reunited with her. As soldiers facing combat know, the proximity of death can be a powerful aphrodisiac, and Michael's near encounter with death may have intensified the desire he felt—remembering how his sweetheart responded that morning when he awakened her to say goodbye, nudged her and whispered, "Got to get up, sweetheart, it's 5 o'clock." Even though she wanted her sleep, she let him know that she was ready to make him linger. She drew him to her and molded her body to his, stroking expertly and bringing him to full attention. He had never known a woman who would offer herself so freely and resourcefully. His arousal was instantaneous. But like most mornings, he jumped out of bed, driven by an imperative more compelling than tumescence. He valued his position as an electronics engineer, and losing it would mean having to leave China. On the odd morning, when he let her have her way with him, the reward was always exquisite, worthy of an aubade, a song of lovers parting at dawn. But on this fateful morning duty prevailed. Juan looked up at him and giggled as if to say, *"You're missing out, Mike. Don't you know what's passing you by?"* Determined, he went into the bathroom, showered and shaved. When he came out, she was again sound asleep.

Now, on his way back to her in the taxi, he put away thoughts of Juan and focused on what he was passing through, the heart of Beijing, which never failed to arouse his wonder and admiration. It was his dream to be here ever since he took an Asian studies class in high school. His teacher, Mr. Wang, a native of Beijing, had instilled in him a love, curiosity and yearning to know China and its long turbulent cultural and political history, along with its diverse ancient religious preferences, spiritual philosophy and social ideology—Buddhism, Daoism and Confucianism. And now he was speeding along the wide Dongchang'an Jie Boulevard in this magnificent, fascinating and strange mega city. Traveling in an eastern direction, the taxi soon reached the vast expanse of Tiananmen Square situated on the right, with Mao's Memorial Hall visible in the square's southern half and the Monument of the People's Heroes at its center. *This most famous square in China,* he thought, *is grandly and strategically framed on the west by the thoroughly modern and colossal Great Hall of the People, the seat of China's government. And to the east it is bordered by the China National Museum.* The thought came to him, *How peaceful Tiananmen Square is now.* But he could not look at it without also remembering what happened there in the summer of 1989, though the Chinese government had tried hard to make the world forget. Michael was just a youngster then, but he remembered how upset he was when he learned how harshly the authorities dealt with the student unrest and the repression and bloodshed that ensued.

Having taken in the square and its surroundings once more as he always did when he got the chance, Michael threw a glance to the left, exactly opposite Tiananmen Square. Here the beautiful Zhongshan Park and the Workers Cultural Palace flanked the boulevard with the Gate of Heavenly Peace between them. But more fascinating to him than the park or the Cultural Palace was the famous walled city lying behind them—the vast and mysterious Jîjìn Chèng (Forbidden City). It was so named because it was off limits to the common people for 500 years. Being the seat of government of two dynasties of emperors, the Ming and the Qing, it also contained the Emperor's pleasure palace. Emperors seldom left their palace, only if they absolutely had to.

These monuments of cultural development and achievement flew by quickly. They were replaced by some high-end Chinese and foreign hotels along a now tree-lined boulevard. A little further along, his taxi veered right and rushed by the cavernous Beijing East Train Station with long lines of taxis stretched out

9

Uta Christensen

in front of it. Michael hadn't yet had the opportunity to use the train station, although it fascinated him. He had wandered in there one day, just to see it, and was almost overwhelmed by the huge cavernous expanse of the entrance hall. As he stood in the middle of this impressive edifice, he watched thousands of people scurrying back and forth—many sitting on its tiled floor eating, drinking and waiting for their trains. Michael didn't think it would be any time soon that he would depart from this station, for he was tied to his job and had no vacation time in sight yet. But as the taxi sped past the train station, he began daydreaming of the magnificent historical sites, representing thousands of years of culture, he would visit one day. Having read a number of books and articles, he knew which historical sites he wanted to visit. The pictures included in some of these books excited him, and he hoped to travel around China from north to south and east to west once his contract ran out. If it wasn't renewed in two years' time, he would take at least six months to visit as many sites and natural wonders as he could.

Then the taxi turned left and headed in a northerly direction toward the narrow side streets that the Chinese call hútòngs, along which traditional private homes (sìhéyuàn) still stood like walled compounds. That was how middle class Chinese lived before developers started building fancy apartment high-rises. But many Chinese families still coveted these one-story compounds with their large open social space behind the high wall that bordered the hútòng. These courtyards were generally surrounded on three sides by low-roofed, u-shaped houses. Juan preferred living in a traditional dwelling like the one her parents had owned in Nanjing. Here in Beijing she was renting one wing of such a house, consisting of two large rooms, from an elderly couple. Michael's own living space was a studio apartment in one of the centrally located high-rises. Though he still had his studio, he had recently moved into Juan's two-room apartment.

When he first met Juan and she spelled out her name, he thought that it couldn't be that of a woman. It sounded too masculine, for Michael pronounced it as Spanish speaking people would. But Juan taught him the right way to pronounce it so that

10

it came out like the English name Jan. She had also told him the Chinese meaning of her name: very delicate and soft but tough silk. *How appropriate!* He reflected. *Like the fabric itself, she is soft and delicate. But is she also tough like the fabric? She seems devoid of hardness. But one never knows. Perhaps I will find out someday where her toughness lies.*

Just as that thought passed through his mind, the taxi came to a halt. Michael jumped out, paid and disappeared through the massive gate into the courtyard. He needed to be with Juan now. She seemed to him the only anchor that could ground and stabilize him emotionally and mentally that day. He needed to discuss every detail of the accident with her. *Maybe she could shed light on the mystery of why it had happened,* he thought. *Of course she can't provide answers to the questions of why it was done to me or who could have done it or why someone would want to snuff out my life. But her insights may be helpful nonetheless as I try to puzzle it out.* The car crash didn't make sense to him. He had been in Beijing such a short time, not long enough to have made mortal enemies. Was it simply because he was a foreigner? He needed to find out if there were people driven by fanatical animosity who targeted foreigners. During orientation sessions his company had provided before he left California, there had been no mention of xenophobia in China or any accounts of foreigners being hunted down by Chinese on the streets of Beijing.

As Michael entered the semi-dark bedroom, Juan was still asleep, sprawled across one side of the bed with the covers flung back. Beneath her transparent silk nightgown, her splendid body was revealed. He hesitated a few seconds, asking himself whether he should or shouldn't wake her. For several moments he watched this dearest of females in repose. Her long slender marble arms were bare, the exquisite shape of her body and legs somewhat concealed and yet revealed through the fine silk. Her small head was turned so that her face pointed away from him. A wealth of long black hair was spread out across the white pillow. *If I were an artist,* he thought, *I would want to catch this gorgeous sight and immortalize it.* Then he quietly undressed, removing everything but his shorts and undershirt, and slipped into the bed beside her. He wasn't sure whether she was still asleep or whether she had already sensed his closeness. But then, suddenly, she turned around so fast, so unexpectedly and thrust her face in front of his like a viper ready to strike, while she let out a rippling laugh because she knew she had startled him. Michael was almost dazzled by the quickness and lithe grace of her move. She was always a little unpredictable in her physical moves, and he could only guess what motivated them. His inability to unravel her mystery might have made him uneasy, even unwilling to trust her entirely, but he didn't permit his uncertainty to become doubt or fear. Of course he could trust her. But still he wondered: *What will she do next? What will she say next?* And now she was the one demanding answers, "Michael, what are you doing here? Are you real or are you a ghost that's haunting me?"

"Sweetheart, it's really me. I have come back just to be with you. I couldn't stand being without you. So instead of going to work, I came back to you."

Now she seemed perplexed.

"Don't kid me, Michael. You have never done this before and never would unless something happened. Ah, you lost your job. They don't need you anymore because everyone has sur- mised how much in love you are. So you can't be trusted. Am I right?" She was being playful, but she wanted an answer.

Despite everything that had happened to him, Michael smiled at her and hugged her briefly, but then said very seri- ously, "No, it's something more disturbing."

"What is it, Mike? Tell me. Don't create this unnecessary suspense." She almost seemed a little angry now, perhaps because she realized how far off the mark she was.

"Juan," Michael was very serious now, "something dread- ful happened to me a couple of hours ago, a very serious car accident. My car is totaled. I could have been killed, but I was really lucky. A car drove into me at high speed while I was in an intersection. I tried to accelerate, but couldn't move out of the way fast enough. The next thing I heard was this deafening crash of the impact. Then my car tipped over. I blacked out, and when I came to I found myself still strapped in my driver's seat in the overturned car on the wrong side of the boulevard with its wheels against the curb. The car had skidded across until something stopped it," Michael ended a bit breathlessly. Her eyes had opened wide, and she was staring at him in disbelief.

"Who was the other driver? Did he stop to help you? What happened to him? How about your beautiful car?" Her questions rattled off like from a machine gun. "Please, Mike, tell me everything. I am so concerned. Are you injured in any way and how do you feel now?"

"Oh, sweetheart, I feel good now that I'm with you. You need to help me in figuring out how this could have happened. I am quite certain that it was a deliberate attempt to harm me. To answer your questions: no, I don't know who the driver was. It was a hit-and-run kind of accident. By the time the police arrived he was long gone. It was bystanders who pulled me out of the car. I know I would have been seriously injured or maybe killed if the oncoming car had struck my car further forward, next to the passenger seat. No, I'm not injured, at least I don't think so, and I feel quite OK now that I'm with you. I called work to let them know what had happened. They said it was OK that I don't come in today. The only thing I could think of was being with you right now. I thought you would be the only person who could comfort me and help me figure out what all of this means."

After describing the accident to her, Michael experienced a sense of unreality, as if he had just made up some story to scare Juan, just to see how she would react. It was just a fleeting thought because as soon as he stopped talking, Juan grabbed his head with both her hands and kissed his lips tenderly. When she drew back, her face assumed a very serious, thoughtful expression.

"Mike, I am very scared. Some dreadful things have happened to me in the past, but this is the worst. I love you dearly and someone wants to take my loved one away. That someone or these people almost succeeded. It terrifies me, and I wish I could tell you how or why this could have happened. We really need to think about this. Did you actually see the oncoming car? What kind of car was it? Was there anything special about it? Did you notice any car following you while you were driving to work? It was very early in the morning, so I assume there was little traffic. Did you notice any cars behind you?" During the few months Michael had known Juan, he couldn't remember ever seeing her so anxious and intently focused as she was now.

"Sweetheart, I don't really know the answers to most of your questions. What I do know is that it was a black SUV that raced toward me and hit me, and I told the police that I thought the front end had some heavy bars, like a strong protecting steel grid surrounding it. I didn't remember that right away, but then it came to me as the policeman was questioning me. Perhaps, as time goes by and the lingering fog clears from my mind, I'll remember more details."

She nodded and said in a gentle soothing voice, "Don't try now. You've been through a lot. You need to relax and recover. Take your undershirt off and lie back. Close your eyes and try not to think disturbing thoughts. Let a peaceful feeling take over your mind and body. Maybe you can sleep. You need some rest to restore you and put this terrible event behind you. I'll join you, and for the next two hours we'll be free to enjoy our peace together. Nothing will disturb us, and you'll be restored, reborn with a different spirit. Your mind will be clear and we'll then talk again. Since I'm engaging in the same exercise, I might experience some revelations, too. We might both be surprised what will come out of it." Michael tried to do exactly as Juan instructed him, surrendering himself entirely to her guidance. He shifted his attention away from recent events, let his mind be still, but as he looked at her, he couldn't deny himself the pleasure of remembering how she had come into his life. It stirred him with wonder and joy reflecting on how, six months before, a moment had brought them together.

2

Juan

It was a Sunday morning, a beautiful spring day, and he rose early to make the most of it. Upon waking, he decided that he was finally ready to see the Great Wall. Just a week earlier, he had taken delivery of his beloved car, shipped from San Francisco to Guangzhou and from there by truck to Beijing. Having his own wheels gave him the freedom to go when and where he chose, enjoying the countryside and all the sights.

Access to the Great Wall lay just 70 kilometers northwest of Beijing at Badaling. While he was already eager to see the Wall, the urging of a Chinese co-worker and colleague, Wu Zuguang, prompted him to visit it without further delay. "You must see it, Michael. It's one of our great historical and cultural achievements. You can drive to Badaling where there's a viewpoint 1,000 meters high. It's the Great Wall's most photographed vista. If you arrive early, you won't have problems finding a parking space." And then he added with a hint of pride, "We maintain the Wall at Badaling. It has been reconstructed for several kilometers in either direction north and south. That includes the wall's facing, the roadway on top of the wall, the parapets, the stairways and guard tower lookouts. It's easy walking. You'll enjoy it."

Driving to Badaling, Michael was full of anticipation, but he had no way of knowing how momentous for him the day was going to be. He intended to walk a considerable distance on the Wall, seeing as much as he could and trying to visualize the long process of its completion involving millions of convicted and conscripted men. Hundreds of thousands of them died building

15

the Wall. As with any great structure—the Dom in Cologne, the Golden Gate Bridge, Hoover Dam, Salisbury Cathedral—there were always human sacrifices, but nothing could compare with what the building of this enormous protective Great Wall had cost in human toil, suffering and deaths.

At a point in the road leading to Badaling, Michael was tempted to make a detour because a sign directed him to the Ming Tombs of the Ming Dynasty emperors. He had read that this dynasty lasted more than 270 years. The emperors' tombs were located in a beautiful wide, half-circular-shaped valley ringed as a backdrop by an undulating mountain chain. But then he thought he should reserve this major historical site for another day's outing.

At Badaling he found a dozen empty buses already in the parking lot, their drivers congregating on the asphalt and chatting together. The buses had disgorged their sightseers, and Michael could see people strolling high up on the 26 ft. wall. Only their heads and shoulders were visible above the ramparts. He got his ticket at a booth and walked over to the Wall's access stairway. Reaching the top of the Wall, the sight of mountains stretching far into the distance took his breath away. He saw ahead of him a steep incline in the wall that he intended to scale to get an even better view of the mountainous vista that lay beyond. He had always imagined that the wall, with its 19 ft. width at the top, had a good roadway that would be quite smooth and could easily be marched along and even driven on. *But maybe I will find out otherwise*, he thought. When he reached the top of the incline, a whole new vista opened up. As far as he could see looking west, the Great Wall twisted and turned like a giant serpent winding its way up to a high mountain pass. It was grander, more majestic and overwhelming than anything he could have imagined, an unbelievable human achievement considering how long ago it was built. After taking photographs, he walked on and came to another demanding ascent—a very steep stairway with narrow steps, roughly paved with bricks, enabling the visitors to scramble up to a higher level. So much for his idea of a roadway that would allow carts, horse-drawn wagons or horse-mounted military to use the wall. That disappointed him, for he had been visualizing heavy military traffic in times past.

He started climbing the steep rough steps with other sight-seers. When he decided to take a rest after climbing for awhile, he looked back and then up ahead to assure himself that he had made it halfway up. Suddenly, above him, like an apparition, a beautiful young Chinese woman, more like a pure young girl really, descended toward him. At a glance he saw that she had a slim, well proportioned body. She seemed taller than most Chinese women, but that could have been just an appearance because he was looking up at her. Her legs were slim and well revealed by the very tight blue jeans she wore. Her hair, her gorgeous mane, was straight, black, long, and cascading over her shoulders with loose curls at the ends. Even though Michael didn't see her close-up, he noticed that her face, in contrast to the raven hair surrounding it, was of a radiant paleness. She bore herself with regal grace, and her beauty was so astonishing that he was mesmerized, utterly captivated in an instant. Later, after he came to know her as a person, he believed that he had already fallen in love with her even as he first beheld her there on the Wall, a beautiful stranger. He assumed that she must be some wealthy man's daughter, whom no ordinary fortuneless admirer could ever hope to meet.

But even as this thought crossed his mind and he felt the pain of anticipating a state of hopeless yearning, she literally fell into his arms. It happened when the heel of one of her shoes caught between two bricks of a step as she was descending toward him. Seeing her stumble and fall forward, he bounded up the two steps between them and caught her with his arms around her waist and pushed her and himself with her, back into the staircase so that they wouldn't fall together. For a moment, he held her in a close embrace, and she looked at him with a terrified expression induced by the sensation of falling. He would never forget her look of intense fear. Then he disengaged himself, took both of her hands to help her sit down on a step and sat beside her. Momentarily, he thought, *What a show we put on for the other tourists—a young Caucasian man leaping up to grab a beautiful Chinese woman in broad daylight.* When he saw that she had nearly recovered from her fall, he stood up and offered her his hand. She took it and let him help her up so that they were facing each other. Surprised and embarrassed, neither knew what to say. He regained his composure before she did when he saw tears welling up in her eyes. *Clearly she is frightened,* he thought, *as she realizes how dangerous her fall might have been,* and he thought to calm her.

"Are you all right?" he asked her in Mandarin, and smiled.

She nodded in reply and forced an answering smile.

He went on in Chinese, "You could have fallen and been badly injured or even killed if I hadn't been in your way. "Call it luck if you will, but I believe that higher powers were watching over us and put me in your way. You were fortunate." *And so was I,* he wanted to add but didn't, instead he said, "I'm glad I could help."

She looked at him steadily with wide wondering raven dark eyes glistening with tears. He let her compose herself and waited until she was ready to reply. When she spoke, her voice was soft and distant but not cold. "I thank you very much. I realize you most likely saved my life or saved me from severe injury. It was stupid of me not to have my hand on the railing. I don't know why I did that. It was a very foolish thing and a very scary feeling when I lost my footing and started falling head first down the steps. I'm still shaken." Indeed Michael could see that her whole body was trembling.

"Please come up the stairs with me and let's find a place to sit down. I want to stay with you until you feel OK and can be on your own again," he offered politely.

"Yes, thank you, I think I'd like that," she responded gratefully. "I feel very unstable at this moment. Oh, by the way, my name is Li Juan," she added.

"And mine is Michael Sorensen. I'm from California."

When they reached the top, Michael holding her slender left hand in his and her right hand holding the stairway's railing firmly, they spied, a short distance away, one of the ancient stone guard towers that straddle the width of the wall. "Look," she said, pointing toward the guard tower, "we can rest in there out of the sun. And there will be a stone bench for us to sit on."

As they went into the tower and seated themselves, she seemed to have recovered from her near accident. "Are you a tourist?" she asked, but then added quickly, "But wait, let me first guess. I think your Mandarin is too good for being a tourist. You live and work in Beijing. Yes? It's not too unusual for me to converse with foreigners, but most of them do not speak my language very well, usually just some phrases they've picked up here and there. You understand what I'm saying, don't you?" She seemed a little doubtful, and he hastened to reassure her.

"I've been in Beijing for about 8 months. I studied Mandarin Chinese a little bit in high school and had more concentrated courses at a university in California. Of course, since I came here I have immersed myself in it. I hired a private tutor. I love being able to speak your language. It's so challenging and so unlike the Western languages. However, I know my accent leaves much to be desired; but, yes, I do fully understand you," he had answered a bit self-consciously, all the while being fascinated by and admiring her perfectly shaped face. *It's a face*, he thought at the time, *that everyone must be drawn to just by looking at its perfect symmetry and flawless pale skin; and her eyes are the most stunning part of it—large, black, almond-shaped and expressive.*

"How did you come to Beijing and what are you doing here?" she asked. Hearing her soft voice again, he abandoned his train of thought.

"Oh, it's a long story but I will make it short. Since high school I have loved and longed for China and everything associated with it—its hugeness, its people, its very long colorful history, its accomplishments and its spiritual and philosophical traditions. But it's really one man who turned me on to it, Mr. Wang, a former high school teacher. I took a Chinese history class from him, was hooked and that's why I'm here, as simple as that." In trying to gloss over his early passion for China and his abiding love for its culture, he sounded quite nonchalant, as if he were saying that it's not a big deal.

Juan had responded with an astonishing, free-spirited, bell-like laugh that he would learn to love in the months to come. She sensed that he was unlike other men, who typically tried to impress her with how much they knew or how important they were. He seemed modest and self-effacing, and this drew her to him.

"Answer me one more question, Michael. Are you a famous athlete? How did you get to be so well built? You have such broad shoulders and such a wide chest. And when you caught me, I felt the strength in your arms. Even seeing you below me in the stairway, I noticed how powerful you looked, so different from most Chinese men, unless they happen to be trained athletes. Are you a famous athlete, or do you work out a lot?"

He had smiled at her and blushed a little self-consciously. Of course, he was gratified that she was impressed by his physique, but he was unused to having a woman comment so frankly on it, especially someone he had just met. "You're right and wrong. I'm no famous athlete by any means, but I do work out in a gym as much as I can. I also love to walk and jog. But I can't claim total credit for the shape of my body. I owe a lot to my Scandinavian and Germanic ancestors. I suppose you know about the Vikings and the early Germanic tribes. Their men were strong, bearded and husky." Hearing this description, she laughed again and said, "Yes, I know about them, and I've seen one of Wagner's operas. You look like Siegfried, as I imagine him."

He liked that comparison, but he didn't want to keep on talking about himself. She was a much more interesting subject. He asked her to transliterate her name. When she did, he remarked, "In the West, in Spain and Latin America that would come out as 'Hwan,' a very masculine name."

"But that's not how it sounds in Chinese," she explained. "It comes out like 'Jan,' and she went on to tell him what her name meant—fine, but tough, silk.

"How lovely," he remarked. "I'll bet that fits you."

She looked at him quizzically but nodded affirmatively.

"Pardon me for asking. I should have thought right away that your name must have some deeper meaning. I've noticed that most Chinese names or expressions have some underlying meaning that may not be obvious to a foreigner."

"Yes, there are underlying meanings in many Chinese expressions and names but not all words." Juan was trying to relieve what she thought was his embarrassment.

He quickly changed the subject, "Could I ask you a favor, Juan? Would you walk with me a bit farther along the wall before we have to part? I want to see what condition it is in beyond the reconstructed section. Maybe we could walk the old wall for a distance if we are allowed to. And maybe we could leave the tourists behind and just enjoy undistracted the untouched original wall, the wind, the sun, nature's peacefulness, the birds circling high above us and the vast mountain vistas. Maybe we could then contemplate what went on over the many centuries of the Wall's existence. Would you like to do that? Though you don't know me, I hope you'll trust me."

"Of course I can trust you," she replied, smiling warmly. "You just saved my life. And yes, I'm happy to walk with you beyond the reconstructed wall. I've been out there before, and there were no signs or barriers to keep people out. That part of the Wall is crumbling, but one is more in touch with ancient times, when the Wall was built. It's the real thing, the Wall as it was created."

They strolled side by side beyond the reconstructed segment, passing around an ineffective barrier, along the rough, uneven, partially grass-covered roadway atop the Wall, past broken ramparts and half-collapsed watch towers. Frequently they looked about at the distant verdant mountains with a slender light-colored thread stitched jaggedly through them into the far distance. At an especially scenic point, he set up his tripod and took a picture of Juan and himself with the convoluted mountains in the background and the undulating, high-climbing Great Wall imposed on them.

"I know I'll treasure this picture for years to come," he had said wistfully. "This is a stroll I'll never forget. Thanks for letting me experience this, Juan. I'll send you the picture if you'll give me your address."

"Oh, I'd like that. How precious it will be. I'll love looking at the man, the white knight, who rescued the damsel. Doesn't he often appear in your fairytales?"

"'How do you know about our fairytales? I didn't think Chinese children would read them. They would seem strange to them, wouldn't they? You've a wealth of your own children's literature, don't you?"

"Ah, yes, but we can buy the Western fairytales of the Brothers Grimm and Hans Christian Andersen in the big city book stores. And children, curious children, want to read them. I was one of them. I loved them. They transported me into a very different reality. Most of them are very romantic, yes?" she said, half questioningly, with a dreamy expression, and Michael simply affirmed by nodding his head while Juan continued. "I love fairytales and folklore, but my real passion is history. I was a history and economics major at Beijing Uni. Ancient Chinese history was my favorite subject.

He was impressed. Not only was she sublimely beautiful but knowledgeable as well. Michael wasn't intimidated by intelligent, well-informed women. They excited him, and Juan was the most exciting woman he had met.

He ventured a guess, "So you must be a teacher."

"No, not a teacher," she answered with a laugh, "but I'm always ready to learn more about things that interest me and ready to share what I know with people who are interested."

"I'll bet you could teach me a lot about this Great Wall. It's hard to imagine something this long built by human hands."

"About 5,000 kilometers. We Chinese call it the 10,000 Li wall. It zigzags and doubles back a lot. Because of its length, it crosses northern China through widely different landscapes—enormous grasslands, large tracts of agricultural lands, extensive deserts and several mountain ranges."

"I've read that it was meant to keep out the barbarian people of the North, the Mongols mainly."

"Yes, but as you probably know, that wasn't always successful because in the distant past we were ruled by a Mongol dynasty, starting with Genghis Khan's grandson, Kublai Khan, the first emperor of the Yuan Dynasty, in 1279 A.D., and our very last dynasty was Manchu, the Qing Dynasty, from 1644-1911. You might wonder why this wall follows the terrain so closely. As we see it right here, it runs up and down mountain crests in a crazy zigzag fashion. The reason for the twists and turns is that it was meant to control mountain passes through which northern barbarian raiders could easily cross into China. That is the main reason why the wall takes so many turns, and sometimes it even doubles back on itself. The result is that it crosses almost twice the distance from east to west than should have been necessary. The Chinese think of the Great Wall as a mighty dragon winding through the land. Over the centuries, myths have built up around the Wall. You may know that one of the modern myths is that the Great Wall is the only man made object visible from outer space. Astronauts, I have learned, proved this myth wrong, but it is still believed in China that under certain special conditions the Great Wall can be seen from space by the human eye. I think, however, that this modern myth will have to be revised in Chinese history books." Juan took a deep breath and then continued. "Do you know that there is also a different, more somber name by which the Great Wall is known?"

"No, I don't. What is it? I can't imagine it."

"Because of the millions of political prisoners and con-scripted workers who died building the wall, some people call it the Long Graveyard, the longest in the world. I could go on and on, Michael, but I'm afraid of boring you. So I'll stop."

"That was a great introduction to the Wall. No, please don't ever think you're boring me. Never think that. I'd like to hear more about it and the other historical sights of China as well." He spoke so enthusiastically that she knew he was sincere.

* * *

As they walked back to the Badaling parking lot, she men-tioned that she would be catching the bus.

"I have a car," he told her. "Won't you let me give you a ride?"

"Well . . ." she responded, "maybe I should just take the bus. It'll drop me off close to where I live."

"Please let me drive you," he begged her, wondering if perhaps she was hesitating because she didn't want to become involved with a foreigner.

"You're sure it won't be any trouble?"

"Absolutely sure. I'll drop you off wherever you live."

Finally she agreed to go back with him, and that was all that mattered.

* * *

They didn't converse much as he drove until they came to a fork in the road with a sign indicating a turn off to the Ming tombs. Suddenly Juan cried out excitedly and pointed to the sign. "That's where we should go, Michael," she said with much enthusiasm, and added quickly, "You need to see the valley of the tombs that belonged to the Ming Emperors. Only three tombs have been excavated and are open to the public. I would like to show you my favorite. The grounds are beautiful and that tomb is a must-see. Please, Michael, you won't regret it. I can tell you quite a bit about the tombs."

Glancing over at Juan, he saw her sparkling eyes and excited expression and he was eager to please. "Yes, let's go there," he responded without hesitation.

* * *

His ready response seemed to please her. She said, "I see that you're a man who can make decisions on the spur of the moment. I like that. You don't dither or waste any time."

"Wrong," he said laughingly. "I'm usually not that sponta-neous. I'm making this decision just because of you. I saw the excitement in your face and couldn't resist pleasing you. But I did see the road sign to the Ming Tombs this morning. Naturally I was curious, but I promised myself that I would visit the tombs later, so I can give them my full attention. But now that I have a private guide, I should go and see them."

"Oh, Michael, you'll be surprised by what you'll see." He had just made the turn, and Juan carried on, "We are now entering a seven kilometer-long road that was called during the reign of the emperors the 'Spirit Way' or 'Shen doa,' which no common people were allowed to walk on. It's the formal access into the valley of the Ming Tombs—a ceremonial avenue with several fine monuments. We will pass an elaborate stone archway, a front gate pavilion painted in red and gold, followed by 18 sets of guardian-like, life-sized stone animals and stone officials and a three-arched gate, known as the Dragon and Phoenix Gate. After that we'll approach the Great Palace Gate where even the emperor's officials had to dismount and stay behind. The Spirit Way also passes by a mythical tortoise-dragon-like creature. It bears the largest stele in China on its back with inscriptions of commemorative announcements. I have read that the spirit way was designed to be deliberately winding to shake off ghosts, which, it was believed, can only go in a straight line. Most of the Ming emperors were buried in this valley with their empresses and sometimes also with many concubines. The story goes that these empresses and concubines, and even some of the emperors' retainers, were buried alive to follow the emperor into death."

Michael shook his head and commented, "What a cruel selfish practice! Something to think about when visiting the tombs. How many are there?"

"There are 13 in this beautiful broad verdant valley, but only three have been excavated. We'll go to the Dingling Tomb of the Emperor Wanli, also known as the Tomb of Stability. His was the first excavated, I believe, in 1956. His tomb is also known as the Underground Palace. You'll soon see why. His main pavilion above ground is a very impressive stone structure, painted in the imperial colors of red and gold. It's a work of art." He found her enthusiasm infectious, and thought, *What a wonderful tour guide she would make.*

25

As they stood on the shady and beautifully landscaped grounds in front of the imposing red and gold gate, decorated with fine stone carvings and a magnificent bronze lion in front of it, Michael gasped, "How gorgeous and how imperial! Wow, the work that went into this gate alone, at a time when building equipment was still very primitive. When was Wanli buried? "

"In 1620 A.D. with two of his wives."

Walking on, they came to a gigantic marble double door of incredible thickness. Both panels of the door were open. Juan was quick to explain, "These marble doors were shut and sealed through an ingenious locking system after the burial and had never been opened until 1956. During the excavation, chests of jewelry and fine artifacts were found near the coffins that are now in a museum."

"It's really wonderful to hear all this from you. I wouldn't have gotten as much out of visiting this tomb had I come by myself."

"But wait what you'll see next," Juan said quickly.

After entering through the massive marble door, they descended a long flight of stairs into the underground depth of the marble burial vault. It had three burial chambers, each with walls and ceilings of pristine, light-colored marble. Michael stood there, awestruck, taking in the elaborate and spacious lay-out of the vault with its elegant simplicity.

"Oh, Juan," he finally said, "I'm so glad you coaxed me into coming here. Being with you made all the difference. You know so much about your culture, and you make me so much more aware of its richness and beauty. I thank you for opening my eyes to it."

"It pleases me that you can appreciate what you see," she replied, smiling warmly. Suddenly she turned, flung her arms around his neck and kissed him lightly on both cheeks. He was too surprised to react immediately and just stood there without moving. Of course he would have loved to embrace her tightly, but he hesitated, fearful of offending her, and when the moment passed, she disengaged herself and smiled mischievously as if to say, *I thought you were more spontaneous.*

* * *

On their way back, as they neared Beijing, he thought of ways to prolong their time together. It was painful to think of the moment when they would have to part. He invited her to have lunch with him, saying, "I'd be very grateful if you would select the place. I've no doubt you can guide me to a real Chinese restaurant, not one that caters to foreigners. Please do me that favor. I know that you can show me a place that I'll want to patronize regularly. I would really appreciate your guidance."

Seeing through his pretext of needing her, she laughed heartily and accepted his invitation. "Yes, I'll be happy to lunch with you. I'll take you to a very authentic Chinese café, one of my favorites."

. . . .

3

. . . .

A Revelation

And so their relationship had begun. Having lunch with her that day, he couldn't have imagined the intimacy he would come to enjoy, the pleasure she would be giving him at moments like this, easing the stress of recovering from his accident by stroking his chest as she lay beside him. She was coaxing him into a different reality, and he was content to relinquish himself entirely to it.

In the months that had passed since their first day together, they became friends as well as lovers. She had opened herself to him, enabling him to discover the deeper aspects of her personality, her likes and dislikes, her hopes, dreams, fears and heartbreaks. Seeing how responsive he was to her needs and feelings, she in turn sought to please him. As a lover, she gave herself completely and initiated him into realms of pleasure he could not have imagined. As a friend she was always sensitive to his needs, teasing him gently when he was open to it, consoling him when he had problems. As lover and friend, she gave freely without ever giving him a sense that she was clinging or needy. She was secure in her own skin, in touch with her inner core. Michael believed that neither of them would ever feel diminished in the relationship.

Knowing in whose hands he was, he suspended his thinking and gave himself over to her gentle caresses. Sweet sensations began coursing through his body, and he felt them slowly engulfing his entire being. As she gently stroked his penis, he felt himself dissolving into it. That's where his existence now dwelt as her mouth enclosed it and worked it until he came, and nearly passed out in ecstasy. As he came down from his heights of passion, and while still gasping over waves and waves of delightful feelings, he drew her up to him. Her head rested on his chest, and he gently stroked her hair. For several moments they lay still, their moist bodies cemented to each other.

"Ah, sweetheart," he sighed, "you're spoiling me. How did you know what I longed for?"

"I just know," she replied simply, but with a knowing smile. "It's my gift to you. I couldn't have given it to you any other way at this moment." In response, he gripped her so tightly that it seemed he would never let her go. How he yearned to express his gratitude for what she had just given him, an exquisite, deeply moving climax to his daydream of heightened enjoyment reliving the experience of first meeting her.

Enclosed in his embrace and loving it, Juan smiled and stroked his hair. Then she freed herself, sat up and reached out to cover his nakedness with the sheet. She suddenly stopped smiling and said, "Michael we need to talk. I had a revelation while I was meditating and you seemed asleep or, as you said, were daydreaming. It suddenly came to me who might be after you, and perhaps even after me."

All of Michael's senses were suddenly sharpened. He quickly sat up and wrapped the sheet around himself. "What are you talking about?" he demanded.

"You know that I worked for a few years at the Blue Moon Night Club."

"Yes, I do—and?"

Juan continued calmly, "Within a short time I became a valued employee because I attracted the male customers like honey attracts wild bears. They came to chat, socialize and dance with me. I didn't just socialize with one man the entire evening; I gave part of my working hours to many of them. At first I was just a regular employee, a hostess. But then a special position was created for me to do what I seemed to do best—socializing, engaging people in conversation and drawing them in, sort of like what a geisha does in Japan, entertaining customers in a gracious manner. I actually became an important attraction, and the business I brought in increased the club's income substantially. Customers came regularly and brought their friends. They stayed late and bought lots of drinks. I had fine conversations with these gentlemen, and they obviously enjoyed chatting with a well-educated woman."

And a damned attractive one, Michael thought.

"You probably know about the *hetaerae* in ancient Greece. They were prostitutes but well educated and able to converse with their clients about philosophy and politics. I was no prostitute, but I can converse with men about whatever interests them. Customers were willing to pay for that, even without sex." Juan took a deep breath before she continued while Michael sat still. "By the way, the two owners of the club are prosperous, influential businessmen, and I've even heard rumors that they might have underworld connections. They were very upset when I told them I would be leaving soon. I thought then, they are just trying to flatter me. The club, they said, wouldn't be anything special if I left. They would certainly lose customers. I didn't give them the real reason why I left and just lied that I couldn't handle the late nights anymore, that it affected my health and that I had to become a day person again. I saw that they were very determined to keep me, for they offered me more money, quite a bit more, which was tempting. But I said I couldn't do it any longer."

"Oh, sweetheart," Michael replied, "was it because of me that you left the club? I know that you quit about the time I moved in with you. Was it because of our relationship? You told me then that they chose to let you go."

"Yes, they finally let me go, albeit reluctantly. But that wasn't and still isn't the end of it. I didn't tell you about this, but they've been calling me repeatedly for several weeks. They want me back. They said they would give and do anything to get me back. They even pleaded on the phone. But I kept on saying 'No.' Then I changed my phone number. Pretty soon they called at the new number. I have no idea how they got it. They must have all kinds of connections and can find out whatever they want to know. Now I'm wondering if they had me followed. If so, they would have found out about you, and maybe they guessed that you're the reason I left. Maybe they think that if they get rid of you, they can get me back. They seem to think they own me. And now, having them on my trail, so to speak, I feel like an escaped slave. They have my scent and my secret, my relationship with you, and they're determined to impose their will on me. I'm scared. I'm really scared. Maybe it's time for us to leave Beijing and go into hiding to preserve what we have, our love for each other. I'm willing to leave everything behind." Juan was clearly beside herself with fear and anxiety. She needed him to reassure her, help her think clearly.

But at first he was unable to think of what to say, stunned by the revelation that this woman he adored might be in danger. Moreover, there was a chance that whoever was threatening her had made an attempt on his life. And so should they leave Beijing and go into hiding? Momentarily at a loss for words, he stared at her and shook his head.

This was not the reassurance she needed. When he went on shaking his head and said nothing, she burst out pleading, "Please, Michael, talk to me! What I told you is just a conjecture, just a hunch. I can't say for certain that it is absolutely true. But you've asked me to help you figure out who might hold such dire animosity and hatred toward you that they would try to kill you. I didn't suspect that the club owners could be so ruthless, but maybe they are. They were very angry when I kept on refusing to go back to the club. Maybe they hired a hit-and-run driver. Maybe they'll try again to kill you. If they do, they'll do it discreetly. They'll hire professionals who won't leave a trace of their involvement. Oh, Michael," she said, while tears streamed down her face, "I'm so afraid for you and so sorry I've put you in danger."

"Don't be, Juan," he said, pulling her to him and holding her gently. "It's not your fault. What you've told me is very disturbing. I need a minute or two to digest it. What you suspect may be the truth. We may both be victims. Those men have no right to take away your freedom. If they do, they're criminals in my view, and it looks as though they'll even commit murder to have their way. You hinted that these club owners may have underworld connections. I haven't heard about a Chinese mafia, but I wouldn't be surprised if one existed. Wherever there is money to be made and people who will stop at nothing to get it, there will be a mafia. Japan has the *Yakuza* and I know Russia has a really nasty network. The mafia was run out of Sicily, but just about every country has one."

"Oh, Michael, I'm so frightened and I feel so bad for having brought this upon you. I should've never started a relationship with you. Without me, you would be a happy man, free to do all the things you told me you were planning on doing. I'm so sorry." She looked utterly miserable, her eyes downcast and tearful.

He kept on holding her in his arms and murmured, "Sweetheart, we belong together and we can solve this problem together. We'll give each other strength to create a new life for ourselves, and no one will stop us. Are you up to it? I am."

He spoke with a lot more confidence and certainty than he felt. In fact, he had no idea what he was going to do. When Juan said that they should leave Beijing, he was so startled that he was unable to answer. To leave Beijing meant leaving his job, breaking his contract. How could he even consider it? He was married to his job and had a clear agenda he meant to follow when his contract ended—six months of travel throughout China. Was he willing to give up everything for this woman? He adored her, but how well did he really know her? He was about to terminate a relationship with another woman, Annie, his fiancée back in California, with whom he thought he'd been in love and who told him in her letters how much she loved him and yearned to have him back with her. She would be heartbroken, and he wished that he could somehow avoid giving her so much pain. But what he felt for Annie could not be compared with the passion that bound him to Juan. It was all-consuming. Would she always feel for him what she seemed to feel now? Even as this question crossed his mind, he told himself that he would take the chance. It really wasn't a matter of choice. The love he felt for her left him no alternative. He remembered the words of Luther: *Ich kann nicht anders.* Like Luther he could make no other choice.

Now, having committed himself to Juan, he had to think clearly about how they were going to deal with the obstacles they faced. Michael arranged himself on the bed so that he sat face to face with Juan. "Yes, I see that we need to talk seriously about how we could get away from here. At this point I don't really know. For one thing, how difficult would it be for you to get out of your job quickly? How would you do it? Could you just leave? As for me, I only have one idea and that is to pretend I'm more seriously injured than I thought. I could go to my boss with my arm bandaged up and wearing a neck brace. I would be lying, of course, which makes me uneasy." *In fact, lying didn't come easily to Michael. He was no prevaricator, but having committed himself to a course of duplicity, he became creative in working out a fraudulent scenario.* "But if I did it the way I described, I could request a medical leave of absence. I would plead with them to let me fly home immediately to get the medical care I need. I would tell them that I want to be treated in the States, by my own doctor and get a referral to a specialist. And I would emphasize my concerns about the vertebrae in my neck. If you and I feel certain that we want to flee, that we want to stay together, I will get an airline ticket today so that I can show it to my personnel department. I will also call the insurance company and tell them a report about the condition of my car will be on the way from the police and the auto mechanic who evaluated it. I will ask them to contact me once I can give them my new address. I should get some money out of the collision. And we both need to do something about our apartments. I suppose you will know how to go about yours and I'll take care of mine today. Oh, I must not forget the most important thing: you should get train tickets to X'ian, leaving tomorrow morning. I'll give you the money."

Juan's eyes were fixed on Michael's face and she absorbed his every word. Having been dismayed by his hesitation to respond earlier, she was reassured and impressed by his decisiveness. His plan seemed to be workable, and she was ready to follow his directions. The prospect of getting away excited her, but she couldn't help being a little anxious.

"Darling," she replied, still looking into his eyes, "I'm impressed by how quickly you came up with a plan, and I'm ready to go with you wherever you feel is best. I'll take an extended leave from my job and tell my boss that I need to look after my ailing mother. My landlord will be fine with having to rent my apartment to someone else. There is nothing holding me here. I think I can accomplish everything today that you proposed I should do. But I wonder if your boss will be convinced that you need to leave Beijing. Won't he advise that you seek medical care here? And there might be other things that may come up and hinder us. Maybe we should think about it a little before we barge ahead."

Now she was the one hesitating. But having wrestled with his own doubts and having decided to escape the danger that threatened them, he hastened to reassure her that they were making the right move. And he was elated by the prospect of escaping with Juan. As always, the question of whether or not she would always feel for him what she seemed to feel nagged him a little, but at a moment like this he felt reassured. Maybe what happened this morning wasn't a total disaster. It had bound her to him, and now he had a clear purpose to make a life for them together. Yes, she was his now.

In spite of everything, he was optimistic, even joyful. And suddenly he was so exuberant that he startled Juan by hugging her and exclaiming, "You're such a wonderful woman! We'll make it because we're devoted to each other. Nothing can stop us. But we need to act quickly to protect ourselves from people who wish us harm. My greatest fear is that they will barge in here and kidnap you. They must know where you live and that I'm living with you. They'll dispose of me and take you. I'm ready to die for you, but I can't bear to think of you in the hands of evil men."

Juan responded by putting her arms around him and clinging tightly. "Yes, darling, we must act without delay. I cannot bear to think of you being harmed trying to protect me." Noticing how his body was responding to his contact with her, and, in spite of her anxiety, she laughed and said, "I love your body."

$$\cdots\cdots\cdots\cdots$$

4

$$\cdots\cdots\cdots\cdots$$

The Escape

Michael and Juan went their separate ways to accomplish the tasks they had set for themselves. Juan gave him the address of a pharmacy that also sold medical equipment where he could buy his neck brace, bandages, medical tape and a sling for his left arm. They went about their business—placed telephone calls and saw the people they needed to see—just as they had planned. Everything went smoothly. Michael got his medical leave and Juan a short leave of absence. She told her employer that she needed a leave to attend to her mother who had suddenly been taken ill. They came together at Juan's apartment in the late afternoon. Juan came back earlier than Michael. From groceries in the fridge, she cooked a quick meal and they ate as soon as Michael came back. They told each other what they had accomplished. Juan had purchased the train tickets for the next morning, destination X'ian. Michael was squared away with his company. He told her that he showed them the airline ticket, which he later in the day canceled. His boss gave him permission to leave for his medical consultations in California and expressed the hope that his injuries could be treated, and he had added, "Michael, I hope you will be back with us soon. Best of luck to you."

"Do you still feel OK with what we're planning?" Juan asked him a little anxiously as they munched their dinner with little appetite. She still couldn't quite believe that they were going to do it. But Michael had come back to Juan's apartment all bandaged up. He looked weird but the get-up seemed convincing. She worried, however, that he might be exposed as a fake. If someone saw him without his get-up and reported it to his company, he would be fired outright, and no one would hire him, at least not in China. But she tried not to worry that this would happen. *How wonderful it would be if we were truly free and could leave with clear consciences*, she thought.

"I do, sweetheart," he replied, and, mirroring her feelings, he added, "but, to be honest, I don't like the deceptions our escape entails. I wish we didn't have to lie and fear discovery. But we must protect ourselves. I don't see any other way to escape. I do know now for certain that I love you very much, that I can't be without you. I believe that I'm doing the right thing—for me, for you, for us." Michael spoke coolly and rationally about the need for deception. But when it came to declaring his love for Juan, he spoke quite passionately. He reached over the table for her right hand and kissed it tenderly.

Juan nodded to show that she agreed and trusted him, but then he saw tears rolling down her cheeks. "Sweetheart, don't cry. Let's be happy. We know we have dedicated ourselves to each other. Haven't we?"

"I'm happy, darling," she responded and added, "these tears are tears of happiness and joy. Sometimes when I'm moved to the core, because something wonderful is happening, I burst out in tears," she said, smiling at him now through her tear-filled eyes.

After they finished their simple meal, Michael got up from the table first. He took both of Juan's hands and pulled her up to him and kissed her softly and tenderly. To his surprise, Juan responded more passionately, kissing him deeply, almost demandingly. Taking it as a challenge, Michael responded in kind, giving his passion free rein. The two were so engrossed in devouring each other that they didn't realize how dark it had become in the meantime. When Michael withdrew momentarily, he took a deep breath, then picked Juan up and carried her to the bed. She protested, "No, darling, not now. We have to pack. We have to get ready and get away."

"Yes, but it can wait a little. Our loving each other has first priority." They had already reached the bed, and he lowered her down gently while still kissing her. At the same time he pulled up her skirt and tried to push down her panties. He himself had grown so engorged that he could not manage to get his pants off. Sensing his frustration, Juan got up to assist him, unbuckling his belt and stripping off his trousers. Throwing off her clothes, she pulled him over to the bed and pushed him down gently. He understood right away that she wanted to be on top with his hands on her breasts. She rode him long and hard, and when he felt her shuddering into her climax, heard her moaning, he let himself explode inside her. Happily they had arrived almost simultaneously at the blessed terminus.

They dropped off to sleep with his arms about her and her head on his chest. When they woke up, it was late in the evening. They both jumped up at the same time and shook their heads, looked at each other and started laughing at the same time.

"I can't believe we did this, sweetheart," he said. "We must be crazy. Let's get cracking. We're still in danger. It could be this night that they'll come for us. I'll straighten up the two suitcases I brought over from my apartment. Everything is just thrown in there. If I'm done before you, I'll help you. And I suggest we should leave right after we're finished with packing."

"Oh, thank you. I might need your help." Then she looked at him quizzically. "But where will we go? The train doesn't leave until eight tomorrow morning."

"Juan, don't you agree that we should get out of here? We can sleep some more in the train station. I've seen people doing it. We'll take a couple of blankets and pillows along."

"Oh, I guess you're right. Maybe we should do that," she agreed, reluctantly.

It was Michael with his innate sense of organization who ran the packing endeavor. It took them just under an hour. Several times, when he looked across the room at Juan hunched over her suitcase indecisively, he said to her, "Sweetheart, do you really need that? Think of just the most necessary items. We want to keep our luggage at a minimum. Otherwise traveling will be too cumbersome."

Juan nodded and resumed sorting out her clothes. She kept on talking to herself almost like a child. "No, not this one," and she put it aside. "Yes, this one, this one and this one," she continued.

Michael listened to her talking to herself, half amused, half annoyed. But he didn't interrupt her, or tell her to step it up. He figured he would have to help once he had his things in order.

All packed by midnight, Juan phoned for a taxi. "In ten minutes it will be there," the dispatcher said.

"Darling, the taxi will be here in ten minutes. Let's take everything outside and wait by the gate. I've already said goodbye to my landlords. We can simply leave." With one last, nostalgic glance at their love nest of the past months, they moved out to the narrow lane to wait there for the taxi. Michael had his neck brace on, his arm in the sling and a large Band-Aid across his left cheek. He wore a dark blue sporty fabric hat, the rim shading half his face, a parka, jeans and jogging shoes. Juan wore flat loafers, the tight blue jeans she had worn when Michael first met her at the Great Wall's dangerous stairway, a knee-length raincoat, and a wide-rimmed felt hat. Her face was hardly visible.

They arrived at the train station within 15 minutes. As Michael had described the scene to Juan, droves of people were settled down on the floor of the cavernous train station hall. They looked around a bit, dazed at first. Spying an open floor area across from them against the wall, fairly close to the door that led to the train platforms, Juan said, "Darling, let's go over there," and she extended her arm in the direction of the unused space. "We can rest against the wall instead of just sitting or lying on the floor."

"That's fine with me. OK, let's go." Juan was pulling one fairly large suitcase and Michael two medium size ones. On top of two suitcases they had strapped a blanket and a pillow.

As they reached the spot they had staked out, Michael touched Juan's shoulders gently while asking, "How are we doing, sweetheart? Are you up to this adventure?"

39

"I'm OK." She lifted her head so that he could see her face under the wide rim of her hat, smiling faintly at him. "Don't worry about me. I'm tougher than you think. I wouldn't do this by myself, but I feel very secure with you. I love you, darling." Michael kissed her on her left cheek, ever so gently and stroked her right cheek with his free hand. He loved stroking her facial skin. Marble smooth and white, it always felt like the finest velvet.

They settled down on the spread-out woolen blankets. The pillows they put up against the wall. They both felt tired now, not from any strenuous physical work but from the stress of getting ready. All day long, they had waited anxiously to begin their adventure, and now that it was beginning, there was nothing more they could do. Resting in anticipation of their next move, Juan dropped off to sleep. But sleep didn't come to Michael until the early morning hours. Throughout the night he kept lying very still but his mind was active. His thoughts were on Juan. Since their relationship began, Juan was seldom out of his thoughts. He mostly focused on the pleasure they gave each other and their absorbing conversations. But in spite of all the time they spent together, she remained mysterious. Of course, he reflected, *All women are mysterious. That's why men fear them and try, usually without success, to impose control.* But Juan was more mysterious than any other woman he had known. She was an enigma. He didn't wish to control her, but he yearned for more understanding, even as he yearned for a greater understanding of China itself. In an effort to learn more about her, he had asked her late one evening to share with him her family history and memories of growing up.

She was reluctant and prompted him to tell her first about his own family. He did so, beginning with his ordinary childhood and teenage years in an average stable family, with a younger sister as the only sibling, and a father who taught civil engineering at a two-year community college. His mother was putting herself through university, hoping to earn a bachelor's degree in literature. When he had finished, she nodded thoughtfully and said, "It sounds as though you weren't unhappy growing up. I wish I could say the same." Clearly she didn't want to share painful memories, but she could see that Michael was eager to listen.

5

A Family Portrait

"I was hoping you wouldn't ask me to talk about my family or how it was for me growing up. There are things, ugly things, I'd like to put behind me and forget if I could. And I hope you won't think less of me when you hear them."

Oh, Juan," he assured her, "there's nothing you could tell me that would diminish my love and respect for you. Please tell me your story."

"The names of my father and mother are Li Gang and Li Sola. When I was very young, I and my brother, Li Yong, who was two years older than I, thought we had an ideal family. My parents had their own business, and we were well off compared with people around us. They owned a furniture business. Most of the pieces they sold were made in the shop behind the store. Father employed several cabinet makers. He knew the trade himself. He was an expert craftsman but didn't actively work in the trade anymore. He mainly supervised his workers. Mother managed the showroom and did most of the selling. She was a very good sales person—friendly, attentive, giving advice readily and exhibiting very good taste as far as furniture was concerned. She had studied feng shui in her early years. You may not know it, but feng shui is quite an art in China. It aims to put people in harmony with their environment, such as villages, towns, parks, buildings, houses, apartments and furnishings."

"Oh yes, I have heard about the underlying concept, but only with regard to interior decorating," Michael replied.

"Yes, I understand that's more or less how this art is perceived in the West. But it is much more inclusive in my culture. It strives to identify the most auspicious positions for furniture, dwellings, public spaces and even communities. I can see myself being involved in this art that tries to teach understanding of how energy flows and how it affects us. Customers were attracted when they learned that my mother was proficient in this art. Her knowledge was a great asset to the business."

Juan paused momentarily, took a deep breath and then continued. "In the early years I know our family lived in harmony. I very much loved my mother. She was short, a bit rotund, which is unusual for Chinese women, with big breasts, which is even more unusual. She felt very soft when she embraced me or I embraced her. She was chatty with strangers, but also knew how to listen to people and she had an easy smile. I loved my brother, too. He was very smart, always into math and the sciences. My father was strict with us children but fair. In comparison to my mother, his temperament was opposite to hers. Not a man of many words, he was rather quiet, kept much to himself, and we, the children, often had to coax him to open himself up to us. But once he did, he could be fun. He was a good story teller because he was an avid reader. His parents had made sure that he learned to read and write because he was a smart boy. They were hoping he would one day become a government official or a scholar. But he also liked to work with his hands. He liked to shape things. Wood was his favorite material because it was easily transformable."

Juan stopped again. She looked at Michael questioningly. He had been sitting very still listening to her story. "Yes, there was harmony in our house. But that soon changed. It's not a happy story I have to tell. Are you sure you want to hear it?"

"But of course. I want to hear everything," he said eagerly, and added, "So far it has been very interesting. How will I really get to know you, if I don't know anything about your family and your upbringing?"

"Very well. When I was 12 and my brother 14, everything changed in my family's constellation. Our business continued to prosper, but our family life was thrown into turmoil. Father brought this about. I always thought my parents loved each other. I had been convinced of that, but what happened in my 12th year turned all my beliefs upside down. One weekend, on a Sunday afternoon, my father came home with a fairly young, very nice slim attractive woman. He introduced her to us children as Auntie Liu Jie. She greeted us in a friendly way, but, at the same time, in a somewhat formal manner. I thought right away, *This is strange, I have never heard of this auntie. Why have we never been introduced to her?* I looked at my mother, but her face didn't show any emotion. I immediately felt awkward in this woman's presence. Father was all smiles, but mother kept very quiet. When auntie greeted her, mother just nodded. She stayed seated; she didn't even extend her hand. And that again seemed strange to me because mother was such a people person, always very cordial.

"On weekends, father kept on bringing Liu Jie by our house. She ate her meals with us and pretty soon seemed a regular member of our family. But I could not help detecting a constant awkwardness in the atmosphere. Father, contrary to his nature as we had always known him, was usually outgoing now, talkative and sometimes even boisterous; whereas mother, contrary to her nature, became habitually reserved. And then after a few months, auntie moved in permanently. I never heard any arguments between my parents about this new arrangement as auntie quietly became a permanent member of our household.

"At age 12, I knew little about love relationships and what was going on between men and women. I was quite sheltered. But I was very perplexed about our family's new triad of father, mother and auntie. Our house wasn't very large. Some situations were quite embarrassing. We all had to use the one and only bathroom in the house. I didn't know who to ask about what was really going on or who to confide in. Eventually thinking that my smart brother would know more, I asked him.

"'Yong,' I said one day when only he and I were in the house, 'tell me, why are we forced to share our space with this stranger?' By now I had figured out that auntie wasn't related to us. I was sure my brother knew it, too.

"He answered my question very bluntly and shocked me: 'She is our father's mistress, and she means now more to him than our mother does. They are lovers.'

"I gasped, deeply disturbed by this awful revelation, but I realized at the same time that Yong must be hurting too. Otherwise he wouldn't have been so blunt and harsh, knowing that I didn't have a clue. *He is harboring a buried anger that eats at him*, I thought, *and he's making me feel it as well*. At first I simply refused to believe it. So I said, 'You can't be right. Father would never do that to Mother.'

"'Yes, he would. He has done it already. I saw him going into her bedroom the other night. That was the first time. Last night I stayed up deliberately quite late, and the same thing happened. It's a fait accompli.'

"Angry now and still clinging to my denial, I shouted at him, 'What does that mean? Don't use those fancy expressions I don't understand.'

"'Can't you guess, dumbbell? It's done. It can't be undone. It's irreversible. We all, including mother, have to live with it. Of course, she could leave him, but she never will. Never, I say, because of the business and also because of us.'

"My anger was still increasing, and I yelled again at him, 'What are you going to do? Are you just going to accept the situation? I hate it and I hate my father for destroying our family. Mother is not who she used to be. She has lost her sparkle. She is not herself. I've a hard time being intimate with her. She never confides in me. I swear right now that I will never speak to father again. I feel very hurt. And I won't be friendly to this auntie either. Maybe she will leave when she has figured out how much we dislike her.'

"I really had worked myself up into an emotional state, especially after Yong said, 'I don't like it myself but I really don't care that much. In a few years I'll be out of here. Maybe dad will send me to a boarding school before that, if I plead with him. But I doubt he'll want to spend the money. Just cool it, sis.'

"I was so angry at Yong now, as well as father and auntie, I just raced out of the room, slamming the door behind me. For the rest of the day, I stayed in my bed. When mother came home and into my room later on, I just lied to her and said I had a stomach ache.

"I wish my parents, especially my mother, could have talked to me confidentially and explained the situation. But I guess people at the time didn't know how to be open about things like that. Looking back, I think that my mother had become dysfunctional over time and was perhaps always kind of frigid when it came to sex. I also think that mother and father may never have found fulfillment in that area of their relationship. But then I asked myself many times, *Why in the world didn't father just have a mistress on the side and be discreet about it? Why did he have to put the whole family through this incredibly awkward charade and especially humiliate mother? Why wasn't anything explained to us children?* I think I suffered much more from the change in my family than my brother, and still do today."

Juan paused then and was a bit exhausted from having to relive her family's destruction. Before she could go on, Michael interrupted, raising his hand as a signal to stop. "Telling the story is too emotional for you, Juan. Why don't you stop; and, if you want to, you can tell me the rest later. I don't like you to get worked up like this. I can see it still hurts very much, which I can understand."

"No, I want to go on. I don't want to pick up the thread some other time. The story won't be much longer. There isn't that much more to tell."

"OK then. If you're sure, I'll listen."

"Well, I haven't talked to my father since I had that talk with my brother. It's going on 12 years now. Eventually the situation changed somewhat, maybe brought on by my stubbornness, or maybe my mother couldn't handle it anymore. I don't really know. Communication broke down completely in my family. After one year, my father and 'auntie' moved to another apartment and are still living there today. But my parents never got divorced, and they're still in business together. It's all very strange. Don't you think so, darling?"

"Very strange indeed," he replied, "hard to believe. No husband in a Western household would ever do that. Men may have mistresses, but their relationships with women outside marriage is kept as secret as can be. No man would ever bring the mistress into the family as your father did. That's taboo because it's destructive to the family. And I can certainly understand how it affected you, my poor sweetheart."

"But darling, there's more. I need to tell you what happened to us children. Yong was the first to leave home at 18, and home meant our mother's house. He didn't stop talking to our father as I did. But their relationship was never as close as it had been. When it was time for Yong to go to university, father was willing to see him through it. He supported him financially. As for me, there was no university education in the plans—no support for it from my father. Strangely enough—and very disappointing—mother didn't use her influence in support of me even though she knew I had the smarts and the drive for a higher education. Instead, when I was 17, my father tried to hook me up in marriage with the son of a well-to-do friend of his. This was all done with my mother's collaboration. I was still very sheltered then and naïve. When I was introduced to the young man, I liked him. His name was Gao Xin. He was handsome, and he liked me, too, I thought. He was very charming around me. I think he was 21 then. Our relationship was well chaperoned. It seemed like eventually it was going to be a traditional betrothal. Then one time, Xin's parents, Gao Dishan and Gao Anyi, had to travel to Hong Kong for one week. They wanted Xin and me to come along because they were eager to show us 'this great cosmopolitan city.' They promised my parents that they would take very good care of me, that they wouldn't have to worry about anything. So we went and we stayed in a beautiful, expensive hotel. I had my own lovely room and loved it. We went out to the finest restaurants in the evenings where there was dancing. During the day, when Dishan, the father, had to pursue business, he took Xin with him. Anyi, the mother, and I spent a lot of time together sightseeing and shopping; or rather, she did the shopping, but I accompanied her and was amazed by all the beautiful things I saw. Anyi was kind to me. She bought me a lovely cocktail dress. It made me look very beautiful, I thought, when I tried it on in front of the mirror in my room. While we had dinner, Xin always danced with me. When he first saw me in my new dress, he said he was dazzled. 'You look gorgeous, Juan,' he exclaimed, while his father applauded. 'It's only thanks to your mom,' I said demurely.

"'Oh, no, no, no! It's you, Juan. Let's go and dance.' And he grabbed my hand and pulled me out onto the dance floor. That was the first time Xin acted differently. He danced passionately, held me very tight in his arms so that I could feel his entire body. He whispered in my ear, 'Oh, my lovely Juan.' Then he brushed my cheek with his lips. This new, very affectionate behavior thrilled me but also scared me. *Be careful, Juan*, I told myself. His behavior on the dance floor was just the beginning. He kept putting his hands on me, giving me hugs and touching me. I don't think the parents noticed or had any clue. That's when I started looking forward to our departure from Hong Kong. I couldn't discuss the situation with anyone, certainly not with Xin's mother. But during one of our last evenings in Hong Kong, Xin behaved himself like a perfect gentleman, was very cool, correct and respectful. I was relieved, and my warmer feelings and respect for him returned.

"I was therefore amazed by what happened the night before we left Hong Kong. It was late. We had all gone to bed, and I was dropping off to sleep when I thought I heard a soft knock on the door. When I thought about the knocking, I told myself that I had already been dreaming. So I turned over in bed and ignored the knock. But then it sounded again. I thought maybe my mother was trying to get hold of me, that she had rung the hotel. Maybe the desk sent someone up to let me know. But I still waited. Then the knock occurred again, louder and seemingly more urgent. I got out of bed and went to the door. I opened it gingerly and was surprised to see Xin. He said, 'Please Juan, let me in. I need to tell you something.' When I didn't, he begged me, 'Please, Juan.' I firmly said, 'No, Xin, it's too late. I was already asleep. We can talk tomorrow.' 'No we can't. That will be too late.' 'Please go, Xin. I don't want to shut the door in your face. Please go and talk to me tomorrow.'

"He didn't go. Instead he pushed the door open so forcefully that I, standing partially behind it, was knocked to the floor. He looked down at me and saw that I was just about ready to scream. He quickly shut the door with his foot, threw himself on top of me and clamped one hand over my mouth. I was terrified. Our eyes met. I saw hunger and rage. He must have seen fear in mine. I tried to shake my head in a 'No' gesture, but couldn't move it. His hand was truly like a clamp, holding my head down and imposing himself on me. I freed my arms from under him and tried to pound the sides of his body. That didn't seem to hinder him. His face looked angry and contorted. I was really scared by then. I had never seen a man so completely possessed by desire. I sensed that he would let nothing stop him. If I had been able to speak, he wouldn't have heard a word I said. Then I felt his free hand grabbing my nightgown and pulling it up. I tried to raise up one knee to block his hand. That was my mistake. I had previously kept my legs straight and very tight together. But now with his free arm, he pushed my knee to the side and placed his knee on top of it. With his hand he now gained access to my private parts. I felt his fingers working my genitals, adeptly, knowing just where to touch, where to put pressure and where to massage gently. Soon, without wanting it, heat and irresistible sensations rose in my body. I had never experienced anything like it in my young life. The feeling was totally disarming. Before I knew it, Xin had thrust himself inside me, and I felt pain and a sensation of something tearing. Suddenly, my mind became very clear. I was being raped. At that point, I felt an incredible strength coursing through my limbs. I started squirming under him and scratched and pinched him with my long pointed nails and with my hands. He finally had to take his hand off my mouth to try to subdue me. I immediately sank my teeth into his neck and I caused so much disruption with my squirming body that he finally withdrew himself. I don't think he got any satisfaction out of raping me, no pleasure.

"When he jumped up and closed his pants, I sat up and saw the bloodstain on my white nightgown. That's when I poured out my own rage. 'You beast, get out of here, now! We are through! I don't want to see you again!' With a stupid, apologetic little grin, he went out the door and closed it gently behind him, and I got up and locked the door.

"I did my best the next morning to be friendly with Dishan and Anyi. I ignored Xin. I never talked to him again. We flew home that day. I didn't even look at him once. He was loathsome to me. The first thing I did when I got home, I told my mother that I didn't want to see Xin again. I asked her to tell Dad. I spoke very firmly. She seemed perplexed. 'Didn't you have a good time with the Li's? They are very nice people.' 'Everything was fine, mom. Mrs. Li was exceptionally nice. But I just don't want to have a relationship with Xin. I'm serious about that.' It was then like always. The communication ended there. I didn't know what my mother suspected. But I knew I couldn't confide in her. She would have told Dad and it would have become a scandal. He probably would have blamed me, knowing how stubborn and unforgiving I was. So the whole affair was laid to rest. I didn't see Xin or his parents again. But from then on I felt I needed to chart my own course and let neither my mother nor my father interfere. The next year I enrolled myself in university and took on the evening position at the Blue Moon to pay for my tuition. That one experience with Xin taught me a bitter lesson. Even people who seem very nice can betray and use you. I realized that I shouldn't and couldn't trust anyone."

As Juan ended her story, Michael could see that she was emotionally exhausted. A wave of compassion washed over him and nearly carried him away. "Sweetheart," he said gently, holding her hands, "thanks for confiding in me. What an awful, humiliating experience you had to go through, but it made you tougher, more resilient and self-reliant. I love you all the more for choosing me as your confidant," and he kissed her softly, first on her forehead, her cheeks, her throat, and then her lovely delicate lips. Desire wasn't prompting him now, only a yearning to protect her, give her comfort, and heal her pain.

6

The Journey Begins

When Michael awoke at seven in the morning, he squinted at first and then looked around. Feelings of unreality crowded him. Seeing a multitude of people—people of all ages, from infancy to very old age—spread out on the vast floor in an unorganized fashion, like refugees after a massive natural disaster, he shook his head as if to clear it of a persistent haze. *How did I get here?* he thought at first. He happened to look down at Juan. She was still sleeping, curled up next to him. Then he realized where he was. He remembered the long wakefulness he had experienced and the memories surrounding Juan and her family that had come back to him before he finally fell asleep.

He placed his hand gently on Juan's arm that was positioned as if she were reaching out to him. "Juan, sweetheart," he whispered. "It's time to wake up."

She opened her beautiful, night-dark eyes, still full of sleep. "Where are we? Still in the train station? I slept very well."

"Yes, we're still in the station, but our train will leave in less than an hour. Let's see whether we can freshen up a little, throw some water on our faces, before we hit the platform. Please, you go first while I watch our luggage. I'll go when you come back."

Instead of getting up, Juan turned toward him and hugged him tightly. "I still feel good about our getting away. It's going to be a good journey. I'll try to be the best guide I can be," she said excitedly, sounding almost like a child.

"I feel good, too, sweetheart. But let's get a move on now," he urged.

When Juan returned, she was carrying a little cardboard tray with lidded paper cups of hot green tea and a couple of sweet buns. She walked very carefully and stealthily picked her way between outstretched bodies. As she came over to him, she wore a big smile. *How wonderful that she is mine*, he thought.

When Michael came back to the space where they had slept, Juan had already folded up the blankets and strapped them and the pillows to the suitcases. He quickly looked up at the large departure panel to see which platform they had to go to. It was number 12. They set off with Juan pulling her suit-case and Michael pulling his two cases. She carried the little breakfast tray.

Their train came in at 7:45. It had come overnight from a northern province, from the city of Shenyang, and disgorged throngs of passengers. Hundreds were waiting impatiently to board the train. The crowd was very mixed and included a number of farming peasants—men, women and children—from outlying areas. Carrying their livestock in cages and produce in large baskets, they would board the hard-seater carriages. There were also students and business people, men and women, heading for the soft-seater carriages. The more well to do, and almost always the foreigners, would ride in the soft-sleeper car-riages. Michael and Juan were in a good position. They boarded the train among the first passengers. They had a compartment reserved in a soft-sleeper car that could seat as well as sleep four. If they were lucky, they would have it all to themselves. And they were lucky on that leg of the trip. It was theirs alone for the next eight hours, on a stretch of more than 800 kilome-ters that would end in X'ian.

When they were seated by the window opposite each other with the little window table between them, they drank their hot tea and ate their sweet buns in silence. Now that they were leaving Beijing and heading into an uncertain future, they ate quietly and pursued their own thoughts. After a little while, Juan reached over and placed her hand on Michael's hand. As

53

he looked up, she smiled brightly at him, "Darling, how are you feeling? We are off for sure now."

"Oh, I am feeling just fine, but I'm still experiencing a sense of unreality. It won't quite sink in yet that we have cut ourselves loose from everything that grounded us—our jobs, our living quarters, friends and the city we know so well. But don't worry. I'll soon be up to our adventure. As you know, I can adjust fairly quickly." She nodded to affirm her faith in him. He had spoken slowly as though weighing his words and reflecting. When he went to freshen up in the train station, he had taken his bandages and neck brace off. As he sat before her now, healthy looking, youthful, strong and handsome with his chestnut brown hair and square energetic chin, she felt joy in her heart. She wanted to talk to him about their future beyond the journey they were currently on, about going to America with him. But, at the same time, she felt she shouldn't broach the subject now. *It's too soon*, she told herself. *I need to wait for the right moment. It will be good when we're away from Beijing, when we're experiencing some wonderful historical and natural sights. It will put us both fully into the spirit of adventure,* she imagined.

Michael was now looking intently out the window and watching as Beijing, the familiar place, receded into the distance. He wanted to take in the landscapes of China, especially the important, centrally located, historically rich and fertile Yellow River Valley they would travel through later on that day. As long as it was daylight, he promised himself, he didn't want to miss anything.

After a while, Juan sought to focus his attention on her. She touched his hand and said, "Shall we lie down and take a little snooze? We could fit together in one of the upper bunks if we snuggle up. It would be cozy and sleep inducing to hear the monotony of the train's churning wheels against the steel tracks and feel its eager forward motion like that of a team of spirited horses." She felt she had said enough to express her desire for something more pleasurable than a nap.

"Sweetheart, I'm always ready to snuggle with you, but I was going to sit here and watch the landscape flying by. It's all so new to me. I don't want to miss anything. You can climb up and take your nap. I'll be here. I won't go anywhere. I'll just watch. I know you've seen all of this before, so it's not that interesting to you. You know the conductor will be coming through to check our tickets. Please make yourself comfortable, but first come here and give me a hug and a kiss."

She moved over to his side, placed her long slender arms around his neck and said coyly, "I love you, darling. I know I could go with you to the end of the world."

He placed his arms around her waist and gently kissed her lips. Juan returned the kiss hungrily, devouring him. So engrossed were they tasting each other, murmuring and moaning with pleasure that they didn't hear the light knocking on the compartment door. The conductor was a cheerful little white-haired man with a sparkle in his eye, sympathetic and perhaps a little envious, remembering his own stolen moments of pleasure as a young man. Peering in, he said, "Hey you two lovebirds, I need to collect your tickets. Just spare me a few moments of your time. After that I'll leave you alone."

Hearing the man's voice, Michael and Juan let go of each other, and looked a bit sheepishly at the intruder.

"I'm sorry," Michael said right away and rummaged in his jacket pocket and handed over the tickets.

"Thank you, sir, and I promise I won't bother you anymore," the conductor said with a knowing grin.

After the interruption of their tender pursuit, Juan was unable to rekindle their intimacy, for Michael's attention was again drawn to the landscape speeding by outside the train's window. Beijing was now out of sight. They had already entered Hebei Province to the south of the capital and were heading toward the undistinguished provincial capital of Shijiazhuang with a population of over two million. Whereas Beijing is cosmopolitan, slick and modern, Shijiazhuang is quite countryish, has less money and is less fashionable. Hebei province is one enormous stretch of farmland, but it also became famous because of an important archeological find in the 1920s. At first, what were thought to be uncovered dragon bones in Zhoukoudian, to the southwest of Beijing, turned out to be not the bones of a mythical creature but those of Homo Erectus, a precursor to modern humans, dating back 500,000 years. It was then thought that humans originated in Asia until it was later refuted.

When the train slowed and finally came to a belching halt, Juan woke up and stretched. She felt very refreshed and called down to Michael.

"I am awake, darling. Where are we now?"

"We've just arrived in Shijiazhuang," Michael responded, and added, "I can't believe the mountains of coal that were piled up next to the railroad tracks just before we entered this city. I have never seen anything like it."

Juan was now sitting on the edge of the upper bunk bed with her slender calves and feet dangling down next to Michael. "Oh, that's nothing unusual because just about everything is fired with coal in this country—power plants, all heating and cooking facilities in private homes, private and commercial furnaces, as well as braziers used on the city sidewalk food stalls. These mountains of coal will be a very common sight as we travel through the cities and towns. I know, I know what you want to say. That it causes too much pollution. But we don't have oil, just large amounts of coal deposits, and we can buy coal cheap from overseas, mainly Australia. So that's what we have to use."

"I understand. But tell me is there anything special about this city that I should know?"

"No, nothing special, just a museum. But very near it is the much smaller city of Shengding, an historically important place. It's known for its beautiful pagodas. You see them jutting prominently above the town. It also has a number of Buddhist monasteries, popularly known as temples, like the famous Dafo Temple, dating from sixth century A.D. I know you would love to stroll among the pagodas and temples and revel in these historical remnants. But where we are heading today, you'll see much grander historical sites. I promise you, you'll be in for some overwhelmingly grand sights." As usual, Juan sounded excited when she discoursed about historical places. She jumped off the upper bunk and stood before him with her arms and hands, palms up, stretched out to the side and her eyes bright with enthusiasm, in a posture of intense animation. "Really," she exclaimed, "you'll see it's all very grand and imperial. The sites are wonderful, breathtaking, so ancient and with such ingeniously conceived monuments, designed and built as the finest achievement of art and imagination." Her sense of wonder shone in her face.

"Yes all of it, I'm sure, will be phenomenal and breathtaking," he replied. "Your country had a high civilization not just through centuries but through millennia. I'm looking forward to seeing as much of it as I can."

She now sat down by the window opposite him. "I won't go to sleep anymore until we reach X'ian. I promise. I have to point out to you the wonders of the Yellow River Valley and the ancient imperial cities. It wasn't always Beijing from where the emperors reigned, you know. There are a number of ancient imperial cities in this central part of China."

"That's very interesting, sweetheart, but let's come down to earth for a moment. We need some lunch, don't we?" Michael interjected. "We can either step onto the next platform when the train stops and buy something from the vendors or we can go to the dining car. What do you think we should do? I'm in your hands. You're the expert."

"Let's do the dining car," Juan replied. "I think the food would be safer there, especially for you. But let's see whether we can make a reservation for the time when the train moves out."

Just before Michael was about to open the compartment door, he enclosed Juan in his arms, held her very tight and whispered in her ear, "Sweetheart, I'm so happy to be able to be with you. You're wonderful. I love you with all my heart."

"Do you really?" she said as if surprised, and let out her rippling laugh. It reassured him that she was happy, too.

They ate their lunch, and by then the train was on a roll again. When they entered their compartment, they were happy to see that they didn't have to share it with other passengers.

"How great that we still have our privacy," Juan cried out with delight, and laughing at the moment they entered. "Our little private hideaway is still unspoiled and offers us all kinds of delights."

"It seems like luck is with us. Maybe it will remain with us to the end of this journey and beyond," Michael added hopefully.

They settled down opposite each other once more. "This wasn't the best of lunches we just had," Juan commented. "The fish was overcooked and too bony, the vegetables a bit soggy, and the rice too sticky." She laughed again.

"And don't forget the table's greasy oil cloth," Michael pointed out with a bit of disgust in his voice. "I couldn't believe the waiter would draw a number in the grease with his finger to indicate the meal's charge. I was surprised I could actually read the number he had drawn."

"Don't be upset or disgusted about it, darling. The farther we penetrate into the provinces, the less refined and sophisticated the eating places will be. You've already been spoiled by Beijing's gourmet dining," Juan said with a laugh.

"And so have you," Michael countered, "Otherwise you wouldn't have commented on the overcooked fish, the soggy vegetables and the gooey rice." Now they both laughed heartily.

7

The Yellow River Valley

It was still two or three hours until the train would enter Henan, the next province, a virtual treasure trove of historical sights and artifacts.

"Darling, listen to me. We'll soon cross into the famous Henan Province, and I've a confession to make. I hope you won't be cross with me," Juan said hesitatingly.

"What's your confession? Let me hear it. It had better be something exciting or naughty," Michael said good-humoredly.

"In Beijing I bought train tickets for two railway segments. One from Beijing to Luoyang and the second one from Luoyang to X'ian," she replied a bit sheepishly.

"Why did you do that?" Michael wasn't upset, but definitely curious.

"Because near Luoyang is something very special I want to show you, something you shouldn't miss. I've been there once and was overwhelmed. It's such a monumental place. I promise you it will take your breath away. We'll have to stay overnight in Luoyang, and in the morning I'll take you to this ancient awe-inspiring place. Our train leaves tomorrow at three in the afternoon from Luoyang, and it'll get us to X'ian at 5 p.m. We'll have plenty of time to wander through that breath-taking place and absorb its spiritual vibrations. That's all I want to say because it's supposed to be a surprise for you. I won't even tell you the name of it." Juan sounded excited, and as Michael looked at her closely, he detected a blush of pink on her cheeks that seemed to have risen out of her V-neck blouse and suffused her face.

Without giving him time to comment on what she had just revealed, either to commend or chide her, Juan asked Michael hastily, "Do you want to hear a bit about Henan Province we are going to cross into soon? I don't mean to give you many details, just some information in general. Please interrupt me if you get bored with it."

Michael could sense that she was very keen on telling him, and smiling at her he answered, "I love to hear you lecture, sweetheart. What could be more rewarding than to hear history so splendidly presented by the loveliest and most passionate woman alive, who also happens to be my beloved. Tell me more, sweet professor."

"Thanks, darling, you're very kind, and I'll try not to bore you." She took a deep breath and continued. "So once we cross into Henan, the train will stop at Anyang, the capital of the ancient Shang Dynasty that reigned from about 1600 to the middle of the 11th century B.C., more than 500 years if you can imagine that. Though modern Anyang is not very interesting for sightseers, it is of great interest to archeologists. In the late 19th century some farmers unearthed a few fragments of bone, tortoise shells and bronze objects that were inscribed in a primitive form of modern Chinese writing. It was then speculated that the area around Anyang was the seat of the Shang dynasty. It is now quite certain that modern Chinese writing was developed from these ancient pictographs. So if you and I were out to discover the various capitals of China beside Beijing, here we are speeding toward the first one that we know of. By the way, at the time of the Shang, China may have been the most advanced bronze-working civilization. It had already transitioned from the Neolithic or New Stone Age to the Bronze Age. Its people were able to work with bronze, and fashioned tools and weapons. By the way, the Shang rulers were not emperors but priest-kings and may have used bronze vessels in their rituals."

When Juan finished her account of this early piece of Chinese history, Michael was amazed and impressed, as always, by how much information and vivid details she had stored in her memory from studying her country's history. He was certain that he would not do nearly as well in recounting American history off the top of his head. And besides, what was American history in comparison with that of China?

Hoping that she would reveal more of herself as she discoursed, Michael prompted her by saying, "Tell me more, sweetheart. I love to listen to you. You're really a very impressive historian."

Looking at him skeptically through narrowed eyes, Juan responded, "It's sweet of you to describe me that way. But I don't think such extravagant praise fits me. You don't really know me yet, and I don't see myself that way."

"Well, if you won't see yourself that way, allow me to do so. And I insist that I know you better than you know yourself," Michael countered, prompting Juan to smile in her peculiar sphinxlike, skeptical manner and remain silent. Her smile was a little unnerving because he couldn't interpret it, and it seemed to signal withdrawal. Unwilling to let her withdraw into silence, he prompted her to continue telling him more about the history of the Yellow River Valley, for he had a sense that they were soon to cross the Yellow River. He was reassured by a change in her expression, which became no longer skeptical but clearly pleased by his sincere eagerness to hear her history lesson.

"I know you realized that we'll soon cross the famous Yellow River that takes its name from the large amount of yellowish-brown silt it gathers on its way through mountains and vast stretches of countryside. It's a very important river in Chinese people's lives. It has provided them with wealth and well-being, but it has also brought them great tragedies. Over millennia millions of people died from the river's great recurring floods, especially before the dikes were built. In recent history, during World War II, when Japanese invaders broke the dikes, they created severe flooding of the entire valley. But I want to go back to early history. After Anyang, the train will stop at a minimetropolis as we think of it. It's the city of Zhengzhou. Despite its ancient history, this city has few historical sites to show. Because it is a major railway transport junction, it has grown and modernized rapidly, but it's not unattractive. Zhengzhou is clean and has wide, tree-lined boulevards and some upscale shopping areas fanning out from the railway station." Halting for a moment, Juan took a deep breath and continued.

"What is more interesting than Zhengzhou is the nearby ancient capital of Kaifeng. It was the thriving capital of the Northern Song Dynasty that reigned between the 10th and 12th century A.D. Today Kaifeng is still a walled bastion and has some interesting historical sights, but being situated just south of the Yellow River, it could not escape the river's periodic flooding that worked to people's as well as dynasties' detriment. After centuries of flooding—on average of once every two years—the original Song Dynasty's capital now lies buried eight to nine meters underground beneath today's city. If we were to stop at Kaifeng, you would notice that it has no skyscrapers. The reason is that these tall buildings require deep foundations. They are not allowed to be built for fear of destroying the city that lies unexcavated below."

Juan suddenly stopped her lengthy discourse and looked at Michael to be sure he was listening. He kept his eyes on her, but frequently glanced out the window. When she stopped talking, he reassured her immediately that she had his full attention. "Oh, wow," he exclaimed. "How interesting that an entire ancient capital lies buried under a new city. I've never heard of it before. Since today's city is built on top of the ancient one, won't it be difficult if not impossible to uncover the old one? But how very interesting it would be to see and stroll through a thousand-year-old city," Michael mused. "I still can't believe how fortunate I am to have you with me. You're virtually a walking history encyclopedia." Whereupon Juan threw back her head and let out her charming laugh.

"Yes, you are so right. It would be interesting to walk the streets of this old Song capital. Maybe one day, when China becomes exceedingly wealthy, the archeologists can excavate the underground city and have it once more come alive for people interested in ancient history. But there is one more site I want to tell you about," Juan quickly added. "If we were to stroll through today's center of Kaifeng, close to the ancient pagodas, we would see an historical place where once a synagogue stood. The synagogue is gone, but we can still visit the Sacred Heart of Jesus Church, the Dongda Mosque and the Old Guanyin Buddhist Temple with its recumbent Sakyamuni in the Reclining Buddha Hall. You may be surprised to hear that these four religions were well represented in Kaifeng. It was the first city in China where Jewish merchants settled when they came via India along the Silk Road during the Song Dynasty. Today Kaifeng still has a small Christian community, a much larger Moslem community and the traditional Buddhist community. The communist regime permits people to practice their religion of choice."

"You're really enlightening me," Michael exclaimed. "You're more than a guide. You're opening my eyes to a vast field of knowledge. What you're giving me is a precious gift. Thank you, sweetheart." Michael suddenly got up, grabbed Juan's hands and pulled her up to him into a tight embrace. "If only I could give you something in return. As I told you when we first met on the Great Wall, I believe that higher powers watch over us. I now know that the events of the last few months, including even the car crash and our escape, were meant to have happened. Otherwise, I might never have been on this exciting trip with an enchanting young woman and my heart filled with love for her." He kissed her forehead, cheeks and neck gently at first, then her lips passionately. Juan, although she let it happen passively at first, soon returned his kisses with no less passion while underneath them the train's wheels were turning tirelessly, rhythmically, and noisily on the old railroad tracks. They weren't aware of how close they were to Anyang. But then, as the train approached the city, it slowed down considerably. When the brakes were applied, an unexpected jolt unsteadied the young couple, who had spaced out of time and reality. Still in their tight embrace, they lost their balance and fell onto the soft-sleeper seat next to them with Juan underneath and Michael on top. In that position they could have both easily given their ignited passion free rein, but Michael was the one who controlled himself as he realized how easily someone could enter the compartment during their tryst. He disentangled himself and got up quickly while Juan looked at him, puzzled by his hesitation. Then she giggled when she spied Michael's bulge that he quickly tried to hide with his hands. "What's wrong with you, darling? You don't have to hide it from me." And she reached out to stroke him enticingly.

Flustered and reddening with embarrassment, he said "What if someone comes in here?"

"Oh, don't be silly. I doubt anyone will come in here, a least not for a while. The conductor has already come and gone. But it's so funny to see you being so cautious. Please forgive me for laughing. I wouldn't want to embarrass you."

"It's all right. I forgive you. I agree it was funny what happened to us. But I'm afraid I wouldn't be able to stand the embarrassment if anyone were to see us. That's all."

* * *

By now they were sitting again properly opposite each other. For awhile they were silent, and Juan gazed out the window without focusing on the scenery. Then she looked at Michael and seemed to be considering something. Finally, as though she had decided that it was an opportune moment, she asked him in a playful tone, "Darling, do you remember when you said a while back that you didn't know how to give me something in return for being a fine tour guide for you?"

"Yes, certainly I remember that. Why are you bringing it up?" Michael looked at her curiously, wondering what she was thinking.

"I now know how you can make it good and give me something in return," she continued, still rather playfully and with a charming smile while her intense dark eyes held his.

"Well, how? I want to know." Michael felt most eager to know and said, "You make me really curious, sweetheart. Let me hear it."

Now that the moment had come for her to reveal her most fervent wish, Juan seemed slightly embarrassed. She began a little reticently. "How you could really make it good would be if you promised . . ." and here she hesitated ever so slightly, and then quickly blurted out, ". . . to take me with you to America."

Now it was time for Michael to laugh out loud. "But Juan," he responded without hesitation, "how can you make such a request when you know that I'm going to do that? I wouldn't go back and leave you here in China unless you wanted to stay. I love you, and I want you to be with me always. I mean it. I'm totally committed to you. Before I met you I had a fiancée back in California. Her name is Annie, and I'm sorry I didn't tell you about her before now. But I've written to her and broken off our engagement. I told her that I've fallen in love with someone else."

"Ah, poor woman," Juan replied sadly. "How disappointed she must be to lose a man like you. Are you really sure you made the right choice?" For all his avowals, Juan still needed some reassuring. *A man who can break off an engagement is changeable; and the woman he has chosen to replace a previous love, he can leave her as well,* she thought.

"Oh, Juan, I've never been more certain of anything. You're the only woman I love." He wanted desperately to make her believe him. But she was skeptical and needed still more reassuring. She said, "Perhaps I shouldn't have brought up the subject of my coming with you now. Are you sure you want me to come with you?"

"Absolutely, sweetheart," he responded passionately, "I want you to be with me always. I felt I couldn't talk to you about coming with me until I had made a decision about my and Annie's relationship. I made my decision some time before we left Beijing, but I put off writing to Annie. It was a hard letter to write, but I finally wrote it and mailed it to her the day before we left. I see it now that I should have told you right at the start of our relationship that I was engaged, but I was afraid that you would think less of me. I was falling in love with you and didn't want to lose you."

She nodded thoughtfully and seemed to accept his explanation. Before she could respond, he went on, "I hope that you brought your passport. Before we arrive in Guangzhou you will need to obtain a visa to enter the United States. I forgot to remind you during our hasty retreat. If you were planning to travel to California with me, you should have brought your passport."

Juan blushed a little and replied, "Darling, I believe everything you've told me, and my heart is jumping for joy, but I have to confess that I don't possess a passport. I never needed one. I've never been outside China, but I'm so excited that I'll soon see and experience another part of the world." Her lovely pale face was flushed with emotion and tears glistened in her eyes.

"Yes, you'll be seeing another part of the world. But I'm a little concerned that we haven't shared some important things until now. I didn't tell you that I was engaged, and you didn't tell me how much you wanted to go with me to California. We need to be more open with each other. Please promise me that you won't keep things from me. Please say it."

"I will honestly try," she responded demurely.

"But, sweetheart, trying is not enough for me. Can you say, 'I will discuss with you whatever is on my mind that concerns you and me.' He pressed her.

"I promise I will," Juan solemnly assured him.

Though she hadn't repeated his words verbatim, he had to believe her, and he reached his right hand across to her so that she would take it into hers to seal their pact. She took his hand, smiled and shook it.

"Now we need to think about getting you a passport. You'll need to apply for one in Guangzhou. That's your last chance. You need to do it right away as soon as we get there. It's too bad because it may take some time for you to get it. You can't get a visa from the American Consulate in Guangzhou unless you have the passport. You understand, don't you?"

"Yes, I do. I'll go to the authorities the day we arrive in Guangzhou."

Michael added, "And I'll go with you. I'll pay extra if it will help expedite the process. In my country that is possible, maybe in yours, too. If we're lucky, you'll get it in a few days."

8

The First True Imperial City

The train stopped just briefly in Anyang, maybe half an hour. From there it was still about three hours until they would reach Luoyang. Michael and Juan stepped out onto the platform as soon as the train came to a halt. They wanted to buy some steaming-hot green tea and pastries if they could find them among the vendors' offerings. One vendor was selling, besides the tea they were looking for, what appeared to be a delicious homemade raisin-filled coffee cake. They bought four pieces that would tide them over until they were settled and had supper in Luoyang. They took their afternoon tea into their compartment and placed the cups and the paper plate with the cake on the little window table. Then they stepped again out onto the platform and walked hand-in-hand up and down to get some exercise. They didn't talk but just took in the colorful bustling spectacle on the platform with droves of vendors trying to hawk their wares, railroad officials strutting up and down answering questions, directing passengers to their respective train cars, and late arriving passengers running toward the train. Juan and Michael kept walking until a conductress blew her shrill whistle that signaled the train's departure. They had to run a little to reach their car and were pleasantly surprised that no other passengers had settled into their space. They would still have their privacy, perhaps all the way to Luoyang unless passengers boarding the train in Zhengzhou had seat assignments in their compartment.

67

When the train started rolling out of Anyang's station and gained speed in the verdant countryside, they enjoyed their still-hot tea and polished off all four pieces of cake. When they were done and felt satisfied, Michael said, "Sweetheart, forgive me for saying so, but for me everything seems so strange, so unreal. I have a hard time getting into the here and now. To me it still feels as if I were on a dream journey that may or may not end well. Nothing seems to feel real to me—our hurried departure from Beijing, the only place I knew in China until just yesterday, and now it lies far in the distance. I suddenly find myself on this train and hardly remember how I got here. I am speeding across this vast country, and being brilliantly introduced to its long colorful and turbulent history by an expert guide I hadn't even hired. Even the car accident and the subsequent charade of faking injuries are also part of this dream. I can't believe that I actually did that. I have always been taught by my parents that the greatest virtue is honesty. I now realize I've sorely let them down." Michael stopped for a moment because the thought had suddenly entered his mind, *Could it be that my beloved has the power to corrupt me?* But he discarded that thought quickly and heard himself say, "The only thing that is real to me is you. You have already become so much part of me that I can't imagine it could ever be otherwise. And if anything were to threaten our togetherness, I would fight with everything I've got to keep you." Michael was musing and reflecting, and he added, "Do you feel as I do?"

"Yes, I do because I love you," Juan responded simply, and she added, "I think I understand your feelings of unreality. I feel somewhat the same, but since I'm still in my country and I've made this train journey before, it seems perhaps less unreal." As if to reassure him that she felt as he did, she suddenly got up, knelt down in front of Michael and slipped in between his spread-apart thighs. She pressed her head gently against his chest, and folded her arms around his waist. He was touched by her sensitive and reassuring gesture. He looked down at her glossy black hair and stroked it gently. They stayed like this for quite awhile until Juan lifted her face to his. She looked at him steadily. Then her eyes moved across his face as if she were studying every minute detail of it and as if she were trying to take his features into her heart and memory so that she could always conjure them up in their entirety.

Feeling a bit uneasy, Michael suddenly broke the spell and asked, "What is it, sweetheart? You seem so pensive. You seem to be wondering about something. I hope you're not wondering whether you have made a mistake to run away with me, a stranger and a foreigner to boot." He tried to say it rather light-heartedly.

"No, I've no doubts. I know I made the right decision." After a short pause, as if she were wondering what it would take to reassure him, she took what seemed like an evasive tack. "What I'm wondering about at this moment is whether you would like to hear about Luoyang now or a little later?"

A little startled by her quick switch from their relationship to China's ancient history, Michael shook his head as if to get a better grasp on their present reality that Juan was replacing with an ancient bygone one. He had been hoping that what he'd told her about his sense of unreality could lead to an in-depth discussion, but it appeared to him that Juan didn't want to go there at this time. So he said, hiding a slight disappointment and always ready to please her, "Yes, sure I'm eager to learn about Luoyang. It must be important if it's connected to the 'breathtaking monument' you will show me tomorrow morning."

She was pleased by his acquiescent response. Still kneeling in front of him, she placed her head against his chest and said, "I'm so glad you'll let me introduce you to Luoyang. It has a colorful and very long history. Then, releasing her arms from his waist, she got up and seated herself opposite him as she had been before she embraced him.

She began, "Yes, I really want to talk about Luoyang before we get there. If you can imagine the time span of it, Luoyang was the capital of 13 dynasties until the Northern Song dynasty moved it to Kaifeng in the 10th century, a city I've already talked about and that we'll come close to on our way to Zheng-zhou. So this fact makes Luoyang one of China's true ancient dynastic cities. Some say it was the center of the Chinese universe. Of the dynasties that reigned there, the great Tang dynasty was the most outstanding and long lasting. Can you believe that at one time Luoyang was home to 1,300 Buddhist temples? Two magnificent palace complexes, those of the Tang and Sui Dynasties, stood at Luoyang's center. But the city was sacked by invaders from the North in the 12th century and never recovered its old splendor. For centuries, the city remained with only distant memories of its greatness. Its population kept on diminishing until only 20,000 inhabitants were left by the early 20th century. Today it has a population of over one million and resembles other modern Chinese cities, choking air pollution, roaring street traffic and a lot of concrete construction. Now there is little evidence of the once-splendid ancient capital." Juan paused for a few seconds and then added, "I think, for a starter, this should be enough information about Luoyang. What do you think, darling?" But then she quickly added as an after-thought before Michael could answer, "Tomorrow afternoon, before we board the train to X'ian, we can, perhaps, walk the old city complex and look at the interesting 700-year-old Wen Feng Pagoda and the old Drum Tower and walk among the old historical and traditional Chinese courtyard houses that are still lived in."

"That sounds all very interesting and I'm looking forward to it. But where are we going to stay tonight? And where is this grand historical monument you are so eager to show me tomorrow morning? You didn't mention it. Is it not in the city of Luoyang?" Michael felt a little perplexed and overwhelmed.

"Oh, I'm sorry I forgot to mention that what we are going to see tomorrow morning lies outside the city. We'll be going there by bus. It'll be a short bus ride. But tonight, we'll be staying at Luoyang's Mingyuan Hotel, only a short distance from the train station. I called the hotel the day we left Beijing and made a reservation for one night. I hope you approve."

"Of course, I approve of whatever you've arranged and I'm grateful. I wouldn't have known what to do. I just feel that I'm not contributing much to this journey," Michael said, feeling a little too passive, even impotent. She was so completely in charge.

Juan understood immediately and said, "Oh, I think you're feeling a little controlled. You would like to be the master of this journey, wouldn't you? I think I understand. I can tell you that I have made no further arrangements except the train trip to X'ian after leaving Luoyang. From then on we have to decide together what we're going to do. And, by the way, I haven't traveled beyond X'ian, so I won't be this great expert anymore. But wherever we go in China, I will most likely still be able to tell you some historical facts about the area. However, I won't be as familiar with the history of other sights we'll be seeing as with those we have seen and will be seeing the next couple of days," Juan responded, trying to reassure Michael. Though she thought she understood him, she wasn't sure how willing he, as an American male, was to be led by a woman. She only knew how Chinese men still tried to be the traditional leaders and masters in anything outside the house.

"I'm sorry," Michael responded quickly, "I think you misread me a little. I couldn't be happier with what I have learned from you so far and the arrangements you've made for our journey. You're very capable of handling everything. I can see that. But I'm glad that we'll work together on the rest of the journey after we leave X'ian—of figuring out where to go, where to stay in Guangzhou and how we'll get beyond it to Hong Kong."

"Yes, we'll do that. But thanks for telling me that you're happy so far. It's important to me."

"I certainly am, sweetheart."

"What do you want to do next, darling? I know you're waiting for the crossing of the Yellow River, which should be coming up soon. Maybe you would like to sit close to the window and watch the river crossing and our arrival in Zhengzhou. I'd like to stretch out on this seat and rest awhile by meditating. I feel a bit exhausted. But I'll try not to go to sleep. If you see something special, don't hesitate to ask me what it is."

"OK, that sounds good to me. You just rest peacefully and I'll watch the scenery fly by.

And indeed they crossed the river sooner than Michael had anticipated on a broad, new-looking concrete bridge. He looked down into the dark yellowish-brown water and could see why the river had been given the name it has. At the time they passed over it, the river was flowing languidly, a rather narrow main channel of water within its high dikes on both sides. It didn't seem a deep river. It had small rivulets in between the sandbanks of the broad sandy river bed. Neither did it seem a navigable river, definitely not for big boats. Michael remembered that he had read something about the Yellow River while studying at the University of California. It said that this river, after it leaves the mountains, flows through a vast highland, called the Loess Plateau, where it picks up the yellow silt. When it enters the great valley that the train was passing through now, the river, having slowed down because of the relatively flat terrain, deposits much of its silt before it reaches the eastern seaboard to the north at Bo Hai Bay. He also learned then that the riverbed has become elevated in relation to the surrounding countryside due to thousands of years of silt deposits, and that the river used to be much more voluminous before modern China built a succession of dams and industries along its 5,500 km flow. He had also learned that this Yellow River, the second longest in China, like most major Chinese rivers, had its origin in the snowy and glacier-rich Tibetan highlands.

Michael was still engrossed in recalling what he'd read about the river—its documented capriciousness in flowing languidly much of the year, then becoming suddenly a raging torrent and spreading its life-giving and life-taking water across the broad fertile valley—when the train slowed down and the outskirts of Zhengzhou came into sight; and here, as just outside every other Chinese city, there were mountains of stored black coal piled up along the railroad tracks. Not until the long train slowly entered the station, huffing and puffing like an ancient winded dragon that had been snaking its way through the land and was now going to take a rest for a short while, did Juan, sensing the slowdown, wake up for their arrival in Zhengzhou, a major railroad hub with a massive train station.

"Oh, what a good rest I had," she said, as she stretched her lithe body upward, sideways and backward. "And you didn't even interrupt it one time. You're happy with what you saw, darling?" she asked a little drowsily.

"Yes, thank you, I am. I saw a lot and even remembered that I once read about the Yellow River's silt and where it picks it up—in the vast high country called Loess. And what I found amazing is that the riverbed has risen over millennia because of the enormous silt deposits so that today's riverbed is actually higher than the land around it. I had never heard of anything like this before, and today I saw it, and could believe it when I saw how heavily laden the river water is with silt."

Juan nodded her head affirmatively. "Yes, I know about that, too. It's one of those unusual phenomena. The topography and the makeup of the Loess soil are just right for the accumulation of silt to occur."

Meanwhile, the train had come to rest at the platform that was crowded with people. "In this city, we will for sure lose our cherished privacy," Michael predicted. "Look at all the passengers crowding in on the train, will you?"

"Yes, I think you're right. Remember, this city has a population of over two million. I may have forgotten to tell you that it's considered to be a small metropolis. But let's get out and walk a bit outside until the train is ready to take off."

"Yes, good idea. But it won't be easy to work our way through the crush in the aisle outside our compartment." Michael was already close to the compartment door as he said this, and Juan was right behind him. Through the glass sliding door, he could see people bunched in the passageway, and a couple of men looking at the compartment number. As he opened the door, two Chinese men stared at him as if they had never seen a Westerner.

"Excuse me, I think this is our compartment," one of them said politely in English.

His eyes opened wide and his jaw dropped, when Michael answered him in almost perfect Chinese. "I'm sure you are right. Please come in and make yourselves comfortable. We are just going for a walk on the platform."

"Oh, thank you," the astonished man said while Michael and Juan squeezed out the door.

Both men appeared to be businessmen, clad in dark blue suits, white shirts and colorful ties. Michael said to them, "We'll see you in a little bit. Make yourselves comfortable. Our seats are on the right, as well as the bunk above."

"Oh, thank you for sharing your space. Very kind of you," said the man who had spoken before, and he bowed at the waist to Michael.

* * *

By the time Juan and Michael reached the platform, much of the crowd had dispersed. The two walked briskly up and down again holding hands, as they had in the last train station, and stayed outside until the platform master's shrill whistle blew. The train seemed much more crowded than before with passengers visible in all the windows. Some of the windows had been opened and passengers were leaning out to chat animatedly with their loved ones or friends who had accompanied them to the station. When Juan and Michael finally boarded the train, the passageway to the compartments was hardly passable. They had to squeeze through. Passengers were still trying to get settled in their compartments. They seemed to have more luggage than they needed. All the compartments where now completely filled.

Michael whispered to Juan, "We've been lucky so far with all the privacy we've had. That's been lost now. But this next leg of the journey is fairly short, isn't it? I'm glad that you've already told me so much about Luoyang because it would be a bit embarrassing for you to recite all these historical facts and tidbits in front of the two strangers. And tonight at dinner you can tell me about tomorrow morning's marvelous sight you'll take me to, won't you?" he said eagerly.

"Yes, the next leg will only be two hours," Juan responded and then added happily, "Now you see how well I timed everything. You're so right. I could hardly give you a long historical spiel with those two stiff businessmen present. And, you know what?" she added with a little giggle, "we'll have to behave ourselves. No fooling around anymore."

"I'm afraid you're so right on that score," Michael responded ruefully.

"But I'll try to keep you diverted," she said. "When we go to dinner I'll tell you about that wonderful monument. It'll be better than having me hold forth like a tour guide on the bus."

"You are right, sweetheart." And just before they entered the compartment, he patted her sleek, beautifully shaped rear that he always admired every time she walked in front of him. She had perfect gluteal symmetry.

Michael was startled to see that the two fellow passengers seated next to each other were now dressed in black and red striped silk pajamas. He couldn't help staring at them more than he should have, for he had never seen anything like it. No Western traveler, man or woman, would ever exchange his or her day clothes for sleepwear while sharing a train compartment with strangers. But the two men smiled and bowed, obviously pleased with themselves as they met Michael's inquisitive stare. He thought their getup to be rather hilarious and stifled an impulse to laugh out loud. He noticed that their business suits, shirts and ties were lying carefully folded on the upper bunk. He regretted not being able to talk to Juan about this strange custom and whether it was commonplace. He thought he might try to communicate with her in English, which they had largely avoided until now. But one of the men did know a little English, and Michael certainly didn't want to embarrass them. So he thought, *Apparently it's nothing unusual because I haven't noticed a startled expression on Juan's face.* So he just relaxed and overlooked the formal businessmen's most informal attire.

When Juan and Michael found out that their two companions were on a lengthy business trip to Kunming in the distant Yunnan Province, in China's deep Southwest, Michael could understand that they wanted to save their perfectly pressed outfits for their arrival in Kunming. He had also noticed that their luggage was quite small, and the suits they were wearing were most likely the only ones they brought with them. The switch in clothing made sense to him now, and he could accept their very casual outfits.

Most of the two-hour train trip was spent by Michael and Juan in almost whispered conversation, while their companions also conversed in very low tones. And Michael, sitting again close to the window, frequently looked out to take in the land-scape that was still largely rich, flat agricultural land, as far as he could see.

9

The Longmen Caves

The two-hour train ride seemed sooner accomplished than Juan and Michael had expected. They were presently entering Luoyang. They passed again mountains of piled-up coal at the city's outskirts, to Michael now a very familiar sight, and entered the train station with a belching locomotive. The station was moderate in size and the platform was not crowded as in Zhengzhou. They got off the train quickly, having said a brief good-bye to the two businessmen and bowed to them while wishing them good luck on their journey. Juan and Michael stopped briefly on the platform and arranged their luggage for easy handling on the way to their hotel. But then Michael, to Juan's surprise, embraced her quickly and tightly, planted a soft kiss on each of her cheeks and whispered in her ear, "Another milestone accomplished, and tonight we're going to sleep in a real bed, thanks to you. That'll be wonderful." Juan put her arms around his neck, looked him straight in the eyes, smiled, and nodded her head in affirmation. Then Michael noticed that people in the closest train car were tapping on their closed windows while laughing and waving at him and his beloved good-naturedly, while others shouted, "Good luck," out of the open windows and others whistled at them piercingly. Michael noticed that they were all young faces who, unlike the older generations, weren't too afraid, too formal or too inhibited to express themselves. Slightly embarrassed, Michael let go of Juan. They turned to face the people in the train windows and waved to them good-naturedly. The passengers waved back. This good-hearted attention brought joy to the lovers' hearts, and Michael thought it was a good omen. They soon turned their attention again to their luggage and left the platform quickly.

Out in the street, in front of the train station, Juan held up her map and said, "The Mingyuan Hotel is not very far away at all. We just need to take the first right turn and another right into the next street, and we'll be there. We don't need a taxi, we can just walk, don't you think, darling? Oh, I also see something else on our map. On the way to our hotel, we'll come by the Jinyuan bus station that, I'm sure, is the one we need to go to tomorrow morning. I'll talk to the hotel receptionist to find out about an early morning bus to the monument."

"That sounds excellent and easy. So let's head out."

It was shortly after 5 p.m. when they signed in and were pleased with their spacious and nicely furnished room with private bathroom. It felt very civilized to them. As soon as the door closed behind them, Michael let out a shout of joy. He lifted Juan up in his arms and virtually threw her onto the bed and himself next to her. Both laughed out loud and shouted together, "We have it made for one night." As Michael moved closer to her, Juan sat up and shook her head. "Let's wait until tonight, darling. We'll have all night to frolic on this bed. Just think how enjoyable it will be. Think about it and store up your passion for a little later. I suggest that we both take a shower and freshen up. It's already 5:30. Let's go to dinner around seven and then come back early to this room unless you want to take a stroll into town before turning in for the night." As usual, Juan had taken charge, and Michael was willing to be managed. He said, "That'll be fine with me, sweetheart, let's decide on the city stroll after dinner and after you've told me about tomorrow's outing. Does that feel all right with you?"

"Yes, sure. So am I going to take the shower first?" she asked coyly.

"Sure, go right ahead. I'll rest a little. Want me to scrub your back?" He was already half at attention anticipating their evening love feast and was only too willing to be served a preliminary course of showering, scrubbing and stroking in full nakedness. But she wasn't quite ready.

"No thank you. Not now, darling," she answered with a laugh, "But tonight I may surprise you."

* * *

Right at seven that evening they entered the hotel dining room on the first floor. Hardly any diners were present yet. Michael and Juan were allowed to choose their own secluded dinner table in a corner of the vast restaurant. When the waiter came, he asked them right away if they wanted the 'water banquet.'

"No. No, thank you," Juan answered.

"Wait a minute, sweetheart, what did he say and what does he mean by a 'water banquet?' Maybe we should try it. Do you know what it is?" Michael bent his head close to Juan's and looked questioningly at her.

"Oh, it's a famous Luoyang specialty. It's a 24-course meal with several soups, other dishes and desserts. If that sounds excessive, we can order regular dishes from the menu. But if you want to experience something special or if you are very hungry, we'll have the water banquet. I've had it before, so I'll let you choose. To be honest, it was a bit too much for me at the time I was here. I can recommend the barbecued squid. It's delicious."

"I'll go with that." he replied, "Even though the water banquet sounds tempting, I don't know whether I could handle a 24-course meal. Our Thanksgiving dinners are excessive but they don't come close to 24 courses. It sounds a bit overwhelming. Yes, I prefer to go for the barbecued squid, some veggie dishes and rice. That'll do me fine. So, what do you think?"

"It sounds perfect for me, too, and I'll order for us."

Their dinner was wonderfully tasty. They splurged that night and had a bottle of white wine with their dinner to celebrate their successful escape.

Michael looked at his glass and shook his head as though marveling at something. Then he said, "I cannot believe it that we were able to get away this easily. We did it, and we're going to be all right. I think we are safe, sweetheart." But after a few seconds' reflection, he said, "Don't you also think it would be difficult, after this long distance we have come, for anyone to keep pursuing us?" He was deliberately sounding hopeful, and he wanted her to agree.

Juan thought for a moment before replying. "To tell you the truth, I don't really know. And to tell you another truth, the events of a few days ago, although they're behind us, have really shaken me to the core. I do feel better the more distance we can put between us and Beijing. To answer your question more precisely, yes, it feels as if we're more secure the further we get away and the more time elapses."

"That sounds pretty good to me. Let's think positive and let's drink to our future together because I love you. I feel so extraordinarily lucky to be in your company," Michael said with a smile that expressed his confidence and pleasure in the moment. He raised his glass. "Here is to our life together and all the wonderful experiences we'll have." Juan raised her glass, too, but with a slight hesitation that Michael didn't notice in his ecstatic mood, and he toasted again, "Here is to us and our future, sweetheart."

"To the future," Juan said seriously and looked at him with her intense black unfathomable eyes while they clinked glasses and Juan said, "gan bei." Now they had to empty their glasses in one fell swoop because that's what her Chinese toast meant. And when they set their empty glasses down, both of them breathless because the full glasses were a good long draft, they both burst out laughing. Michael grabbed Juan's head and planted a soft kiss on her glowing red lips. "That seals our pact. Now you can't escape anymore, my beautiful swan," Michael said with a laugh while Juan nodded in agreement and said facetiously, "I'm afraid I know," followed by her disarming bell-like laugh. He wondered whether she'd ever seen *Swan Lake*. Probably. No doubt it had been danced in Beijing and elsewhere in China. As though reading his thoughts, she said, "And you don't need to worry about my becoming an evil black swan. I'll always be your white swan, and you'll be my prince."

Michael was delighted to hear their commitment reaffirmed. He sought to enhance his delight by focusing on the pleasure he anticipated hearing her discourse on the site they would be visiting the following day. He asked her, "And how about the wondrous sight we will see tomorrow? Will you tell me about it now? I'm overflowing with expectations."

"I will, darling, I will. I remember that I promised you that it would be tonight during or after dinner. So here I go. The great historical sight we'll visit in the morning is called Longmen Caves. That site is very, very special to me. It is a shame that these natural limestone caves and the treasures they contain have been ravaged over the centuries but much is still there that is untouched. It is now a UNESCO World Heritage site. Can you imagine that, over a time span of 400 years, more than 100,000 images and statues of the Buddha and his disciples were chiseled into the limestone cliff walls on either side of the Yi River? They have also called it a sutra in stone. The statues and images were first begun by stone artists of the Northern Wei Dynasty, after their capital was moved from Datong to Luoyang in the late fifth century A.D."

Because Juan paused a few moments, Michael butted in, "But Juan you can't be right in mentioning 100,000 statues and images, the latter I assume are carved into rock surfaces. That is a phenomenal number. Are you sure about that? I can't wait to see this sight." He was immensely interested.

"Yes, I'm dead sure. Can't you imagine that a small army of chisellers could create that many statues and images in a time span of several hundred years? I can," Juan replied with conviction.

Michael chuckled and replied, "Well, if you're that certain and sure of yourself, I must believe you."

"And here are a few more tidbits," Juan continued. "There are 1,300 caves altogether that contain 2,100 grottoes and niches, a number of pagodas and myriads of rock inscriptions. It has been said that the artwork of the Longmen Caves represents the high point in China's Buddhist culture. The sad part is that the major losses of art pieces occurred not through erosion over many hundreds of years but through looting by Westerners in the 19th and 20th centuries. Many masterfully carved heads were cut off and ended up in Europe or North America. Even entire statues were removed and taken to the West. Two magnificent murals, depicting a royal procession, were taken off a cliff side and ended up in two American museums. As I've mentioned, the art of religious stone carvings started with the Northern Wei Dynasty in the late fifth century and ended with the more advanced three-dimensional stone carvings of the Tang Dynasty in the mid eighth century. The Wei carvings are less voluptuous and less three-dimensional than those of the Tang. We'll talk more about the cave art when we look at it." Michael nodded and was digesting this while Juan quickly continued. "Oh, by the way, I mustn't forget to mention that some stolen artifacts are slowly being returned and heads are being restored to their severed necks. Also, many statues suffered defacement during the dark days of our Cultural Revolution. Not much can be done about that as far a restoration is concerned." Juan leaned back in her chair and smiled. She was breathless.

"Oh, sweetheart, how interesting this all sounds. I can't wait until tomorrow morning. Let's be sure to catch the earliest bus. Thanks so much for your excellent introduction to the caves." She really had kindled his curiosity, and he responded enthusiastically.

"You're most welcome, darling, but I suggest that we take the 8:30 bus, not the earliest one. If I remember correctly, the caves are only 16 km away. So it's only a short bus ride. Let's go and get the bus tickets now at the reception desk. I'm sure they'll have them."

After finishing their dinner a little after eight, they decided to skip the evening stroll through town. They postponed it to the following afternoon. After obtaining their bus tickets at the reception desk, instead of taking the elevator to the fourth floor, they raced each other up the stairs. Michael won the race and was already holding open the door to their room when Juan appeared out of breath at the top of the stairs. She made it through the door and into the room, threw herself onto the bed and pretended to be wasted. Michael followed suit and stretched out next to her.

"Let me just take a few deep breaths," she panted. "Then I'll make a suggestion you might like." Her speech was hardly audible. But she caught her breath shortly and suggested, "Let's take a shower together before taking over the bed."

"Great idea!" Michael cried out as he jumped off the bed and proceeded to tear off pieces of his clothing, one by one somewhat provocatively, as if he were performing a striptease. Juan lay on the bed in a fit of laughter. Michael was a sight because his stripping wasn't exactly graceful. When completely naked, he disappeared into the shower, and beckoned her, "Follow me, sweetheart."

Juan threw off her clothes and joined Michael. "Come on let me soap you down, sweetheart. This will be luxurious. I'll allow you do the same with me." When they were both foamed up all over, they came together, right in the center beneath the shower head.

"Oh, what sybaritic bliss!" Michael exclaimed. "Never have I been soaped down by a beautiful young woman, except my mother, perhaps, though I can't remember how beautiful she was," Michael chuckled. "I do remember that she was always very gentle with me. I loved her light tickly touch. The few times my father took care of me were not nearly as enjoyable." To coax him back to the present and make him put away his childhood memories, Juan placed herself in front of him while the shower head was still raining on them. In quick persistent kisses, she covered his mouth, neck and chest. Michael quickly abandoned his early memories and focused entirely on their moment together, relishing the joy of anticipation.

He let Juan do what she wanted to do. From his chest, her kisses moved downward ever so gently. She knelt down on the shower floor, fondled and kissed his genitals while he felt himself growing to immense size and could hardly contain himself. He drew his beloved up to him then, met her lips in a long passionate kiss, while bracketing her waist with his hands and lifting her slender body up until she could clasp him between her thighs, opening herself up to him. Still kissing passionately, he placed his hands over her delicate hipbones while initiating a slight rocking motion. He felt such sweet tender feelings and yearned for them never to end. But inevitably their motions became more forceful, more passionate as if naturally seeking a final height and resolve. The water was still streaming over Michael's back when he and Juan came to rest breathlessly, clinging together as one being in their mutual bliss. It took a while till they came back to reality. She was still clasping him with her thighs and gazing into his eyes. Then, as though they'd just discovered something astonishing, they broke into a resolving laughter. Carrying Juan, still clasping her thighs around his hips, out of the shower, he set her down on the floor mat. And grabbing the nearest towel, he rubbed her down gently. She relished his touch, his gentle stroking, and let it happen gratefully in a feeling of utter well-being. Afterward she did the same for him. When they sank down onto the bed, still naked, they fell asleep almost immediately.

It seemed hours later when Michael woke up while Juan was still sleeping soundly and peacefully next to him. He had no idea what time it was and he didn't care. Looking at her in the dim light of the dawning day, he recalled events during an earlier part of their relationship. There had been one occasion when it was not clear to him whether their togetherness would last. It was the night he first set foot in the seductive atmosphere of the Blue Moon Nightclub.

It was weeks after he and Juan had met at the Great Wall. At first they dated a number of times, going out to early dinners because she had to start her evening work at seven, or to Sunday brunches. Sometime later they spent Monday and Tuesday nights together which were her nights off. When she confided in him where she worked, he decided to visit the club without letting her know to watch her and to take in the scene. He would watch her at work from a secluded corner. He had not been to this night club before, though he had heard of it in conversations with co-workers. They had smiled knowingly and told him that the Blue Moon was a place that offered a

range of pleasures. They painted an elegant but almost deca-
dent picture.

Entering the nightclub, Michael noticed its plush and elegant furnishings and discreet lighting. He spied Juan immediately among the other beautiful girls. He could not have missed
her. She stood out splendidly. She was dressed more tastefully
than the others, in a slim deep red, very simple silk gown that
reached down to her high-heeled gold sandals but had a slit on
one side of her legs. Her long black hair was braided and grace-
fully pinned up at the top and back of her head with a large
pure white lily decorating the right side of her head just behind
the ear. Her clinging dress revealed the superb lines and shape
of her body. Her makeup was such that her large black almond
eyes and her delicate bright red lips dominated her face. They
floated like islands in the pearly lake of her skin. Watching her
from a distance, he had a hard time reconciling this enchanting
female with his beloved, charming, sensitive, almost girlish-in-
her-laugh Juan. Her transformation into an alluring, siren-like,
desire-arousing female seemed to him almost unbelievable.
Since she appeared so different from the Juan he knew and
loved, he was not surprised that he wasn't jealous initially. It felt
to him as if he were watching a stranger. But as he watched a
hefty grinning businessman trying to thrust his paunch into her
and he saw how artfully she maintained a space between them
as she guided him across the dance floor, he stifled an impulse
to go out onto the floor and cut in. But presently she walked the
man back to his table where two of his associates and one of the
hostesses were sitting. The girl was engaged in a lively conversation with one of the associates who was fondling and kissing
one of her hands. Juan immediately left them and walked back
to her station by the bar. Presently, a remarkably tall, handsome
and well-dressed Western man approached and said a few words
to her with a slight bow. She nodded her head and let him guide
her to the dance floor. Juan and her elegant, imposing dance
partner made a handsome couple. To Michael they seemed to
be engaged in a serious conversation while they glided across
the parquet floor.

Michael tried to detach his feelings for this woman from the role she was playing in the club. For now, she wasn't his Juan. He remembered a scene from Shakespeare's *Troilus and Cressida* he had seen on stage, in which the hero watches as his beloved submits to another man and says, "This is and is not Cressida." So it was for Michael as he thought, *This is and is not my Juan.* He tried to detach himself from this geisha-like person she had become, who was not the same person he came to know and was in love with. His situation called for an Orwellian doublethink, but he had a hard time managing that. He was beginning to feel miserable.

Since Juan did not know that Michael was visiting the Club that night, she was startled to find him there drinking at the bar, where he had been watching her for close to two hours. He sensed that she was embarrassed, though she tried to cover it up and maintained with him momentarily the same formal but friendly manner she had shown with her many admirers that evening as she greeted him. In those moments he wished he hadn't come to spy on her. *Would she be so offended that he would lose her?* This terrible thought crossed his mind. But to his surprise, Juan suddenly changed her manner and let out her trilling laugh that disarmed them both and said in that sweet voice he found so intoxicating, "Oh, Michael, what are you doing here? How come you didn't let me know you were coming? I would have loved to dance with you, of course more pleasurably than with all the other gentlemen. And only you and I would have known why. That would have been thrilling. Don't you think? I might have wondered what the other gentlemen would have thought had they known that all my real favors are bestowed on you. Of course, I'd rather dance with you than with any of these other gentlemen."

She seemed to him to be in a merry, coquettish mood, perhaps brought on by having gotten into her role for the evening. He had noticed how she, whenever she danced with a customer and as she floated in his arms, seemed to give herself to him. Her lovely face was directed up to his, and she seemed all ears and attention as he talked to her intently and she sometimes responded in kind. He knew that many of the men who frequented the club, because it was expensive and exclusive, were well-to-do, well-educated foreigners and many of them could converse in Mandarin. He could now understand that they would be fascinated by Juan, and if they came to know her as he did, saw how bright, cultured, and well-educated, as well as alluring she was, they would be captivated, too. And as he watched her over a period of hours working her magic, he saw how the men lingered to drink and dine for hours, each one having gotten perhaps only 15 minutes of her time but feasting on the sight of her even as she danced with and was fully attentive to other men. At the end of the evening, it was expected of the patrons to leave a gratuity for Juan when they settled their bill with the maître d'. Their gifts to her were generally quite generous.

By the time Juan discovered Michael in the club, it was close to two in the morning, and the club would close shortly. The band was getting ready for the last dance, and Juan begged him to dance with her. Now that she had discovered him, she didn't want to lose him. She knew that several admirers of the evening might still ask her for one more dance. But she just wanted to be with Michael. He did dance with her but was painfully aware that for the moment Juan was someone else—a cool, gorgeous, sophisticated hostess, not the woman he had come to love. Their closeness, their intimacy, was out of place on the dance floor of this opulent setting. He decided there and then that he would not set foot in the club again while Juan was working there. He even began to doubt that she loved him and that she was really his. The thought crossed his mind, *Was it just a fancy of hers to bestow her love on one man when she lent her beauty and her exquisite presence to many men five nights out of every week?*

"You must come more often to the club, Michael," he heard her say. "We can dance now and then during the evening. The rest of the time you can make acquaintances and have good discussions with the patrons you'll get to know. Most of them are interesting worldly and educated men. It would be nice for me to float in your arms several times during the night. It's such a different feeling with you. I feel one with you. The other men don't mean anything to me," she said, obviously trying to reassure him.

He could sense that she meant what she said, but he didn't want to be part of what seemed to him a charade. She wasn't really his during her working hours, and he knew he had to stay away. He didn't want to hurt her feelings. But there was no way he could say 'yes' to her suggestion. Anxious and unwilling to offend her, trying to be tactful, he said, "My sweet Juan," he started somewhat formally and hesitantly, "I'm sorry. Even though you are inviting me, I feel I would be coming back to the club the way I came tonight, just as an onlooker. Do you understand? I just wanted to experience you in your work at least once. I wanted to see what you give to others, how you work your temporary magic. But I would feel out of place as I felt it tonight, to be honest. I don't mind waiting for you until you come back to me after work. I will receive you with open arms because when you come to me, you'll be different. I like to think that when you are with me that's the real you. I don't want to lose sight of that real you. I know this is just a job for you, one that you actually enjoy, because you can play a part as a sophisticated actress would. And you play your part exceedingly well and convincingly. You connect with men as a social being one hundred percent. And when I discovered that, it struck me as an admirable quality because you bestow temporary joy." While he spoke, he watched her face. Her eyes stayed fixed sharply and penetrating in his. He almost felt them mesmerizing him. Her expression was very serious and her posture was straight and erect. He sensed that she didn't like what he said. But he also guessed that she was digesting what he'd said, that she was weighing it carefully and was possibly trying to look at the situation from his point of view. He felt he couldn't say anymore and waited for her to respond. Soon they would part and go to their separate living quarters, and he was fearful that she might be angry and want him to stay away from her. But after a few moments, she responded thoughtfully, choosing her words with care, as he had done.

"My dear Michael, although I won't see you here anymore, I do understand what you're saying. You can't reconcile what I am at night and what I am to you when we're together. Your need is to have exclusivity, and I do understand that you must stay away. From your perspective, to be here at night, would be painful for you and hurt our relationship. I took your words hard at first, but when I put myself into your shoes, I understand, believe me. Maybe it's time for me to find other work. I know my feelings are strong for you. You have a way of making me truly happy when we're together without interference from others. What do you think, Michael?" Her words were an eye opener to him. He saw how sensitive she was. She understood his feelings and accepted them without judgment. And clearly their relationship meant a great deal to her.

"Please, Juan," he said, "Don't do anything rash because of me. Let's continue our relationship and see where it will take us. Let's carry on the way we have. I don't want to restrict you or demand anything from you. You and I need to come seriously together out of our own desire and need, and if we leave it that way, a deeper relationship will happen naturally. Please continue on as you have been doing, I mean in your present job. I know that I love you, and my heart will always be open to you." He stopped talking then because he saw tears welling up in her eyes. She appeared extraordinarily moved.

Presently, she dabbed her eyes with a tissue she pulled out of a hidden pocket in her gown, and responded, "I love you, too, and know that you respect my right to make my own choices. All other men I've known, starting with my father, have felt that they have the right to impose their wills on women. You're not like any man I've met. You don't try to dictate what our relationship will be. You offer me the freedom to make my own decisions about it, and I'm so grateful that you don't try to put any pressure on me. Thank you from my heart. I know what you've said is true. If we are patient and don't change anything by force, time will do its work and will show us the way. So let's leave everything as is for the time being."

She changed then right before his eyes. She suddenly seemed serene, and her face was even more beautiful to him than before. They were standing off to the side of the now empty dance floor and neither of them knew how much time had gone by. Even though there were still some patrons at the bar, most of the guests had left. It was a precarious situation for Juan and Michael. At that moment, Juan saw Zhang Xun, one of the owners of the club, regarding her curiously from the bar across the room. She knew he was a man who believed that he had the right to impose his will on women, including of course any hostess who worked in his club. She would have loved to fall into Michael's arms and kiss him on the lips, but she didn't dare. She was afraid even to touch his hand or arm affectionately while her boss was watching. So she told Michael later. Now, lying beside her in the hotel bed, Michael recalled how she had signaled with her eyes that they were being watched by the man at the bar and how he sensed that it was time for him to leave. Yes, they had come far in their relationship since that night in the Blue Moon. Tonight they had drunk to their future and reaffirmed their commitment.

He placed his hand gently on her arm and heard her sleepy voice, "Darling, you're awake. Have you been awake for awhile? Can't you sleep?"

"I fell asleep at the same time you did. But then I woke up and got caught up in a long reflection that lasted until now," he replied quietly.

"Oh, darling, I hope it was something beautiful you thought about, some experience you cherish more than anything else." She probed delicately.

He hesitated a little. He didn't want to go over that past experience with Juan and answered evasively, "Yes, it was something beautiful, something to be cherished in view of where I find myself today." At the same time he turned on his side and planted a gentle kiss on her cheek. He really didn't want to talk about past happenings. He wanted desperately to make time stop. If only he and Juan could stay where they were, in the present moment. If only they could make the present moment the only reality. The past was past, and the future was unknowable. All that mattered was the present.

Juan turned toward him. She kissed his forehead, slowly and lovingly, his eyelids, which he had already closed, his nose, his cheeks and chin. Then she pressed her naked body against his until she felt him stirring. At that moment, she turned her back to him subtly indicating what she wanted most. He raised himself on his knees while his hands enclosed her hips. He pulled her up to himself into a kneeling position and slowly, almost teasingly—he could sense her impatience in her wiggly motions—inserted himself. He knew it was her favorite position, that it excited her the most. She had told him once shyly and had called it 'her primordial position.' When he applied his fingers' magic, adding to her other sensations, she was transported into ecstasy.

Reaching their climax almost simultaneously, they both collapsed face down. Michael rolled off, turned her delicate body toward him, and took her into his arms. Sound dreamless sleep followed quickly for both of them.

It wasn't until his tiny alarm clock rattled next to him that they both jumped off the bed. They were confused at first, having slept so deeply. Michael was hoping that he had set the clock right and he wasn't even certain that he had set it after their delightful frolic in the shower. But as he squinted at the clock he saw that it was 7:30 in the morning. They had exactly forty-five minutes to shower, get ready and eat breakfast downstairs before they had to run to the bus station. Michael was about to tell Juan that they had to hurry, but she had already left the bed and was in the shower. He was surprised that she was way ahead of him.

* * *

The bus was already filling up as they ran toward it. They were in the best of moods, especially Michael, for he would get to see for the first time another one of China's great historical wonders. They both laughed at each other, like youngsters, as they flung themselves down into their seats while holding hands. When they were seated, he pressed her delicate hand so forcefully that she wailed in pain. "Darling, you are breaking my hand. It hurts terribly. Don't ever forget how strong you are," she protested.

"Oh my sweetheart, forgive me. I didn't know what I was doing." He gently lifted her hand to his lips as if he intended to mend it with his soft kiss.

Michael then realized that he should be alert and look at the landscape as they headed toward the Longmen Caves. He was lucky that he had been able to grab a window seat for himself. Even though he had offered it to Juan, she insisted that he take it because she had already viewed the scenery.

As he was taking in the scenery, he felt Juan gently tapping his arm. When he turned to her she said, "Darling, the site of the Longmen Caves is quite vast, intricate and very important in what it represents for Buddhism in China. One can get quite confused when one visits the site for the first time. Visitors don't know where to start. The carving art that was going on in these myriads of caves and grottos was abruptly halted in the mid eighth century when thousands of Buddhist sculptures and temples all over China were destroyed by the followers of Confucianism and Daoism. Although Buddhist art and religion continued to be practiced, they never again reached the height they enjoyed during the Tang Dynasty. I think I told you that the Longmen Cave art was created by artists of the Wei, Sui, and Tang Dynasties; and since the art was practiced over 400 years, the earlier and later arts are markedly different. We'll start with the great Fengxian Temple Cave. It exemplifies Tang art, and its centerpiece is a striking 17 meter high Buddha, Bodhisattvas, a celestial guardian, and defenders of Buddha. As you will recognize, when you see the arts of the early to the late periods, the figures over time became more three-dimensional. The Fengxian Temple Cave is the most glorious of the late three-dimensional art. The carved statues stand out in high relief as if freed from their limestone cliff backdrop." Juan stopped, for she thought that she had perhaps given him too much information.

But Michael responded, "Thank you, sweetheart. As always, you have so much information at your fingertips, and you've given me just enough to whet my appetite for more."

"It's my pleasure to share with you what I know. Your interest pleases me. The carvings in this cave were done over a period of three years in the latter part of the seventh century A.D. When we get there you can ask me about what interests you in particular. I'd like to hear from you what exactly you want to know and where your interest lies," she said, making it clear that whatever mattered to him concerned her as well.

He smiled at her. "You're very thoughtful, and I know that you can give me all the information I want."

In another 10 minutes, their bus pulled into a large lot on the west bank of the Yi River that was lined at this point on both sides with high limestone cliffs and caves. The passengers climbed out and went in different directions, some in groups with tour guides, others sightseeing on their own like Juan and Michael. Most of them stood for awhile in the parking lot orienting themselves according to their detailed maps they had purchased, but Juan took Michael's hand and walked him directly to the monumental Fengxian Temple Cave. He was almost overwhelmed as he stood facing the giant statues, lined up against the back limestone wall of what seemed to him more like an enormous grotto than a cave, with the 17 meter or 55 foot high Buddha at its center. The sightseers along the stone walls at the foot of the statues looked to him like Lilliputians in the land of the giants.

Michael became quite emotional beholding the prodigious, almost unearthly art in front of him, while Juan stood beside him reverently and in silence as if in prayer. "Oh my god!" Michael suddenly cried out, "It's really overwhelming! What magnificent creations! What grand achievement! I'm amazed how individualized these statues are, each one with different features and different facial expressions. Too bad that the effects of weathering on some of them couldn't have been staved off. I've never seen anything like it. This is such a mysterious, timeless, mystical and hallowed place. I strongly feel it. They must have been visionaries whoever created these works of art. I wonder whether the Tang emperors envisioned these figures or whether they represent the visions of the artists who created these overpowering representatives of Buddhism. I wonder if these statues were perhaps modeled on living persons of the time."

All the while Michael was uttering his effusive outbursts of admiration, Juan stood very still and seemed to be in a meditative state. When he finished expressing his wonder and appreciation, she said, "I don't know whether all of the statues carry the likeness of individuals who lived at the time. I only know that the face of the giant Buddha was allegedly modeled on the face of Empress Wu of the Tang dynasty. She funded the carving of this statue."

"Who? Empress Wu? I never heard of her before. Can you tell me about her? I'm interested in powerful women who made history and have read about a number of them—Catherine the Great, Queen Nefertiti, Queen Elizabeth I, and Golda Meier among others."

Michael's response pleased Juan, who was happy to share what she knew about a remarkable woman who had shaped Chinese dynastic history. "Empress Wu," she began eagerly, "is a most interesting historical figure because she was the only woman who ruled China in her own name. Even though she was part of the Tang dynasty, during her rule she tried to establish a new Zhou Dynasty which failed. By the way, the historical Zhou Dynasty was a much older one then the Tang Dynasty but a great one. Eventually, when her Tang relatives took over the throne after Wu's death, they resumed the Tang Dynasty for another 200 years. Empress Wu only ruled for 15 years from 690 to 705 A.D. She was hated by many Confucian historians. They maligned her. They thought of her as an aberration. According to them her rule went against the natural order of male rule. It was not until the 20th Century that historians reassessed her reign. They recognized that she introduced many useful innovations and successfully defended the country's borders. They found that as far as rulers of that time were concerned, she did as well as any man."

Nodding vigorously, Michael interrupted Juan and remarked, "I'm glad she did 'as well as any man' in ruling China and was rehabilitated by modern historians. I'm glad for their honesty. But still, also many ancient western historians had biases that shaped their accounts. When it comes to having a sexist bias, you can't find anybody worse than Aristotle, who said that women lack the deliberative faculty. He actually wasn't an historian, but he represented a common mindset. I'm impressed that your modern historians aren't hampered by sexist biases, and I think we've come a long way in appreciating women's abilities to rule successfully."

"I agree with you. I'm happy to hear that you can appreciate that. But let me tell you about her background and how she worked herself into a ruling position. It's not always a pleasant picture because she could be ruthless in attaining her goals. She came from a fine family, was intelligent, beautiful and well educated. She was also very manipulative and determined. She had to be because she started as the emperor's first concubine at age 14. Over the years, Concubine Wu became wise in the ways of the court. After the emperor's death, she disregarded the court's expectations and instead of retiring to a nunnery, she became a second-rank concubine to the next emperor and bore him two sons, his first male children. That gave her more influence at court, and she also became even more determined to gain power by whatever means were necessary. When her next child, an infant daughter, died, Wu had the empress accused of the baby's murder and was instrumental in having her deposed. When Wu was elevated by the emperor to be his empress, she had the former empress and the former first concubine killed. That left Wu with no female rival."

"Oh, how ruthless she was," Michael suddenly interrupted. "But then it's nothing new. It happened in Europe, too. Queen Elizabeth I of England kept her rival Mary, Queen of Scotland, imprisoned and then had her beheaded."

"I don't know her story, but it's interesting. I suppose it happened all over the world," Juan replied. "But I want to tell you just a little more about Empress Wu. Hers is really a long story. When the emperor died, the reins of power were supposed to be taken over by one of his and Wu's sons. Through Wu's machinations, the new emperor, her third son, Li Xian, was eventually replaced. Wu didn't like him as a ruler because he showed an independent mind and was also greatly influenced by his empress. Wu's fourth son, Li Dan, was subsequently made emperor. He was quite young and greatly influenced by his mother. Eventually Wu persuaded him to abdicate in her favor. She then took the throne herself as full-fledged emperor. Wu favored Buddhism over Daoism. She encouraged Buddhist culture, scholarship and art. She had the largest statues carved in the Longmen Caves. And it is believed that the massive, 17 meter Buddha statue carries the features of her face."

All the while Juan was discoursing on Wu, Michael was studying the face of the huge Buddha statue. "Your account of her is fascinating, and I'm trying to detect feminine features in the statue's face. To tell you the truth, I'm not doing that well. To me the face could be masculine or feminine."

"Yes, I agree with you, darling. "It's an androgynous face. But perhaps I've become carried away. Am I telling you more than you want to know, or do you want me to go on?"

"No, sweetheart, I found it fascinating. It's certainly a remarkable part of dynastic history. But I'm wondering now how Empress Wu ended up? What happened to her? Please, tell me the ending."

"As you wish," Juan responded. "Wu's announcement that she was founding a new Zhou Dynasty when she began to reign, to bring back an old illustrious dynasty, did not sit well with the court. Eventually, as her powers eroded, she elevated her son, Li Xian, whom she had years earlier deposed, as her successor and made him crown prince. So he became the legitimate successor to the throne. In a subsequent palace coup, Empress Wu was forced to abdicate and Li Xian became emperor. As a special acknowledgement, Wu was then given the title 'Zetian' which means 'Supreme Empress.' The name, Wu Zetian, is the one she is best known by in the dynastic history. She died in the same year in which she was elevated to Supreme Empress, at the age of 82."

Juan seemed ready to take a break, and after a short pause, she said, "That's it, darling." She seemed exhausted and had nothing more to say. Michael was grateful for all that she had shared and said, "That was more than I could ask for. But I'm curious about the two large statues on the right hand side of the cave. They seem quite different. Their facial expressions are not as serene as those of the Buddha and his disciples. Also their garments seem different. They don't look like robes."

"I'm glad you noticed them. Good observation. They are supposed to represent Guardian Kings of Buddhism."

"Ah, that's very interesting. I had no idea there were such figures."

"So, are you ready to move on, darling? I want to take you now to the finest examples of the Northern Wei carving style, in other words, the early carving style. It can be seen in the Central Pingyang cave, which contains eleven large Buddha statues, not as large as the one we are standing in front of, as well as smaller figures of the Buddha and his disciples. The figures have elongated features. They are not as natural as those of the Tang statues. And the style of the figures is rather two-dimensional."

"I had no idea there were such figures. So we'll be able to see these different styles back to back. Yes, I'm ready to move on." He was truly eager to see more cave art.

"After that I want to show you some of the very earliest cave art that was begun in the very late fifth century A.D., also by the Northern Wei dynasty. You will see rock paintings and bas-relief wall carvings that show beautiful flying apsaras. They're believed to be celestial beings, much like Christian angels. They were supposed to carry newborn babies who died into paradise. They are sometimes also depicted as musicians, flower or incense bearers."

"That's very interesting. So, similar to Christians, who like to believe that they're looked after by angels, Buddhists have had the same need to be attended by celestial beings. I have never heard of them before. Besides the Buddha, his disciples and the Bodhisattvas, I haven't seen or heard of any other significant, divine beings in the realm of Buddhism."

"Well, I don't really know myself. Possibly over centuries and perhaps over a thousand years, religions become more purified, less mythological. We can only gather from what we are seeing here in these caves that at some time in the past people believed in these strange intermediary beings."

"So it would seem. Let's move on to some of the other caves. The magnificent Fengxian Cave, grotto, or temple, whatever you want to name it, we saw first, was certainly deserving of the time we gave it. It must be the showcase of this splendid art complex."

* * *

It wasn't until the early afternoon that Michael and Juan returned to their hotel. They had eaten some small snacks they purchased from one of the vendors at the Longmen Caves. When they entered their cool, air-conditioned room, they realized how hot, sweaty and exhausted they were. But Michael was particularly thrilled because of what he had seen and experienced on their historical outing. He couldn't believe how extensive and filled with precious art these limestone caves, walls and grottos were. He felt grateful that Juan had put Longmen on their itinerary.

They both took showers and subsequently crashed on their comfortable bed, falling asleep immediately. Perhaps two hours passed, and they were jolted out of their deep sleeps by a ringing telephone. Neither Michael nor Juan knew precisely how much time had gone by since they had fallen asleep. It seemed dark outside. It was Juan who jumped out of bed rather quickly and started rummaging in her handbag. She fished out her mobile phone, pressed the on-button and disappeared into the bathroom. Michael thought, *Who in the world would be calling her here? Someone has her phone number.* Then he remembered that she had changed her number some time before they left Beijing. Hardly anyone would have her new number. *So maybe it's one of her family members, possibly her mother*, he thought. *It must be her mother*, he told himself. *Maybe she thinks Juan is still in Beijing. Maybe she doesn't know that she is in flight from danger. Maybe she knows nothing and just wants to know how her daughter is doing. After all, in her mother's mind Juan lives in the huge capital, far removed from Nanjing, her hometown. But perhaps it wasn't her mother. Who else could it be? Had she left her number with someone else?* He wanted to believe that she didn't keep things from him. He had made her promise that she wouldn't. *Surely there is no reason to be suspicious*, he told himself. *Juan will presently clear up the mystery of the phone call when she steps out of the bathroom.* He decided not to think of it anymore, just relax and wait for her to come back.

When she came into the bedroom, her face revealed that she was tense and anxious about something. Her brows were knit, and her mouth was tightly set. But then she smiled and said to him, "It was my mother, darling. She was just checking up on me. She does that periodically. She also likes to tell me what is going on in the family business and with the family. I'm sorry it took a little while until she was through with her newsy stuff. Everything seems to be fine, nothing to be concerned about." While she was talking to Michael, her features relaxed. As soon as she stopped talking, she raced over to the bed and threw herself down next to Michael and embraced him tightly.

"Darling," she whispered in his ear, "I'm so glad to be with you. It's fun to be on this journey. It's only now as I'm telling you daily about the historical background of the sites we're visiting that I realize how much of Chinese history I still remember. I guess it will always stay with me. I used to love learning about it, and it makes me feel good that you have such a great interest in it, too," she ended happily.

"Yes, I have a great deal of interest in your country's history, but not as much as I have in you. You are very special to me, and I want to marry you as soon as we get to my country if you'll have me. Will you?"

She looked at him in amazement, wide-eyed and seeming to wonder if she'd really heard what he'd said. After pausing a moment to choose her words, she replied, "Darling, I feel honored, but also almost blown away by what you've just proposed. We haven't known each other very long. You know that I love you, but marriage is a lifetime commitment. I think you're very honorable in letting me know that you want to marry me. But I beg you to wait until we get this flight from danger behind us. We need to deal with reality—the fact that your life has been threatened because of me and possibly my life is threatened as well. We've become engrossed in seeing a lot of historical sights and imagining the past, but we can't forget the present, the fact that we're in danger. We should've probably gone straight to Guangzhou to get truly away from whatever is pursuing us. Maybe when we get to your country and are safe it will happen. That is, if you still want me then. I do love you, Michael, and being your bride would be wonderful." She was sitting up in bed next to him as she revealed her thoughts to him. When she was done speaking, she bent down to him and sealed her statement with a passionate kiss.

Presently, Michael was able to free himself and replied with great seriousness, "Sweetheart, I said these things and made the proposal now because I want you to know that my intentions are honorable. I'm not just using you. When you leave your country and come with me across the sea, I will not abandon you. I want us to be together. I mean what I say. Please believe me."

"I believe you. In fact, I know this about you: you're the most honorable man I have ever met. All I'm asking is for you to wait until we're safe. I want the same future for us as you do. That's all I can say for now. Please forgive me if I'm not saying enough." Juan had gotten so emotional that she was now almost in tears.

"Lie down here with me. Nestle yourself close to me, and let's lie here in peace. I'm sorry that I got you upset. I won't press you anymore. I think our escape must be more of a strain on you than it is on me. You're contemplating giving up your culture, your secure surroundings, a place where you feel you can make it even if you were to go it alone. When you come with me, there will be cultural barriers as well as language barriers and a certain sense of dependency that you have fought so hard to get yourself unshackled from. Sweetheart, I just want to let you know that I understand and that I don't feel rejected. It's just my love for you that makes me seem controlling at times, and perhaps not as sensitive to your needs and feelings as I should be."

"Oh, darling, you are so sensitive and supportive. I'm so happy to continue this journey with you, and I wish it could go on forever."

They stayed in their comforting nestled position—neither of them wanting to say anymore—until they dropped off to sleep again.

* * *

When Michael woke up out of a disturbing dream, he didn't know how much time had elapsed since they both fell asleep. Since Juan was still sleeping soundly, he stayed very still next to her. Now in his waking state, he made an effort to recall the dream he had just come out of. In it he had seen a beautiful young woman. She was colorfully dressed, slender and with her long black hair trailing behind her in the wind. He decided to follow her, to catch up with her and meet her perhaps. She was walking incredibly fast as if she could sense that she was being pursued. He had a hard time making himself go at a walk just a smidgen faster than her pace to catch up. But he thought, *Even if it will take a long time, I'll catch her eventually.* Her trim waist and fine symmetry drew him on like a panting hound. He realized clearly that there was nothing else he wanted to connect with more than this enticing woman. Life for him had taken on a timeless quality, and he felt that he wouldn't mind if it took his lifetime to meet up with this object of desire. Sometimes he thought he was close to catching her; other times she seemed further away than at the beginning of the pursuit. Soon he became utterly obsessed. He promised himself that when he caught up with her he would give himself fully to her. He would do his utmost to make her understand his devotion to her. He didn't think twice whether it would be a good thing for him to give himself away before he even met the goddess of his dream. The pursuit and the attainment of his goal to possess her meant everything to him. He had already told himself that his life, his former pursuits, his friends, his family meant nothing to him anymore since he spied this irresistible siren.

Uta Christensen

It was a lengthy and arduous pursuit. He was becoming hot and exhausted. Yet he carried on as before. He didn't know anymore where he was. The part of the city he had reached in his pursuit seemed very strange to him. The houses became smaller and shabbier, and, suddenly, he could see the end of the paved street he was on. In the distance there was a dense forest of tall trees. He got worried that he might lose her if they entered the forest, so he began to jog. He couldn't believe that he hadn't thought of jogging before. He would have caught her so much sooner. There was no way she could jog with her high heels.

While considering what he might do if he caught up with her, and jogging along at a fast clip with his shoes making a terrible clapping sound with each step, he suddenly saw his dream woman cross the street and start to veer off into the last side street before they reached the forest. It was at this point that she turned her head and paused as if she wanted to identify who was following her and what the distance was between herself and her pursuer. She also seemed to want to show herself and to see what his reaction would be. She had enticed many men to follow her. All had pursued her, but none had come as close as this one. When he realized what was happening, that the beautiful figure was going to reveal herself, he stood less than 20 feet from her and saw her clearly. She still had her long flowing black hair, but the rest of her front was downright ugly. Her sheer slim dress was faded and bleached out. The colors that seemed so vivid had disappeared. Her front seemed flat and bony. But the worst features were her neck and face. They were deeply wrinkled, the skin mottled, and her face terribly scrawny. She could be 80 years old or more, he thought. He was absolutely appalled by his stupidity, his nearsightedness and his being so easily roped into this charade. How could he have pursued such an old ugly hag? How could he have been feverishly on her heels without realizing what he might be pursuing? Fear suddenly overcame him because he was afraid that her power of attraction might still, even now, as they connected, overpower him.

At that point in the dream, Michael had woken up, bathed in perspiration. He couldn't believe he would have a dream like

102

this when his life, even though it had veered off track in Beijing, had come to be this wonderful, life-transforming experience. Seeing Juan next to him still soundly asleep and so pure and beautiful to behold, he couldn't imagine that there was any connection between her and the vision of his fear-inspiring dream. But what might his deep unconscious be trying to tell him? In his waking state he couldn't see any connection. But he couldn't rid himself of some weird uncomfortable feeling that he feared to ponder at this point. He was relieved when he noticed Juan's stirring and when she opened her eyes.

"Sweetheart, you have been sleeping long and soundly. I was beginning to feel lonely. How I love to look into your eyes. Have you had any strange dreams that you can tell me about?" he questioned her anxiously.

"No, no dreams," she responded sleepily.

He then bent down and kissed her long and passionately. She didn't respond in kind but let it happen. When he embraced her body tightly with both arms, she felt limp to him as a rag doll. *She's playing with me*, he thought. He guessed that she wanted him to stimulate her, to stir up her passion and to persist until she would reciprocate. Strangely enough her lifelessness did stir his passion. *This must be what a necrophiliac feels,* he thought. He got up off the bed, pulled Juan toward him, lifted her up and carried her to an upholstered stool across the room. As he sat down, he tried to draw her to himself and onto his lap. She then suddenly opened her legs, mounted his lap and let him slip into her while her bare breasts brushed against his naked chest and her mouth sought his in a wild exuberant kiss. Excitement flooded his body because she had truly come alive, after being limp and unresponsive. Juan rocked back and forth on his lap, her upper torso and her upward stretched arms swaying rhythmically from side to side while he held her with both hands securely around her waist. That's when his thinking stopped and he became one with her and they reached a simultaneous climax. They sat on the stool entwined for a long time with her head resting on his shoulder. Time stood still.

It was Michael who spoke first, tenderly, "Sweetheart, how I love your passion. It's so hard for me to break the spell, but it's dark outside now. Shouldn't we go and eat somewhere? I've no idea what time it is. The dining room may already be closed. Let's clean up, get dressed and let's see what we can find." He tried to maintain the warmth of the moment even as he made her think about their need for sustenance.

Reluctant to move, Juan moaned and lifted herself slowly off his lap.

* * *

It was nearly 10 at night by then. The hotel dining room was closed, and the large reception desk virtually deserted with only one clerk on duty. As Michael and Juan went out the hotel entrance, the cool night air invigorated them. They practically flew down the steps and started running down the boulevard into the city center. They were both in a heightened mood, laughing as they ran.

"I know a good restaurant," Juan suddenly cried out. Michael was glad to hear that her appetite was working.

"Very good, because I'm hungry," he answered.

"Let's hope it's still open. It's iffy at this time of the evening. It depends how many customers they still have."

But they were lucky and were quickly seated in a restaurant that appealed to Michael. It was very Chinese in its décor with red lanterns hanging from the ceiling. Also, the food smelled appetizing.

They were served quickly. At Michael's request, Juan took on the ordering. When she tried to give him the menu, he said, "I totally trust you, sweetheart. Order anything you like. I know I'll love whatever it is."

While they were eating their Peking duck, Juan said unexpectedly, "Darling, there is one very interesting historical site in the vicinity of Luoyang that I'd very much love for you to see. It's called the Shoalin Monastery or Shoalin Temple. Do you know Gongfu?"

"Yes, I've heard of it, but I don't know much about it. Isn't it China's most famous martial art?" Michael asked curiously and added, "How far is this Shoalin Monastery from Luoyang?"

"About 50 kilometers—and we could go there by bus if you're interested. Let me give you a few historical tidbits, and then you can tell me how interested you are. I'm sure we could grab a bus from here tomorrow morning."

"Sure, go right ahead. I'm somewhat interested. It depends how much you can entice me and how much time we want to spend in this area. We still have to go and see X'ian. Which is more important—our seeing absolutely everything we can or speeding up our journey to Guangzhou?"

"You're absolutely right, darling. We need to set priorities. But let me just quickly tell you a few interesting historical facts and a bit of legend about the monastery and its surroundings," Juan offered.

"I'm ready. I'm all ears," Michael quickly replied and prepared himself to hear another informative discourse.

"What I'm going to tell you is actually more legend than based on historical facts. The Shoalin Temple was supposed to have been founded in the fifth century A.D. by a monk who migrated to China from India. Some time later another Indian monk by the name of Bodhidharma arrived. He was turned away at the entrance to the temple. So he climbed nearby Wuru mountain instead, found a cave, and to calm his mind, he sat and meditated there for nine years. He eventually gained access to the temple, and Bodhidharma gathered disciples around him who, to achieve relief between long periods of meditation, started imitating the movements of animals and birds. These movements evolved over time into physical combat routines with a spiritual component, then called Shoalin Boxing. Today the Shoalin Monastery or Temple is a busy tourist haven. In the past, because of the monks' involvement in uprisings and even wars—always, their supporters argued, in righteous causes—it is said, their monastery was a frequent target of attack. It was last set on fire in 1928 but was later reconstructed at least in part. There is one famous hall, the Pilu Pavilion, where the monks, practicing gongfu, placed their feet every day in the same places. Over the centuries these same foot stances left deep depressions in the stone floor which are still clearly visible today. Nowadays, inspired by the gongfu tradition, there are a number of martial arts schools near the monastery, but little true gongfu is practiced there because it requires many years of patient and very taxing physical discipline along with mental exercises and spiritual studies. So there you have the legend and the facts.

Michael was thinking and didn't answer immediately, but then he said, "It all sounds very interesting, sweetheart, but I think we should skip the Shoalin Monastery." For some reason, he couldn't stop thinking about the disturbing phone call and sensed that they ought to resume their journey without delay. He said, "I feel strongly that we need to move on."

"Oh, wait. I forgot to tell you about a couple of interesting historical features surrounding the Shoalin Monastery. Near its entrance is an ancient cemetery that contains the ashes of famous abbots and eminent monks. It's very unusual and it's not called a cemetery but the Pagoda Forest. There are close to 250 stone pagodas one can walk among. They function as gravestones. Some of them are in a bad state of neglect and some have collapsed over the centuries. It's an eerie feeling to walk through this graveyard. Those little pagodas are much taller than a person and are a bit overwhelming, especially since they are built very close together. Another historical landmark nearby is Wuru Mountain. Up there, at the end of a hiking trail, is the cave where Bodhidharma was supposed to have meditated for nine years." Juan paused for a few seconds before she said, "I'm definitely finished with my storytelling. What do you think now?"

"As I said before, I find all of this fascinating, but I think we should stick to our itinerary. After all, we're on the run. If we were on a leisurely journey of discovery, I would say immediately, 'Let's go.' But I'll think about the detour some more."

"OK, darling, I agree with you that we must not forget we're fleeing from a real threat. Let's talk about it some more in the morning."

At that moment the waiter appeared to remove their empty dishes. He had waited patiently until he noticed the pause in Juan's animated talk and Michael's short replies. He was sensitive enough not to disturb the couple. Here was his chance to collect their plates and to hand Juan the dessert menu. With the menu held in front of her, she waved her hand in a negative gesture and asked for the bill. But then she hesitated and addressed the waiter, "Wait a second, please," and he stood at attention while Juan looked at Michael.

"I'm sorry, darling. I forgot to ask you whether you want dessert. I thought only of myself. I'm sorry. Do you want to order one for yourself? Here is the menu."

"No, no. I'm very satisfied, too. It was a big delicious meal."

Turning to the waiter, Juan told him, "No, thank you, that's it. Please bring the check." The waiter bowed deeply and left.

10

Xi'an

After they returned from the restaurant and were just entering their hotel room, the faint ring of Juan's cell phone sounded. She rummaged through her purse and went into the bathroom. As soon as she closed the bathroom door, Michael looked at his watch. It was half past eleven in the evening. He was puzzled at first, wondering, W*ho could this be? Of course, I'm wondering who the caller is, but I shouldn't pry. If it's her mother, why can't she call earlier in the evening? But then she might have tried a little earlier when we were out to find a restaurant,* he thought. *But who else could it be?* Then it crossed his mind that Juan must have close friends in Beijing that he didn't know about. He remembered how agitated she looked after the last call, and he wondered if she would look that way again. Of course, her calls were her business, but he couldn't help wondering who this caller might be.

It didn't take long until Juan came back into the bedroom. Her cheeks were flushed. She didn't exactly look happy.

"Who would call you so late at night? Isn't that insensitive? Or did you expect that call?" Michael asked curiously. *I'm prying too much,* he thought. *I'm too interested in her calls. That might annoy her,* he told himself. *Ah, she must have friends and acquaintances who like to keep in touch with her.*

Juan seemed to have some difficulty in composing herself, but presently she explained, sounding a little annoyed now as she replied, "Oh, it was just my mother again. I asked her not to call so late because I might be asleep. She said she would try to avoid doing this. I think she feels lonely or abandoned. I feel sorry for her and I love her. But this time I kept it short. And besides, she actually had very little to tell me. Nothing of importance. Maybe she just wanted to hear my voice again. I soon excused myself and told her I was tired. I asked her to call me at a better hour next time."

Michael listened very attentively to what Juan was telling him. He couldn't detect any deception in it. She had ended speaking very calmly and without any hesitation. *If it's always her mother, I can live with that,* he told himself. *I hope that's all it is.* But then he immediately thought, *Why is there always this slight nagging suspicion in the back of my mind that there may be some duplicity involved? How well do I really know Juan?* But again he told himself, *Michael stop it. There shouldn't be any reason to distrust her. So far she has been devoted, caring, loving, upbeat, sensitive, and obviously excited about our being together and our current adventure.*

He didn't reply immediately, and Juan was puzzled by his silence. "What are you thinking about, darling?" she asked him. "You seem miles away and your wheels seem to be turning awfully fast. Is anything the matter? Do you not like my mother to call me periodically?" Juan asked, regarding him quizzically.

"Oh, nothing is the matter. I think I'm tired and want to go to bed now. I just thought this call came too late at night. But you've told your mother to call earlier. So everything is fine," he said, walking over to her and kissing her gently on her forehead.

But their gay upbeat mood was gone. Michael reprimanded himself later, as he was lying very still in the darkness of the room, for letting dark disturbing thoughts intrude and dampen their spirits. He promised himself not to let it happen again over something that was simply nothing.

They undressed and each took a shower. Then they slipped into bed together. Michael was very gentle with Juan that night. Something always pulled on his heartstrings when he was near her. He frequently thought about how difficult her childhood had been. He needed to help her overcome any residual emotional pain that stemmed from an earlier time. Tonight he was careful not to make any demands, not to try to stir up the passion between them. After working through his thoughts and feelings he became very calm and tried to transfer the peace he was feeling to his beloved next to him. He held her left hand and pressed it softly off and on, until sleep carried Juan off before it came to him.

In the middle of the night, Michael woke up, and, as so often happened lately, he couldn't go back to sleep. He recalled what Juan had told him about the Shoalin Monastery and the myth that surrounded Bodhidharma, who was thought to have brought Buddhism to China. He considered again whether or not they should make the detour. What he had heard was interesting, but some inner voice had prompted him not to veer off the course they had set for themselves, and came again to the conclusion that the decision he had made in the restaurant was the right one. *Who knows how many other diversions may come up,* he thought. We need to stick with the itinerary.

In the morning, Juan was not surprised when Michael told her what he'd decided while she was asleep. But in her view it would have been fine to catch the late afternoon train to Xi'an instead of the earlier one. They would have had time in the morning and through the noon hour for at least a short visit to Shoalin. She thought it would have been interesting for him. She knew he had dabbled with aikido and tai chi, so she understood that he was interested in Chinese martial arts. He had also told her how many martial arts schools in the U.S. claimed to be connected with the Shoalin Temple or Monastery. But then it was his decision, and she accepted it without argument. She wanted to avoid any friction.

"That's perfectly fine with me, darling," she said. "I've been to Shoalin and did and saw just about everything a tourist would do and see. I just wanted to go there for you. As it now stands, we are booked on the 10 a.m. train. So we'll have enough time to get our hotel breakfast. I'll go and have my shower right now. Is that OK with you?"

"Of course it's OK," Michael replied, and got up. "But before you slip into the bathroom, I'd like you to come here to me for a moment," he beckoned.

When she stood in front of him, he said in a soft voice, "I just want to wish you a good morning with a kiss and a hug." Smiling in response, she stepped into his arms. He held her tight and pressed his face against hers as if he were intent on not letting her go. "Sweetheart," he whispered, "I'm always so glad when I wake up and see you next to me. I can hardly imagine what life would be without your company. Just to be with you brings me joy and comfort. I couldn't bear to lose you." But even as he said this, he couldn't help but remember the recent phone calls and wondered who the caller might be, if not her mother. Intent on ridding himself of troubling thoughts, he kissed Juan long and tenderly.

When he released her, she said laughingly, "I'm surprised at you even thinking you could lose me. You should stop that. What we have is something very special. Don't you know that?" Hearing her say that made his spirits soar and he smiled at her. "You go and have your shower. I love you very much."

* * *

Everything clicked into place perfectly—their packing, their breakfast, their hotel checkout and their short walk to the train station. Theirs was again a private compartment for the little more than two-hour ride to Xi'an. Juan had already decided that she would give Michael an introduction about the historical background of Xi'an and that she would, if it was agreeable, take him on a city walking tour in the afternoon. She was hoping that they could find a hotel rather quickly on their arrival. Juan had an idea where they could stay but hadn't had time on their last day in Beijing to make a reservation. She thought at the time that they could take a chance and go without one.

As they sat in their soft comfortable sleeper compartment, Juan asked him if he wanted to hear about historical Xi'an and the Terracotta Warriors. Of course, Michael liked the idea. Her discourses had prepared him well for his first-time visits to historical sites. They had made these visits more exciting, meaningful and vivid.

111

"I'd love you to give me an introduction. I know I'll get so much more out of my sightseeing when I've been prepared by you." She sensed that he was sincere and was gratified that he was so appreciative. Immediately she assumed her role as tour guide.

"Xi'an is a big gem in China's history," she began. "Long before Beijing became the center of China's imperial power, there was the city of Chang'an that's now present-day Xi'an. It was once thought to have been the largest city in the world, one of imperial splendor. It was the seat of a number of dynasties. In this city mingled emperors, concubines, courtiers, musicians, merchants and soldiers among others, and many of the world's great religions existed there side by side. At the time, Chinese culture reached a great height of creativity. What contributed to the creativity was that Chang'an happened to be situated at the end of the Silk Road that connected Europe, the Middle East and the Far East through active trade and commerce. Today it is known that the city had frequent contacts with foreigners, even in its early history, because of the figurines of bearded horsemen found in the ancient imperial tombs. Camel caravans unloaded their goods in Chang'an from far-flung places and carried back Chinese goods that influenced the then known world, like gunpowder and silk. But Chang'an, like all great influential centers, came to an end in the 10th century A.D. It was destroyed in rebellions that ended the Tang Dynasty. The reason why today the whole world knows of fabled Chang'an, today's Xi'an, is through the 1970 discovery of the Qin Emperor Shi Huangdi's extraordinary burial site. By the way, Shi Huangdi reigned a long time ago, in the third century B.C. I think it's safe to say that Xi'an, because of that emperor, has become today's most popular tourist destination in China." Juan paused here for a few seconds as if she were collecting her thoughts. But soon she began again. She knew that Michael, always an attentive listener, wouldn't interrupt her.

"Now that I'm thinking about it, I don't want to talk about the Terracotta Warriors burial site until tomorrow morning. There are important historical objects in Xi'an itself. By the way, today's Xi'an is the capital of Shaanxi Province and has a population of 2.5 million. It's a major inland center of industry and somewhat rivals traditional east coast industrial cities like Shanghai. To the north and west, Xi'an is bordered by the Wei River and the rugged Western Hills that are dotted with ancient tombs. The region south of the Wei is fine fertile agricultural land. Does all of this interest you?" Juan suddenly asked because she was always a little worried that Michael might get bored.

"It's fascinating. Just carry on. I am very interested," he assured her warmly.

"So then here are a few facts about the historical features of Xi'an. When the remains of a Neolithic village were found near Xi'an at Banpo, archeologists realized that the area may have been inhabited as early as 8,000 years ago, and this village may have been occupied between 4500 to 3500 B.C. It is also believed that a matriarchal culture existed in the area because female clay figurines with voluptuous bodies, big breasts and obviously pregnant were unearthed there. These figurines may point to goddess worship, which makes sense because the fertility of the land was the most important element sustaining ancient life. Excavations also uncovered remains of houses and other buildings, storage cellars, a few pottery kilns and a large number of graves. You and I could tour this Neolithic village this afternoon as part of our city walk if you like. It's just a short electric trolley car ride from Xi'an."

"Yes, I would be very interested, but carry on," Michael responded.

"Imagine, today's Xi'an, or ancient Chang'an, goes back to the Western Zhou Dynasty that reigned between 1066 and 221 B.C. When the Qin Emperor Shi Huangdi—the one who is famous for his Terracotta Warriors—took over the reigns from the Zhou in 221 B.C, he built his capital a short distance to the east of Xi'an at Xiangyang. However, his magnificent palace, which was never finished, stood within the perimeters of today's Xi'an. Chang'an or Xi'an didn't decline until the 10th century, coinciding with the demise of the Tang Dynasty you got to know

through Empress Wu and the exquisite late Longmen Cave art."
Juan paused again and questioningly looked at Michael.

He was still listening attentively and said, "Carry on, sweet-heart. I'm very interested."

She happily continued, "I have only a little more to tell you about the sights we'll see this afternoon inside and outside Xi'an's old city wall if you're interested. There is the famous Bell Tower that used to ring its large bell at dawn—and the Drum Tower. Its drums were used to mark nightfall. Both towers date from the 14th century. Also China's largest mosque is situated within the city wall. It has fascinating architecture and gardens. The mosque itself is an interesting combination of Chinese and Islamic styles. Outside the city wall, which was built in the 14th century during the Ming Dynasty, are the famous Big Goose and the Little Goose Pagodas. By the way, the city wall, which is ringed by a moat, is quite massive. You'll hear more about it when we walk it later on." Juan now paused again to give herself a needed break, while Michael still sat raptly attentive in front of her not missing a word.

Presently she added, "That will have to do for now. It will suffice for our city tour this afternoon. If you sit by the window now, you can see the fertile agricultural landscape in the vicinity of the Wei River to the north of Xi'an. By the way, we should very soon cross over into Shaanxi Province."

Michael was happy to do as she suggested. "Of course I'll do that. I love seeing the country, and I'm so grateful for all the information you've given me. Now I really have something to look forward to this afternoon. I only wish I could give some-thing in return."

"Oh, darling, it's nothing. I've studied all of this for years, and I've also visited these sites before. I've told you that already. So for me it's no big deal. It's my country of birth after all; however, I know a lot about only a very small part of this country because it's so vast. And most of my knowledge is confined to its dynastic history. If you want to know how to pay me back, I can tell you. You have to tell me lots and lots about

American history when we get there," she responded with an almost bashful smile.

He quickly responded, "Sweetheart, you seem a bit hesitant in asking me to introduce you to the history of my country, which is certainly short from the time European people settled there in comparison to your very long one. Of course, I'll be most happy to do that when the time comes, and we'll go exploring the wonderful sites of the United States, many of which are awe-inspiring natural wonders, like the Grand Canyon, the Great Lakes, the beautiful shores of the East and West Coasts and the Rocky Mountains. They're all breathtaking." When he finished speaking, he got up and seated himself next to Juan. He took her into his arms and kissed her gently on her forehead and the rest of her face. And while she placed her arms firmly around his waist, he whispered, "It couldn't get any better than just being with you, aside from all you've taught me about your country's history. And in the near future we'll both become steeped in my country's history. I can't wait to introduce you to America and to rediscover it myself." He placed his head on her shoulder and they remained for awhile in their silent embrace.

Juan went to sleep shortly after. She curled up on the soft upholstered seat, while Michael sat opposite her close to the window, viewing with great interest the verdant landscape flying by. Juan didn't wake up until the train slowed down just before it pulled into Xi'an.

* * *

As Michael and Juan emerged from the Xi'an train station, Juan suggested the Wenyuan Dajiudian Hotel for them to stay in. "Though it's large," she explained, "it's quite serene. It's located near the Muslim Quarter. I stayed there some years ago. It's quite comfortable for a three-star hotel and not too expensive.

"That sounds good to me." Michael replied and added, "I hope they have a room for us. Let's head there. Can we walk there and pull our luggage?"

115

"I think we can." Juan replied confidently. "The sidewalks are fairly smooth as I recall and should be OK for our little suitcase wheels."

The answer at the hotel reception was negative. "No, I'm sorry, we don't have a room available right now. How many nights would you have wanted to stay?"

"Two nights," Juan replied while the girl concentrated on the computer screen that she seemed to search while Juan and Michael looked quizzically at each other as if to question, "What is it, a yes or no?"

Then the girl said suddenly, "There might be an opening for two nights, but I can't say for sure yet. Can you wait, or come back in an hour?" she said while looking at Juan.

Juan nodded her head, "Sure we can," she said and added, "We would prefer to come back in one hour, but we want to be certain that you won't give the room to someone else. Can we leave an imprint of our credit card? We need to go and find some lunch."

"Yes, that's fine. So, let's make an imprint of your card," which Michael handed to her, "But I won't hold the room longer than two hours at the most."

"Thank you so much," Juan flashed her brightest smile and assured the receptionist that they would be back sooner than in two hours to check on the room. "Oh," she went on to ask, "Can we leave our luggage here for the time being?"

"Yes, ma'am. Leave it right here. The porter will take care of it."

* * *

As they left the hotel, Michael said, "What was that all about? I don't understand. Either they have a room or they don't. It's a puzzle to me. Do you think we should go to another hotel?"

"I think we'll be fine. When we come back, we'll get the room. I think the girl made a mistake at first with her quick negative answer. After that she was just covering up. It's the Chinese way never to admit a mistake. It would have been a loss of face if she had admitted the mistake. I know she has a room for us. Be assured of that. When we come back in an hour or a little later, we'll be able to sign in."

"I hope you're right. I go with what you say. But I still think it's weird."

"Trust me, darling. This is a very different culture than yours, and many things will appear strange to you."

"OK, thanks. I'm learning. Maybe I should have already known about covering up mistakes since I've been in Beijing and around Chinese people for some time."

* * *

Out on the sidewalk, Juan pointed to a little restaurant across the street. "I can't believe it's still there," she suddenly exclaimed. "I had lunch there years ago. And it was good, too. Let's go there. We can't go wrong," She smiled at him, seemed excited and was obviously pleased with herself.

They had a savory little lunch of authentic Chinese food. During lunch, Michael reached across the table and pressed Juan's hand. "I just want you to know that I appreciate how you manage to do everything right for us. I still can't believe how lucky I am to be traveling with you. You're so knowledgeable, and I know you make all the right calls. Thanks, sweetheart, for looking after us so well." He pulled her hand across the small table and kissed it warmly to show his appreciation. When he looked up and into Juan's eyes, he saw them filled with tears. He was astonished. *How strange it is*, he thought, *to see her that emotional over my small gesture of gratitude.* But presently she smiled at him through her tears.

"I'm a silly goose," she said. "Don't worry about me. You're a fine gentleman, the finest I could have dreamed of meeting." He hadn't relinquished her hand yet. He pressed it now, then turned it over and kissed her palm. Then he looked up once more into the mysterious depths of her black shimmering eyes while he felt her hand pressing his tightly.

117

"Let's go and see the Drum and Bell Towers I told you about. They are close by," she suddenly and somewhat abruptly suggested while withdrawing her hand. Then she added, "We can walk to the towers and then head back to the hotel.

"OK, let's go then. You lead the way."

* * *

They walked first to the Drum Tower near the hotel. It was not as imposing a sight as Michael had imagined. He just stood and looked at it but made no comments, while Juan immediately provided a few details. "This Drum Tower is similar to the Bell Tower. They were both constructed in the 14th century under the Ming Dynasty. It's an interesting building, don't you think? It's entirely of wood. The most interesting part of it, as you can see, is that it is topped by three glazed-tile roofs." Juan looked at Michael and waited to hear him respond.

"Yes," he said, "It's quite interesting because of its uniquely Chinese architecture, especially with those three fancy roofs. And so the main purpose of it was for its drums to announce nightfall?"

"Yes, that's right. You remember from what I told you yesterday. But let's now go to the Bell Tower which is the more prominent of the two structures. It's very close by. Come this way." She then added quickly, "By the way, the Bell Tower, as I already mentioned, also dates from the 14th century. It was built at that time in the very center of Xi'an but was later moved to its present location in the 16th century. I don't know the reason why."

Before Juan continued, Michael interjected, "And it has a large bell which was originally rung at dawn?"

"Very good!" she exclaimed with delight. "You also remember its original purpose. The only thing that's changed is that the Bell Tower today doesn't have its great bell anymore."

"Oh, I thought it would still have its bell. It would be nice if it did. We would have been able to hear the bell tomorrow morning at our hotel. But, come to think of it, it would wake us up too early. So maybe it's a good thing the bell is gone."

Meanwhile they had walked down Beijaunmen Street and turned left onto Xi Dajie, a busier thoroughfare. They spied the Bell Tower just ahead of them. It was a two-storey building, 36 meters high.

As they approached the tower, Michael remarked, "How wonderfully graceful the three layers of arched eaves look. Nothing could be more strikingly and fancifully Chinese. I love the intricacies of it."

Juan loved it when Michael expressed his appreciation of Chinese art and architecture and proposed that they walk up to the second floor to gain an overview of the city and its old but still intact surrounding wall.

* * *

By the time they returned to the hotel an hour and a half later, their room was ready for them. Michael couldn't have been happier that it was theirs for two nights. When the door closed behind them, he embraced Juan and said admiringly, "Whenever you arrange something for us, it always turns out for the best. It's great to be traveling with you. And, yes I did like the two towers. They whisked me back into the 14th century. I tried to envision how life was ordered and guided by these towers—by their different sounds recurring twice a day. How they must have enabled the city's people to orient themselves by their sounds. It was also very helpful for me to see the layout of the old city from the Bell Tower."

"You're right. People depended on them. Life was very different all those centuries ago from our world of today. There was much less night life than nowadays. The dawn and nightfall marked the span of the productive day."

"I believe that. But something else I wanted to ask you. Can we just take a short rest in this cool room?" Michael asked with an inviting smile and a glance at the bed.

"No, I'm sorry," Juan responded firmly. "If we put off the sights we agreed on for today until tomorrow, we'll miss seeing the Terracotta Warriors.

"OK, I'm with you. You're the guide and you know best," he answered with forced cheerfulness, thinking how he would have loved to connect with Juan for a short while at least.

"Let's go then. We'll have to take bus 610 from the Bell Tower. The Big Goose Pagoda is situated some distance southeast from the city wall's South Gate."

"Can't we walk there? You know how much I love to walk and get a feel for the place, the city I mean."

"It's a bit too far. We still have to see the Little Goose Pagoda and the Neolithic village this afternoon. If we walk, we won't be able to see all three sites." Juan was clearly determined not to miss anything.

"Hold off, sweetheart," Michael urged her. "A thought just came to me. Why don't we leave the ancient village for tomorrow morning and visit the Terracotta Warriors right after lunch? Wouldn't that be fine? That would give us time after the Big Goose Pagoda to walk to the little one and from there to the City Wall. I would like to have more time for these three sites. Please think about it."

Juan weighed his suggestion for a moment, then answered, "If that suits you better, I'll go along with it. The Banpo Neolithic Village is about 6 km to the East of Xi'an and the Army of the Terracotta Warriors about 34 km to the North-East. We could easily do that tomorrow."

"OK, then. It's settled? And are you sure you're fine with that?" Michael looked questioningly at her. He was a little concerned because until now, Juan had always taken the lead. He didn't want her to think that he was questioning her competence as a tour guide. It was a role she relished and took quite seriously, and everything had so far clicked perfectly into place.

"Yes, I'm very sure. Don't be silly. I'm able to change quickly when something new and seemingly better comes my way," she responded a bit cryptically—letting out her charming peals of laughter. It occurred to him fleetingly that she might be revealing her changeable nature, something to be reckoned with. But he quickly dismissed this disturbing train of thought.

* * *

They caught bus 610 at the Bell Tower just in time. In 15 minutes it took them to the Big Goose Pagoda Square. As they stood in front of the pagoda, a very imposing ancient six-tiered, tower-like structure, Michael was quite overwhelmed by its massiveness and yet graceful eye-pleasing appearance with its six progressively smaller tiers. At that moment Juan said, "Darling, would you like to hear a little more historical information about this pagoda?"

Always ready to listen to her, Michael replied, "Yes, of course, I would like to hear more. What was its original intent?"

"Yes, that's what I would like to talk about. The Big Wild Goose Pagoda, as it was originally called, was built in the seventh century. It was constructed as part of a temple in honor of Emperor Gao Zong's mother. Years later, when the Chinese monk Xuan Zang returned from an 18-year pilgrimage to India, he suggested that the building be used to house the Buddhist sutras he had brought back. He translated these sutras into Chinese. So, instead of a new building, the original five-tier Wild Goose Pagoda was remodeled into a seven-storey, 64-meter-high pagoda. It then became a Buddhist temple and a large monastery was added. Having deteriorated over the centuries, Xi'an's big pagoda was restored in the early 1950s. It offers an excellent view not only of the city but also its surrounding areas. Let's climb up and take in the grand view. Do you want to do that?"

"Yes, let's do that and spend some time way up high to see as much as we can."

As they stood on the top tier with its breathtaking views all around, Michael exclaimed, "What a magnificent view! We can see all of the old and the new city and miles of agricultural land around it. And as you've told me, it's part of China's cradle of civilization. Tonight I'll let my imagination transport me back to its early colorful imperial times and that of the Silk Road with its flourishing commerce between distant lands."

"I'm glad you find this area so interesting. You should also know that monk Yuan Zang's extensive pilgrimage became one

121

of China's best known pieces of literature. It's called *Journey to the West*. If you're interested in history, you may want to find out whether this work has been translated into English. Or, better yet, you could try to read it in Chinese."

"I'd like to read it. I will as soon as I get the time."

After leaving their perch atop the Big Goose Pagoda, they walked the nearly three kilometers to the Little Goose Pagoda. Their walk along Yanta Lu and Youyi Donglu boulevards brought them back close to the City Wall's South Gate. The Little Goose Pagoda, in contrast with the Big Goose Pagoda, was a rather slim delicate building. It had 15 progressively smaller tiers. Michael stood and studied it for awhile. Juan, next to him, waited until she thought it was time to add a little more information.

"Darling, if you can stand a little more information, I'll tell you about the violent history of this little pagoda."

"Sure, I'd love to hear its history."

"Soon after it was built at the beginning of the eighth century, it was almost completely destroyed during a time of war. It was then rebuilt and restored to its former beauty, but then was heavily damaged by an earthquake in the 16th century. I think I mentioned that damage to you yesterday on the train getting here." Michael nodded vigorously, and Juan continued. "It has always been a fragile structure, and it wasn't repaired and reopened to visitors until 1977. I don't know whether you would like to climb this pagoda, but you'll have essentially the same view as from the big pagoda."

"No, thanks. If it offers virtually the same view as the big pagoda, then I'll pass. I would much rather move on to the City Wall. It should be interesting. Maybe we could walk from here to the wall and stroll at least a few kilometers on its top. I think after that we'll be quite tired. Maybe we could have some afternoon tea in a little café and then go back to our hotel. Would you be up for that?"

"Sure, that's fine with me. I'm up for anything you want to see and do. You can count on me."

Every time Juan agreed with his changes in their itinerary so graciously, he was gratified by her willingness to please him. She was never rigid and quite willing most of the time to adjust and go along with his wishes. He also thought at the time how easy it will be to live with her when they became husband and wife. While she was always responsive to his suggestions and preferences, he was usually happy to let her take charge, and he couldn't fault her judgment or the choices she made for them.

So they walked down Youyi Xilu and then turned left on Nanguan Zhengjie Boulevard until they entered the South Gate. Just inside the gate, Juan pointed to the access ramp. They considered for a short while whether to hire two bicycles from the bike hire stand or to walk. They decided to walk on the wall as far as they felt comfortable. Juan told Michael at that point that a walk along the entire length of the wall would take four hours. While Michael enjoyed taking walks, he wasn't up to a four hour trek and said, "Let's just walk as far as we can enjoy it. But before setting out, tell me a bit about the wall, how high it is and so forth."

"I'm very glad to. This wall as you can see is quite massive and is ringed by a moat. It is 12 meters high and 18 meters thick at the base and it's laid out in a rectangle of 14 kilometers. By the way, between the wall and the moat is a parklike strip."

After they had strolled for awhile on the wall's smoothly paved top, Michael pointed to the crowded old city below them and said, "Sweetheart, the grand mosque over there looks very interesting. You mentioned it yesterday. Do you think we could see it after our walk on the wall?"

"Sure we can. It's quite close to our hotel. We can go there on our way back after we're done with the Wall. I'm glad to know what interests you. I haven't visited the Great Mosque myself, so it's also of interest to me." She hesitated here for a moment and then asked, "Could I just tell you first a few interesting points about the City Wall?"

"Yes, I'd love to hear them."

"This wall, built in the 14th century during the Ming Dynasty, was through the centuries not always in good condition. Many of its crumbling sections had to be restored or rebuilt so that we have now again a perfect city wall. But the interesting part is that, a long time ago, there was a much larger wall that enclosed 83 square kilometers instead of today's 14. It gives you an idea of the grandeur of early Xi'an when the Tang Dynasty ruled from the seventh to the 10th century.

Michael looked at Juan and shook his head, amazed by her knowledge. "What don't you know? I'm always amazed by your precise knowledge of dates and square kilometers. How can you remember all of these details? I'm also glad to hear of the much larger old city wall that was here at the time the Tang Dynasty ruled. It gives me an idea how grand this city once was in comparison to what it was under the Ming Dynasty. It's another piece of history I can muse and think about when I lie awake at night."

"Darling, you always make too much of my knowledge and memory. Is it surprising that we remember well what interests us and we've studied thoroughly?"

"That's true, but few people I know are as detail oriented as you are. I just find it phenomenal. You should be teaching in this field you obviously love at a college or university. I'm sure you could learn to lecture in English. You can practice on me while you're learning." Michael spoke with fervor, hoping to excite her with prospects for her future in America. She must see, he believed, that while she could make money in the night club business, she was being used for her beauty and social graces, not appreciated for her gifts of mind. Surely she must realize this, he believed, and he was anxious to hear her response.

He was a little disappointed when she said, "Oh, darling, you're a dreamer. How could I acquire a higher degree at an American university when I still know only basic English communication? I'll be satisfied when I succeed in speaking your language well and maybe get a simple job," she responded in a modest, self-effacing manner.

"But, sweetheart, you need to set higher goals for yourself. Everything is possible with the intelligence you obviously possess; and, believe me, I will help you in every way I can." He spoke fervently and with conviction.

"Thanks for saying all of this—your compliments and plans you would lay out for me. I'm grateful for your concern and for coming up with this fine future vision for me. But can't we put that on hold for now until the time comes when it's appropriate to talk about my future or how you want me to be. Let's just concentrate on getting out of China. The day after tomorrow, in the early morning, we'll take off for Southern China. It'll be a new experience for me as much as it will be for you. Let's not think beyond that," she urged him, almost pleading.

"OK, OK. You're right. I got carried away. We'll talk about it later." He wouldn't pursue anything that upset her. In keeping with her wishes, he would wait for a more appropriate moment.

* * *

When they left the City Wall after they had feasted their eyes and senses enough on the colorful hustle and bustle of the old city below them, they headed toward the Muslim Quarter. They went up the major north-south Nan Dajie Boulevard to the Bell Tower square. From there it was a short distance to the Muslim Quarter that surrounded the Great Mosque.

Soon Juan and Michael stood in front of the mosque's main entrance, which faced west toward Mecca. In contrast, the main entrances to Chinese buildings usually face south. That was the first unique feature of the mosque Juan pointed out to Michael. As they entered the grounds, Michael observed right away that the mosque's architecture was not purely Islamic. "Tell me about this mosque and these grounds, sweetheart. They don't appear very Islamic to me."

"Yes," Juan answered, "it's a fascinating combination of Islamic and Chinese architecture and landscaping. The gardens, as you can see, with their prominent rocks, pagodas and archways are very Chinese. And over there is a traditional Chinese temple feature, a spirit wall, which is believed to keep the demons at bay. Of course, the Arabian part is the great prayer hall with its turquoise roof. But look at the minaret. It's disguised as a pagoda."

Uta Christensen

As Juan paused, Michael said, "It's a fascinating combination. I like it. Tell me more. I want to know how old this mosque is. You'll never see mosques in Western countries built in a combination of architectural styles. They are purely Arabic."

Juan was quick to reply. "To answer your question, this mosque, I mean the grand prayer hall, was supposed to have been founded in the eighth century, but most of the buildings are from the later Ming and Qing Dynasty eras. By the way, this Great Mosque is the principal of the four existing mosques in Xi'an. It serves quite a large Muslim population. In addition, this Great Mosque is supposed to be the largest and best preserved of Muslim sanctuaries in China. It has been renovated several times under various dynasties, and enlargements date from the 16th century under the Mings. As we stroll closer to the main building, which is the prayer hall, I'll point out the beautiful and elegant calligraphy that always adorns the entryways of mosques."

Michael interrupted Juan. "I find it amazing that a mainly Buddhist, Confucianist and Daoist country also supported a religion so unlike theirs. After all, you said that the emperors of the Ming Dynasty initiated and completed the remodel and enlargement of this impressive mosque complex. Apparently, these diverse religions coexisted peacefully in this country. I'm impressed," Michael commented.

"Yes, you're right, that was until the 20th century," Juan pointed out. "Under Mao's communist regime, all traditional Chinese religions and the other world religions represented in China were suppressed. Foreign religions especially were seen as representative of feudalism and colonialism. Mosques, churches, temples and synagogues were converted to non-religious buildings for secular use. In the early years of the People's Republic, religious belief and practice was discouraged and regarded as backward and superstitious. During the Cultural Revolution, religion was condemned as feudalistic, and religious buildings were looted and even destroyed. It was not until the late 1970s, after the end of the Cultural Revolution, when a new constitution was written, that freedom of religion was guaranteed with some exceptions. But the Communist Party of China will still react harshly against special religious groups, like Falun Gong, which are perceived as challenging the party's authority."

"That's interesting to hear. Thanks for telling me that. I'm not surprised. I suspected that something like that was going on under communist rule."

After they'd spent a good long time walking the complex, Michael suddenly said, "I feel a bit exhausted with all the cultural and historical input I've had this afternoon. Let's walk slowly back to the hotel, clean up and rest a bit before going out to dinner. Will that suit you?"

"Of course, if you've had enough for one day, I don't need to talk anymore or drag you to more historical sites. Yes, I'm happy to stroll back to the hotel," she responded with a smile and put her arm through his.

* * *

Back at the hotel, glad to rest their tired feet, they showered, and, clad in their bath robes, they threw themselves on the bed. Upon entering the room on their return, they had pulled the heavy drapes that created semi-darkness.

"Oh, am I glad to be off my feet and be encapsulated in these four walls with the most sensitive and most beautiful woman in the world. This is where I really want to be," Michael exclaimed and laughed while looking into Juan's black eyes, which shone mysteriously in the semi-darkness and seemed to float in her pale translucent face.

"I'm happy, too," Juan responded.

While Michael tried to pull her toward him, yearning to be entwined with her and wanting to hold her in his arms, Juan, in an unexpected move, raised up, threw her robe off and lowered her full body onto his.

"Sweetheart, what are you up to? Don't you realize you're trying to fool around with a tired body? I was just going to snuggle up to you innocently and was hoping to doze off into a short nap," he protested somewhat theatrically.

127

Juan didn't respond in words to his protest. She thought she knew what he really wanted. With her upper body raised up and supported by her arms and hands, she began to gently rub her lower body into his until she felt his erection and guided him inside her. She pressed her upper body down onto his chest and merged her lips with his in a passionate kiss. Then, raising herself up into a sitting position, she rocked back and forth drawing him deeper inside. The unspeakably delightful sensation of penetrating her was enhanced by the visual delight of beholding her perfect breasts above him—offering to be touched and tasted. She provided all the action. All that was required of him was that he maintain his hardness while she rode him to their climax. "Sweetheart," he whispered in her ear delightedly after he came down from the height he had reached, "you are a real magician. You could raise the dead. What wonderful extremes you take us to." She felt his pleasure and laughed in response to his heartfelt tribute.

Utterly spent, Michael soon fell asleep. Juan got up, slipped into the bathroom, put on her clothes, and left the room quietly without waking him; then went down to the reception desk. She had in mind booking a tour to the Neolithic Village for the next morning and to the Terracotta Warriors excavation site in the afternoon. Having made the reservations and arranged for the tickets to be held until the morning for payment and pick up, she inquired about a train trip to Guilin, in the south of the country, for the following morning. The receptionist phoned the Advance Train Ticket Booking Office that was located in the vicinity of the hotel. Getting hold of someone, she inquired about an early morning passage to Guilin for two, soft sleeper. Juan listened attentively and realized that a space would be available on the 8:30 a.m. train. She knew it would be an all-day ride to Guilin, situated in the southern province of Guangxi.

When the receptionist put the phone on hold, she turned to Juan, saying, "Ma'am, two tickets are available on the 8:30 morning train, the day after tomorrow, in the soft sleeper car. Do you want to book now, and how would you like to pay?"

Juan quickly replied, "We want to pick up the tickets at 8:00 a.m. the day we travel and pay by credit card." She was somewhat nervous because she hadn't discussed details of the last leg of their journey with Michael, nor had she mentioned the unexpected detour to Guilin she had in mind. She intended to do that as soon as Michael woke up.

Meanwhile the receptionist passed on the information to the Booking Office clerk. After listening briefly, she put the phone on hold again, and, turning to Juan, she said, "I'm sorry, they won't hold the tickets unless you can give them at least a credit card number."

"Oh, I don't have it with me," Juan responded, a bit annoyed. "Tell them not to book now, and let them know that we'll be by early tomorrow morning to purchase the tickets. Ask them what time they'll be open."

The clerk turned again to her phone while Juan already tuned out. She was eager to get back to Michael. The last bit of information she happened to catch was when the receptionist repeated, "Ah, at 8 a.m. Thank you."

That's all Juan wanted to know. She barely waited until the receiver was replaced. "Thank you very much," she called out, and waved as she was heading quickly toward the elevator. She thought she had dallied too long at the reception desk and that Michael must be already awake and wondering where she could be. She had sensed lately that he was a little irritated when her phone calls came and wanted to know who was calling her. She gathered that he felt he had the right to know. But surely she had the right to communicate with people he didn't know. Their relationship was young, and they hadn't yet established a trust level, so she had to be cautious.

When she got to their room and entered very quietly, Michael was already sitting up in bed. He was looking curiously at her and said, "Where have you been, Juan? I thought you would be next to me fast asleep when I woke up. Did you have some urgent business? You should have told me."

Somewhat flustered by Michael's probing questions, she answered almost timidly, "I went to make reservations for our two tours tomorrow and was able to do so. In the morning we are booked for the Banpo Village visit and in the afternoon for the Terracotta Warriors visit. Making these reservations came to my mind when you fell asleep, and I thought I could take care of them then. I'm sorry that you were worried."

"Oh, that was fine what you did. So we can pick up the tickets tomorrow morning? What time are we booked? And was there anything else?" He still sounded much like an interrogator, but she tried to be patient.

She now spoke very calmly. "Darling, we are booked for 8:30 tomorrow morning and the tickets will be waiting for us at the desk and still need to be paid for. And yes, there was something else I inquired about."

"What was it?"

Juan replied calmly. "I just tried to get some information, but I couldn't make any firm plans because I needed to talk to you first. It concerns our itinerary after tomorrow."

Now he looked at her curiously again. "What about the itinerary, sweetheart? I thought we had it planned. The day after tomorrow, we'll take the train to Guangzhou and go on from there."

"Well," and here Juan hesitated momentarily but then continued quickly, "I have been wanting to ask you for the past couple of days whether we could travel via Guilin. It's such a remarkable place, not so much historically but for its stunning natural beauty. I have never been there, but pictures I've seen of it have intrigued me greatly. I really long to go there, and I was hoping that we could make a two-day detour to see it. I hesitated to bring it up with you." She looked at Michael anxiously, for she didn't know what reply she could expect.

She was relieved when he responded calmly and was wholly receptive to what she proposed. "There is nothing wrong with taking a small detour. Of course we can go there if it means so much to you. Who knows when we will be back in China? I understand. I have even read interesting stuff about Guilin and seen pictures. It looked very lovely. Yes, let's take it in. What did you find out?" *Why,* he wondered, *am I so relieved that she was just thinking about a detour through Guilin. What did I think she might be concealing? Why am I so suspicious?* He didn't like himself at that moment, and when Juan responded excitedly, he put away his dark thoughts.

"Oh, I'm so happy that you will take me there. The train leaves at 8:30 in the morning. We'll have to cross two provinces, Sichuan and Guizhou, before we get to Guilin in the late afternoon. It's situated in the Guangxi province that reaches all the way down to the Gulf of Tonkin. There should be an easy train connection from Guilin to Guangzhou, not the next day but the following day. It would also be an awfully long tiring train ride from Xi'an to Guangzhou without an interruption. It will be good to have a break."

Michael smiled at her now. "Let's do it then," he said, pleased that she was so happy. "We've seen so many human artifacts in the three days and talked about their history. It will be good to concentrate for a change on China's natural wonders. In a country as vast as this one, there must be a great many places to enjoy natural beauty." He paused a moment as if he were thinking of adding something and then said, "Sweetheart, come here and let me thank you for adding still more pleasure to our escape through sightseeing and travel. He was speaking softly to her now, so that she felt disarmed and sat down next to him on the bed. He folded his arms around her and thanked her once more. He felt guilty about his reaction to her sneaking quietly out of the room. *What's wrong with me?* He asked himself again. *Time and again she has demonstrated good foresight, and she always does the right thing. I ought to apologize for my reaction,* he thought, *but then I'd have to tell her what I was thinking.* Still annoyed with himself and trying to shut up his busy mind, he suddenly suggested, "Let's get ready and go out to dinner. It's about time isn't it?"

"Yes, darling."

* * *

After a sound night's sleep they were up at 6:30, in the breakfast room downstairs at 7:30 and at the reception desk at 8.

131

Michael paid for their tour tickets, and he asked the concierge to make reservations for their train trip to Guilin. The soft sleeper seats that Juan had inquired about the previous evening were still available. Michael asked to reserve two seats for the 8:30 train, and he gave her his credit card. He was told that he had to pick up the tickets that day by 5 p.m. at the Advance Train Tickets Booking Office down the street from the hotel, or at 8 a.m. at the train station on the day of travel. Having accomplished all that, he turned to Juan smiling brightly. He stretched out his hand to her. She took it reluctantly. "Why are you doing this?" she asked while he shook her hand firmly. "Oh, that's just to signify and affirm that we have both successfully arranged something for ourselves, and so, in a way, we are congratulating ourselves for an arrangement done well. Do you see what I mean, what this handshake symbolizes?"

"Yes, I see that's a nice gesture, a nice custom. Thanks for telling me," she replied while planting a quick kiss on his right cheek.

11

Ancient Warriors

They arrived at the Banpo Neolithic Village parking lot at 9 a.m. after a 10 kilometer ride in a small tourist bus. The site of the ancient Neolithic community was on a bluff overlooking the Chan River.

While they were still riding on the bus, Juan asked Michael whether he would like to hear a little historical background. As always, he said he would be delighted to listen to her introduction.

She started immediately. "This Neolithic village is of immense importance to Chinese archeologists because it shows how the early agrarians, ancient forerunners of modern Chinese people, lived. The village was discovered in the 1950s when the foundations for a factory were built, and excavations revealed the site of an ancient dwelling place. I already mentioned to you what was unearthed—foundations of houses, pottery kilns, a cemetery, human and animal bones. Also well preserved Stone Age pottery, clay figurines and tools were found. A free standing roof that covers the entire village was built to protect the site. But much still has to be excavated to learn even more about these early people. By the way, Banpo Village is the earliest example of the so-called Neolithic Yangshao culture. Do you remember, darling, what I mentioned about this culture the day before yesterday on the train?"

"Oh, I clearly remember that you said the village was supposed to have been occupied between 4500 and 3500 B.C. and that there were indications these people had a matriarchal culture. You spoke about voluptuous pregnant goddess figurines. Am I right?"

"Yes, you are right. You're a good listener and were probably always a good student," Juan complimented him.

"I'm not so sure about that. But thanks for saying so."

Meanwhile the bus had driven into the parking lot, and the tourists began to pile out. Michael and Juan made sure that they were the last two of the group leaving the bus. They wanted to have a leisurely stroll through the village by themselves as much as they could and intended to read all the signs and explanations carefully. Juan had to read most of the written information to Michael. Having just begun to read Chinese characters, his comprehension wasn't nearly as good as his ability to speak. He had just recently begun to study Chinese writing. And they wanted to talk between themselves about what artifacts and signs of early life they saw. Michael had a lot more confidence in Juan as a guide than he did in the man assigned to lead them. The driver and tour guide had told them that they would have one full hour to view the site. Juan and Michael were fully intent on using that one hour. They took their time as they moved along the wooden paths through the three distinctly separate areas: pottery manufacturing, housing and cemetery.

At one point, Michael commented, "How interesting it is to see such an ancient site. I like to imagine how these people lived and what their daily lives consisted of—what crops they grew, what they hunted, how family life was lived, how they raised and taught their children, what they wore, what language they spoke, what their fears and joys were. While we're walking the village's wooden paths, I want to transport myself back into their midst, but it takes an effort to do so. How about you, sweetheart? How do you react emotionally to a place like this? Do you just look at it as a piece of history? Do you look at it with detachment as most scientists would? Or do you also feel the vibes of the ancient people that permeate this place?"

Knowing his sensitive nature, Juan was not surprised that Michael would ask these fanciful questions and she answered truthfully, "For me it's both emotional and intellectual. When

I'm here, now and as I did some years ago, I do feel some lingering human energy I can respond to, but I also look at it with the eyes of a scientist, an archeologist, and I also view it objectively as a historian would."

"Uh, I see that training would prompt you to try and look at life in the ancient world objectively. Having a more humanistic bent, perhaps I tend to identify with these ancient folk, conjuring them up, and I like to mingle with them and listen to them. Maybe I'm a bit more of a romantic than a realist."

What Michael got as a response was a playful teasing characterization of himself. "Yes," Juan agreed, "you're a romantic, a man of feeling, full of love, amorousness, sensuality, passion and lustfulness."

"Oh, ho, ho—in short, a man with a strong libido," Michael cried out. "Watch out, sweetheart, what might come to light when I analyze you, even without reliving our pleasures of last evening," he countered her assessment of him and ended with his hearty laugh.

* * *

They rode back to Xi'an in silence, absorbed in viewing the fertile landscape. Michael noticed that he had hardly seen any trees since they traveled on the train through the countryside, no grand forests, only small clusters of trees here and there. Almost all land was used for agriculture. *Hardly surprising when there are 1.3 billion mouths to feed*, he guessed.

It was not quite noon when they arrived back at their hotel. They had ample time to go out to lunch, which they took in the hotel's restaurant, then boarded the bus to view the army of Terracotta Warriors. On the bus, Juan offered again an introduction to the next and last historical wonder they were about to see. Instead of talking about the army of clay warriors, she asked Michael if he'd like to hear about the man behind this unusual army.

"I would really like to hear about him," Michael responded immediately.

So Juan began. "The emperor of that time, Shi Huangdi, of the Qin Dynasty, was a brutal ruler, but also one who achieved much that benefited China as a whole. To begin with, he ruled under the title of king, but then became the first to carry the title of emperor after he unified the country. All previous rulers of the separate states that made up China at the time ruled as kings. When he came to power, Shi Huangdi instituted an efficient, centralized government, a model for later dynasties. He standardized measurements, the currency, and, most importantly, writing. This had been a problem because of the many Chinese dialects that existed at the time. He had thousands of kilometers of roads and canals built. He conquered six major kingdoms before turning 40 and then adopted the title of emperor. But, at the same time, he enslaved hundreds of thousands of peasants who worked on his massive road and canal projects, and he had the Great Wall built as a defensive measure. As I mentioned before, untold numbers of enslaved workers perished. He also constructed the extraordinary vault that contained his famous army of warriors just a short distance away from his burial place. His tomb is still not excavated. It will be a massive effort when it gets started because it's believed that it contains an enormous underground palace and other buildings. If you want, we'll talk about the tomb after we have seen the Terracotta Warriors." Juan paused here, but then went on quickly, "Oh, I got a bit off track. You must also know that Shi Huangdi ordered all written texts, including the country's classical works, to be burned. Presumably they contained ideas he didn't want the people to be exposed to. Scholars dared to criticize him for book burning, and he reacted by ordering over 460 of them to be buried alive. So he is mainly remembered as a tyrant and was very unpopular with later historians. He set an example of autocratic rule that seems to be a model to this day."

Here Michael interrupted her. "That's very interesting. Tyrants seem to think that if people aren't able to read, their thinking can be restricted as well. You've probably heard that the German tyrant Hitler burnt books to eradicate knowledge and reshape minds. I'm sure we could discover others who did exactly the same thing."

"Yes, I agree with you. And I can also tell you about another modern tyrant. Like Shi Huangdi, the First Emperor, Mao had academic and philosophical books burned; and he punished recalcitrant scholars. Can you believe, in a 1958 speech, Mao prided himself on having outdone the First Emperor? He mentioned that Shi Huangdi buried 460 scholars alive, but that his own regime buried 460,000 scholars. I can only hope that he was then referring to having sent that many scholars off to hard labor duty on the farms, which was almost like a death sentence to them."

After a short pause, Juan said eagerly, "But let me get back to Shi Huangdi. When he changed his title from King Zheng to Emperor Qin Shi Huangdi, he adopted a tyrant's philosophy that allowed a ruler unlimited power to impose his will. His laws had to be obeyed without question. He instituted a brutal system of punishment for anyone who broke the law, including castration, branding, mutilation, enslavement and brutal methods of execution. He also suppressed knowledge to prevent independent or revolutionary thinking and book burning was just one of those suppressions. It seems like his terrible acts were endless." Seeing Michael frown and shake his head, she said, "Hang on, darling, I've more to tell you."

At this point, Michael spoke up again, "What you have told me so far, I find appalling and fascinating at the same time. Yes, by all means, finish what you have to say about that horrible emperor."

Juan nodded her head and continued: "His early history is interesting. Shi Huangdi, when he was known as Zheng, became the king of the state of Qin at the age of 13, during a period that came to be called the Warring States period. As far as dates are concerned, I'm talking about the third century B.C. Then, through a palace coup, Zheng, at age 21, had his regents overthrown and started waging wars against the other feudal states. When he took prisoners of war, he immediately ordered their execution. When he conquered the last state in 221 B.C., he unified China into one empire. It was then that he became the First Emperor of China and First Emperor of the Qin dynasty. He made the prediction that the dynasty he founded would last a thousand generations of Qin emperors. He was dead wrong. His Qin Empire lasted only two generations. Because of the cruelty of the regime, there were constant rebellions. As emperor, Shi Huangdi was only able to reign 11 years from 221 to 210 B.C."

"Wow," Michael responded. "That is a gripping story. Thanks as always. I need to think about Shi Huangdi and maybe even read more about him. I'm glad his Qin Empire was short. What a brutal, bloodthirsty SOB he was! Please excuse my language."

Perplexed, Juan said, "I don't understand what you mean by SOB. Please explain."

"Well, it's unique to English and hard to translate. It was coined by the greatest poet in English, Shakespeare, and it refers to a very bad person.

Juan now laughed and said, "It's funny because it sounds so strange. Please give me the real meaning," she insisted.

Reluctantly he explained, "The three capital letters SOB stand for son of a bitch. A bitch is a she-dog."

"Oh, I now understand. No man would want to be called 'son of a she-dog,' especially not an emperor." Juan laughed heartily this time and Michael couldn't help joining her. He didn't think he could have ever gotten as much mirth out of these three simple letters had it not been for Juan.

But then Michael turned serious when he reflected on China's power structures over the millennia that ended in a 20th Century Communist regime and said, "You don't think, sweetheart, that the first emperor was the only ruthless tyrant, do you? Hasn't China always been ruled by autocrats even to this day? Look what the current regime did to its people at Tiananmen Square, when the students and intellectuals pleaded for democracy."

"Yes, you're right," she admitted. "I was just a young teenager then and heard about what happened from people who were there. We cannot forget June of 1989, when tanks rumbled through the streets of Beijing and the army moved into the square from several directions and randomly fired into the unarmed protesters. Residents and protesters were shocked by the army's sudden and extreme response. What began with a student protest attracted large crowds of people from all walks of life, angered by widespread corruption and calling for democracy. The government warned of a clampdown, but several attempts to persuade the protestors to leave the square failed. The eventual ferocity of the attack took many by surprise. The attack caused panic and confusion. Students could be heard shouting, 'Fascists stop killing,' and, 'Down with the government.' But the government used the military to clear the square despite repeated assurances from Chinese politicians that there would be no violence. Hundreds and possibly thousands of people were killed in the massacre, but even until today, the precise number is not known." Juan was clearly moved by the pain of remembering that terrible event and how it mirrored the atrocities of Shi Huangdi's despotic rule.

Because their bus came to a halt at a huge parking lot, Juan and Michael had to stop their heated conversation. Many other large busses were already parked there. Michael asked her, "So this is a major, and, perhaps, the most sought after, tourist destination in China? We might be trampled this afternoon among the throngs of tourists. How can we even see anything?"

"Don't worry, it's not as bad as you think. The site is huge. There are three exhibition pits. The people will be spread out and the guides will usher the tourists through as quickly as possible to make room for later groups."

"So we really have to follow a guide?"

"Yes we do. We cannot go off on our own as we did this morning or at the Longmen Caves. But what you'll see will be breathtaking, and the guides are usually quite good. Would you like to know how these Terracotta Warriors were found?

"OK, sweetheart, tell me."

"Imagine, while digging a well east of Xi'an in 1974, a bunch of peasants happened to uncover a life-size army of thousands of soldiers made of clay. This army stood guard close to Shi Huangdi's tomb for over 2,000 years. It's estimated that it originally consisted of about 8,000 figures."

Juan quickly shared this bit of information just before they piled out of the bus. They walked the five minutes with their group to an extraordinarily large hangar-like structure covering the main excavation site.

The guide took their group to Pit 1, the largest and the most imposing with 6,000 life-size warrior figures and horses. They were standing in a deep rectangular excavated pit in battle array facing east. The warriors ranged between 1.78 to 1.87 meters in height and their torsos were clad in armor or short belted tunics. The first three rows consisted of archers with crossbows and longbows. Behind them was a huge contingent of ordinary soldiers who used to hold spears, dagger-axes, and swords. Those weapons are now displayed in the adjacent museum. Accompanying them in the rear were once 35 chariots. Since they were mainly made of wood, the chariots deteriorated a long time ago.

From Pit 1, the group moved on to Pit 2. It contained 1,300 warriors and their horses. The guide told them as an aside, "In a moment, you will have the chance to view five of the warrior statues close-up." After the tourist group had passed the pit, they headed to the five separately exhibited Terracotta Warrior figures: a kneeling archer, a standing archer, a cavalryman with a horse, a mid-ranking officer and a general. Michael found the statues' elaborate and minute level of detail extraordinary and lifelike. The faces, their expressions, the hairstyles, their armor and footwear were truly amazing. He heard the tour guide say that each warrior's face was individually sculpted. The models were believed to have been chosen from the military ranks of the emperor's army. The guide further added, "The torsos of the statues are hollow, but the arms and legs are solid, and the figures were originally painted in bright colors. Of course, when this army was found all figures were broken because the original roof and the layer of soil above, that covered the standing army's underground vault, had long ago collapsed. They had to be painstakingly excavated, piece by piece, and then reassembled. Archeologists, excavators and trained specialists worked for decades on the project of restoring the warriors and horses."

The group then moved to Pit 3 that contained only 72 warriors and their horses. The guide explained: "This group of statues is believed to have belonged to the emperor's army headquarters. These particular warriors were recognized as high-ranking officers due to their more elaborate uniforms and decorations that distinguish them from the ordinary infantry and cavalry soldiers."

When the tour was over, Michael and Juan walked away from the group and Michael commented, "This grand display we have just seen is absolutely mind boggling. I can hardly believe that one man's pride, tenacity, imagination and delusions of grandeur could have created something like this. What do you think, sweetheart? Do you have anything to add that would be of interest?"

Juan responded with a nod and said, "In addition to all of what we've seen and heard, I have a little bit of information concerning the emperor's actual tomb of which the Terracotta Warriors are only one part. By the way, about 20 kilometers distant from the actual tomb, a pair of bronze chariots and horses were unearthed sometime after the Terracotta Warrior find. They are now displayed with some of the warriors' original weaponry in a small museum near the entrance of this complex. We can go there shortly and see the chariot display and the ancient weaponry. But before we go, I want to say a little bit more about the tomb. What I'm going to relate is mainly conjecture. But some of it is taken from historical accounts describing Shi Huangdi's underground palace, its gems and fineries. It was discovered that the tomb has ingenious defenses built in against intruders. The tomb took something like 38 years to build, and as many as 700,000 workers, artisans and artists were required. I've read that the artists and artisans who created the enormous burial site were also entombed in this 'most lavish mausoleum in the world,' as it has been called. So they took their secrets with them. On the way back to Xi'an, I'll point out the prominent mound underneath which the tomb-palace complex still lies buried. It'll take tremendous amounts of resources and the guidance of experts to unearth the tomb without doing damage to the treasures. The government is waiting until it can afford to bring the entire tomb complex to light."

"Oh, my god, you outdid yourself, sweetheart. What you told me was fascinating and also overwhelming. I can hardly get my head around it. We'll definitely have to go back to Xi'an some years from now once the tomb has been brought to light."

Juan didn't respond to this but said, "I almost forgot to tell you that archeologists are conjecturing that Emperor Qin Shi Huangdi may have believed that his rule would continue after his death as it had been in life or that he was terrified of the multitude of spirits of the murdered workers, artists, artisans, craftsmen and scholars. That's why he needed an elaborate number of warriors guarding his tomb."

Michael gasped, "What a megalomaniac he was, perhaps even more monstrous than our modern-day ones like Stalin and Hitler." He hesitated a moment and then said, "Well, that's just conjecture. I don't think Shi Huangdi could have outdone them. He didn't have the killing technology of modern tyrants—gas chambers, cannons, bombers, missiles and nuclear weapons."

"I don't want to comment on that," Juan responded, "because I don't know enough about their history and their deeds to make comparisons. One thing I do know and that is that for all their grand schemes, neither of them left behind such an extraordinary mausoleum as this. But I've read that they were responsible for more staggering numbers of people killed, soldiers and civilians—millions of them. All they did was destroy."

Michael stopped walking at this point and turned to face Juan. He took her in his arms and said, "You are wonderful, sweetheart. I can't believe I found you. I know we're going to have such a rich exciting life together, making new discoveries and having all the pleasure of discussing them." He kissed her briefly on both cheeks because he wasn't sure whether it was socially acceptable for a couple to kiss passionately in a public setting. He would have loved to have lost himself in a long deep kiss at that moment.

As the bus passed a massive, almost pyramid-like mound, Juan identified it as Shi Huangdi's tomb. The tour guide grabbed his microphone at that point, and he essentially corroborated the facts and details that Juan had already told Michael. There were many 'Oh's,' 'Uh's' and 'Oh my god's' in the bus when people heard how fabulous the tomb was. Their responses revealed how much they would have loved to have seen the emperor's vast underground palace complex. Having already received so much additional information from Juan, Michael felt fortunate to have learned more than anyone else on the tour.

Michael was so elated about this historical outing and all that he had heard and seen, that when they arrived at their hotel at 4:30 in the afternoon, he wanted to go immediately to their hotel room and talk some more about everything they had viewed. But then the train tickets popped into his mind. He suggested to Juan, "Let's go down the street and purchase tomorrow's tickets for our ride to Guilin because I don't want to miss out on a compartment for us." But Juan opted not to go with him.

"Can't you go by yourself?" She sounded tired. "I would love to go upstairs and freshen up. I hope we can rest a bit before going out to dinner. Please let it be OK with you," she almost begged.

"Sure, that's perfectly fine with me. I'll be back in about 20 minutes. Then the bathroom will be free for me. Take your time and rest up, sweetheart." He left her at the hotel entrance and went to get the tickets.

When he came back and entered their room, it was empty. He saw the bathroom door closed and thought, *Juan must be in there getting freshened up.* As he came closer to the door, he heard her shout in an angry voice, as he had never heard her before, obviously into the phone, "Leave me alone! I don't need you!" Then there was a short pause before he heard her voice again. "No, I don't. I'm fine and I know what I'm doing." And then it was quiet. She must have cut off the conversation, he guessed.

Michael stood frozen on the spot. He took some steps back from the door. His mind raced. He felt uneasy. He didn't know how to approach the situation. Should he open the bathroom door now and question Juan about the call? Maybe she was talking to her mother again, but it certainly didn't sound like it. If he confronted her now, she would certainly resent his having eavesdropped on her conversation. And in any case, he wasn't about to barge into the bathroom and violate her privacy. But he couldn't help wondering whom she had been shouting at. *No, it couldn't be her mother. She would never tell her mother to leave her alone and that she doesn't need her. So who was it?*

At that moment in his reflections, Juan yanked open the door and rushed into the room, her face revealing anger. She came to an immediate halt when she saw Michael standing in the middle of the room and looking quizzically at her.

"Sweetheart, what is it?" he said. "What happened? I couldn't help hearing your loud voice. Is someone bothering you that much? I've never seen or heard you this angry. Tell me what it is." He spoke softly and wanted her to see that he was concerned but wasn't prying.

His calm manner helped her to pull herself together and get control of her emotions. She wasn't ready to reveal why she was so upset, but she needed to give him some explanation. *What he overheard couldn't have been much,* she told herself. And fabricating an explanation in her mind helped her to calm down.

"Oh, Michael, it's really nothing of great importance, just a bit of meddling with my affairs. I just got angry because I don't want to be disturbed right now when I'm feeling so good, happy and free. I hope you'll understand. It was Mai Mai, a girlfriend of mine who called. She knows that I'm on this journey with you. I confided in her just before we left. We're very good old friends. I told her not to worry about me because I'll be fine. I also told her that I'll get in contact with her when the time is right. She has promised to wait for my call. But she was too impatient and concerned. We had quite a disagreement during our phone conversation, and I got very angry at her. She was getting on my nerves. She was far too solicitous about what I'm currently doing and also about my future. She sounded full of fears. I don't need that right now when I'm striking out happily on my own. I was especially angry with her because she, although I love her dearly, is the worst woman to give advice where male relationships are concerned. She seems very unlucky with men. During her relationship with her last lover, whom she was involved with for years, she had three abortions. How irresponsible can you get? He absolutely refused to use protection, and she couldn't take the pill, so she used a diaphragm but got pregnant three times. Their relationship is over now. He hooked up with a new lover. Good luck to her. Today when Mai Mai called and tried to tell me how to live my life, I felt, with her record of screwing things up, she had no right to insist that she had all the answers. I got very angry, and you probably overheard my last few words. I'm sorry that I lost it. I also feel sorry for cutting Mai Mai off as I did. That's all, darling."

"I see, sweetheart. Why don't you just turn off your cell phone? You get bothered too much."

"Oh, I can't do that. I need to leave it on because of my mother. She needs to have access to me. I need to hear from her, and I need to know how it is going with her. Can't we just leave this alone, darling? It's nothing very important. What's important to me is to know whether you got tomorrow's tickets to Guilin. And did you find out how long the train ride will be? It's quite a distance away. You know we'll be traveling by snail rail." Juan seemed now quite composed.

Michael still looked at her curiously for a moment. He couldn't reconcile Juan's angry voice with the explanation she had given him. If the girlfriend meant well and was just con-cerned about her, why was Juan so angry? He had never heard such an outburst from her. But he really had no choice but to at least pretend that he believed her. He couldn't call her a liar. Moreover, what right did he have to pry into her affairs? He answered as calmly as he could manage, "Yes, the tickets for a soft sleeper compartment are in my pocket. We'll leave at noon tomorrow, and I gather that train ride to Guilin is something like 20 hours long. We won't get in until the following morning. I had only figured on a 12 hour ride; however, it's much longer. But now we can try out the sleeper compartment thoroughly. Won't it be wonderful if we again have it all to ourselves?" In thinking ahead while speaking, Michael got excited about their new destination, and his enthusiasm seemed to infect Juan. As for the phone call, he would accede to Juan's wish and leave the matter alone.

12

The Journey Continues

nstead of searching for a special dining experience, they agreed to eat in the hotel's restaurant. They knew that it served good, wholesome Chinese food, was comfortable, not too crowded, but was overall nothing special, nothing to brag about. They both felt a little tired after the emotional telephone incident and wanted to turn in early. Also they wanted to rise early the next morning.

While Michael was showering, Juan made herself look as pretty as possible with the few mostly practical pieces of clothing she had in her relatively small piece of luggage for such a grand journey as lay before her. She didn't choose the one fancy dress she had at the bottom of her suitcase. So it had to be the face and hair she needed to concentrate on. She wanted Michael to forget what happened earlier in the evening. She wanted to put on her sweetest, most attractive face and attentive behavior to maintain reciprocal warmth and affection and enhance the joy of their togetherness.

When Michael emerged from the bathroom with just a towel wrapped around his loins and looking fresh, healthy, young and desirable, Juan flew to him, hugged and kissed him so passionately that it took his breath away. He was so surprised by her outpouring of love and desire that he forgot to fold his arms around her. They hung limp by his side, and it took him a second to grasp the fact that she was giving herself to him completely.

When she withdrew her lips from his and just gently nuzzled his face, he whispered in her ear, "Sweetheart, what has come over you? I love being treated this way. Keep going. You could warm the heart of Shi Huangdi and turn him from a ruthless, cold-hearted and fear-inspiring despot into someone lovable, though I can't imagine that anyone loved him or that he was able to love anyone. Having your love means everything to me, sweetheart. I thank you with all my heart."

Juan, in return, laughed her happy bell-like laugh as she released him. He quickly shaved and dressed while whistling the whole time.

Their food was good. They sat in a cozy corner in the huge dining room. They allowed themselves a glass of white wine to celebrate a little, and they toasted their successful escape, as well as China's old and new civilization that they would be leaving, and the natural wonders they would be seeing. But Michael was still eager to talk about what he had seen and learned by visiting the prehistoric site. He also talked about how appalled he was by the means Shi Huangdi employed to achieve his end of empire building and maintaining absolute power—denying his people education, enslaving them by the hundreds of thousands, and utterly disregarding their common humanity.

Juan let him hold forth, ranting and raving a bit. She didn't comment much, for she had long been aware of ruthless emperors. She knew that even Wu Zetian, the only female emperor China had in a long succession of dynasties, was ruthless in gaining ultimate power. Wu Zetian rose in her lifetime from second concubine to an emperor's empress and eventually through palace intrigues and even murder to emperor. All Juan could say to Michael was: "Don't be so shocked by China's history, darling. I think you're awed and intimidated by a history like ours because your country is different with its relatively young history. It started early on with a constitutional democracy, had the guidance of inspired and enlightened founders. But, as far as I know, the Roman emperors weren't benign rulers either and neither were absolutist European kings, emperors and dictators. I do think that how countries are ruled is all a matter of evolution. We as individuals are evolving intellectually and spiritually, albeit slowly over time, so are the methods evolving in which nations and their citizens are governed and the freedoms that are allowed to them. You may not fully agree with me, but this is what I truly believe in—the evolutionary process. I also think that the world's great religions have had to a great extent an inhibiting effect on the development of benign and compassionate rule. They inhibit the growth and enlightenment of the human spirit because they maintain institutions fraught with fear and superstition that serve only the interest of a privileged class. Your country's founders were not religious. They separated church and state. The only religion that works for me is Buddhism. Actually it is not so much a religion because it doesn't teach fiction about gods or a God, heaven and hell, redemption and damnation but the right way of living by walking the middle path, the guide of which is the Eightfold Path." Juan suddenly caught herself at being preachy. She immediately said, "I'm sorry, darling. Forgive me. I got carried away responding to your thoughts on Chinese dynastic history."

"Don't worry. I love it when you try to set things into perspective. And you're partly right about religions. In the West, Catholicism supported autocratic rule, but Protestantism had a lot to do with the rise of democracy. What interests me is your country's evolution as a civilization and how much more advanced it was scientifically, artistically and spiritually through Daoism and Buddhism than Europe in the Middle Ages, where people were in bondage to a lot of mindless superstition, and scientific progress was resisted. And now, look at the economic powerhouse your country has become. It may soon overshadow the Western World with its wealth and economic success and perhaps with its military power as well. It already has the largest standing army in the world with over two million men and women in uniform."

Juan saw that Michael had worked himself up into a heightened emotional state. Now she was ready to direct him away from history, the state of the world and the power struggles in ancient and modern times. She could see that it would be a long wearisome exchange of ideas. Although she liked these discussions, she wanted to shift the focus for this night from the macrocosm of the ancient and modern world to the microcosm of their personal relationship. She was ready to terminate the broad encompassing discussion they had been engaged in and to concentrate solely on their love and affection for each other. That's why she suddenly looked at her watch, which Michael noticed.

She looked up at him and said, "Darling, do you know that it's already nine o'clock? Shouldn't we go upstairs, pack as much as we can and get ready for tomorrow? And, of course, I'm looking forward to going to bed with you as always," she added.

Her words had the desired effect of focusing his attention on her and all the pleasure she was offering him with her physical beauty. He called the waiter, paid, and once more, as had happened before, raced Juan up the steps to their room instead of taking the elevator. This time he let her win and let her hold the door open for him.

She stood there triumphantly smiling while ushering him in. As soon as she closed the door, he grabbed hold of her and whirled her around their spacious room in a waltz in such a fine rhythm as if the best Straussian orchestra was playing just for them, while Juan let out one of her high-pitched peals of laughter. On and on they waltzed until they threw themselves breathless onto the bed, lying quite still side by side and looking up at the ceiling while trying to gain calmness and rid themselves of their dizziness. Juan was the first able to speak. "This dance was so exhilarating. I felt like a Muslim dervish, whirling myself with abandon into a trance. If you had waltzed me any longer, I would have truly been in a trance. Your exuberance is so delightful and catching. When it takes us over, I can envision my life with you. It seems so rich and fulfilling."

Michael was touched by the warmth of her outburst. How he adored her when she was like this. Unable to speak and to express himself in words at that moment, he turned toward her and embraced her heartily, holding her body firmly pressed to his and his face to hers for quite some time without kissing as if he wanted their bodies to melt into each other. When he finally released her, they lay on their sides facing each other. Her large black glistening eyes delved ever so deeply into his as if she wanted to extract the hidden mysteries of his soul. Michael felt almost mesmerized by her eyes. It took all his will to pull himself out of Juan's hypnotic gaze. He suddenly sat up, holding his head in his hands. When he felt he had returned to their present reality, he nudged Juan a little. "Let's get real, sweetheart. Let's prepare for tomorrow and let's prepare for the night. What do you think?"

"You're right. I'm sorry I got carried away. See what you can do to me? You can spellbind me."

He laughed out loud then. "It was the opposite. Give me a break. You had me hypnotized for a while. I could hardly get myself disentangled."

"You're so funny sometimes," she shot back. "You've a tendency to take certain things very seriously when it was just playfulness on my part."

"OK. I get you, sweetheart. I'll be careful in the future not to see so much seriousness in your behavior. But for now I'm asking you to get serious. Let's get ready," he said rather sternly, more to get a grip on himself than on her.

He got up and she followed him. He attended to his luggage and she to hers. When she felt she had everything ready for their departure, she said, "Michael, darling, I'll now get ready for bed. Can I use the bathroom for a short while?"

"Of course you can. Take your time."

He lay on the bed relishing the pleasure of anticipation. When she was finished, he wouldn't waste much time preparing himself for bed.

* * *

Soon they were lying in bed in the darkened room. Neither of them made a move. After seemingly a long moment, Michael stretched out his arm and felt for Juan's hand. When he found it he held it tight for awhile. Juan interpreted his testing move as a sign for her to take the initiative. She turned to him. Stroking his chest and abdomen gently for some time, she soon felt him stir, but he remained quite still despite his erection. Suddenly she sat up, grabbed both of his hands and pulled him up into a sitting position. She placed herself into a kneeling position in front of him and pulled his head toward hers, kissing him passionately while he placed his hands on her slender hips. When she finally stopped, he murmured, his hot breath fanning her cheek, "Sweetheart, what are you trying to do to me now?"

"Something special tonight," she replied playfully, raising his expectations.

"What is it?"

"Juan's special. I know you like it," and she turned on her knees in front of him. Then he knew. "You're overwhelming me with your sensuality," he whispered in her ear as he bent over her, gently inserting himself and stroking her most sensitive area. He worked her and himself into an ecstatic state. They climbed higher and higher together. There didn't seem to be an end to their climbing. "Oh, how wonderful," she moaned now and then until they found release at the same time.

They were silent for awhile with his head resting on her back. But eventually she gave way under him and he followed her, and both positioned themselves into a fetal position, spooned together, enjoying a feeling of utter relaxation and oneness.

After a long pause of peace and quiet, each pursuing their own thoughts, Michael spoke up while not letting go of her, "How do you manage to give me such wonderfully intense sensations? I can't remember ever feeling like that. It was absolutely exquisite?"

"You did the same to me, darling. I love this position. It's the sexiest for me. It represents supreme wildness and abandon for me. But I don't want to insist on it every time. I do like variety," she whispered a little superfluously.

Michael chuckled as if he were going to say: *Oh yes, and how I love to give you what you like.*

Shortly after, both fell soundly asleep.

* * *

Michael woke up with a start to some faint noises coming from the street below. He immediately thought that they had not

151

heard his alarm clock. But when he turned to the clock, he saw that it was only eight o'clock in the morning. If they got up now, they would have plenty of time to catch the train. Juan, being awake now, too, gave him right away gentle kisses on his cheeks and forehead. She was the first to get out of bed.

"May I go into the shower first? I need to wash and dry my hair today."

"Oh sure, go right ahead. Don't hurry. We have plenty of time."

While letting the hot water run over her, Juan thought what a wonderfully peaceful night she had had. She had been awake for awhile before Michael woke up with a start. Lying very still, she remembered a partially lovely dream that must have happened toward morning because it came back to her quite vividly. The dream was in full color set in a lush tropical landscape on a Pacific island in a magically blue sea that she and Michael had traveled to. They lay naked under swaying palm trees on a white sandy beach, which they had to themselves. Way out to sea they had earlier spied the fringing reef. Great white-capped waves were, as if by magic, crashing there where they could see nothing but water. The next moment they got up and raced each other into the water. They frolicked in the gentle warm sea water of the great lagoon and chased each other, with Michael catching her more often than she caught him. Whoever caught the other was allowed to dunk the one caught. And so it was up out of the water and down into it again until both felt nearly exhausted. They threw themselves onto the white sand. *We're playing like innocent uninhibited children*, she thought. But suddenly the lush sunny landscape changed. It happened so quickly and unexpectedly that Juan couldn't figure out how it came about. They were not lying now on a white-sandy tropical beach but on a vast expanse of brilliant white snow and ice. How they had gotten from a warm benign climate to a freezing cold one puzzled her. She couldn't remember that she and Michael ever talked about traveling to the Arctic or the Antarctic. But there they were dressed from head to toe in fur clothing; their bodies that were a short while ago naked, were now so heavily clothed that no trace of their physical shapes was visible. Neither of them spoke. They just stared into the vast white distance. There was no talk, no intimacy, no frolicking in the warm water and bright sun. Life seemed drained out of them. And Michael seemed far away, lost in thought with a sad expression on his face. *How did we happen to be here?* She thought. *Was it my wish or his to see snow and ice? Yes,* she remembered, *it was my wish, and she felt very guilty. What have I done?* she thought. Then she began to cry over what she must have done. And Michael, strangely enough, did nothing to console her. Her last thought before waking up was: *I lost him.*

Michael was still asleep then, and Juan kept lying very still next to him as if she were asleep. She thought and wondered what the dream might be telling her. She was having such a good time traveling with Michael in a more interesting and gratifying manner than she had thought possible. They had a tender, caring relationship, gave each other such pleasure, which was inhibited only by a fear that pursuers might overtake them. She wondered if the dream foreshadowed a breakup of their relationship in the future. But she couldn't really envision a breakup and decided to toss the dream aside like a bag of unwanted clothing. However, she couldn't jettison a lingering fear that she might lose him.

Intending to wash away the dream, she jumped into the shower, and when she gave her hair a final rinse, she had nearly succeeded. She would let Michael have his turn in the shower and let her hair partially air-dry. Her face she could do in the bedroom with her hand-held mirror. When she came out so soon, Michael seemed glad. "Thanks for being quick this morning. I appreciate your thoughtfulness," he said in passing.

"Oh, darling, you must be kidding. I was in there far too long. I'm sorry." But he didn't seem to notice what she had said and slipped quickly past her into the bathroom.

* * *

After getting ready, having a long breakfast in the hotel, checking out around 11 o'clock, and rolling their luggage to the

153

nearby train station, they arrived half an hour before departure. They were thrilled to find that they again had a compartment to themselves. When they first stepped onto the platform and saw the droves of people waiting for the train, they thought there would be no chance for them to travel in that pleasurable privacy they had enjoyed before. But they were lucky again. It appeared that most of the travelers were booked into the soft seater and hard seater cars. Michael and Juan noticed when they took a short stroll along the now empty platform that the other cars were filled with people.

Once they were settled in their cozy compartment, Juan said, "I'm glad to be here, to get a move on. I think I told you the other day that I know little of the history of this part of China. But I do know something about Guangxi Province where Guilin is located on the Li River. There are some fantastic natural settings in this province, the mysterious karst peaks of Guilin being perhaps the most prominent natural attraction that lures many travelers to this province. More than anything else, I'm looking forward to seeing these natural wonders for the first time and especially with you. I've wanted to travel to this province since I was very young. But no one ever took me there. My family members are all hard-working business people, as you know. There was no time for them and us children to travel just for sightseeing. Never could I have imagined that I would be making this wonderful trip with you, a foreigner who has come to love China as he loves his own country." At this point she paused a moment, and then added, "Oh, maybe I've assumed too much. Maybe it's not true what I'm thinking," she said slightly embarrassed, pressing eight slender fingers against her lips as if to prevent herself from saying any more.

"Don't worry, sweetheart," Michael assured her. "You haven't said anything that isn't the truth. I do love China, even more now that I've found you, my beautiful companion and lover."

"Oh, thank you. How sweet of you to say that." Juan had overcome her embarrassment and now gushed forth about the landscapes and natural wonders they would see. She promised that she would be at the window with him to see as much as could be seen as the landscape flew by. At that point the train was still in the station but would soon depart.

Meanwhile Juan talked animatedly about what they would see according to books she had read and the colorful pictures she had looked at in the past as she was dreaming of a journey like this. "You know, at first we'll travel through the southern part of Xi'an's Shaanxi Province, all fine agricultural lands. Then our train will move through the fabled Sichuan province of spices, known for its hot peppers and Sichuan's renowned "flamethrower" cuisine as it is sometimes called. It's also known as the four river province. The word Sichuan means 'Four Rivers.' These four rivers are among the mightiest in China, which has more than a thousand of them. Water is this province's most important and most essential element, and the high Tibetan plateau is the birthplace of these long bands of waterways. From Tibet, the rivers spill eastward into the Chuanxi plain. I have read that Li Bing, a famed engineer, active around 400 B.C., harnessed the Du River through a weir system he designed. This system of irrigation has given Sichuan Province more than 2,000 years of prosperity."

"Wow, sweetheart, you know so much, aside from all the dynastic histories. I hope we'll see a lot of the Sichuan landscape. Most likely this afternoon, wouldn't you think so?"

"Oh yes, I think we will. But I want you to know that I only know a little about this vast province, one of the largest in China. We'll be viewing some of it this afternoon, at least the northern part of Sichuan. It's too bad that part of the trip will be at night-time. We'll miss a big chunk."

"Oh, well, we'll still see a lot. But we wouldn't want to extend our trip even more. I'm eager to get to Guangzhou and out of the country. In years to come, we'll come back here and take a long, leisurely trip. I promise you that."

Juan smiled as Michael made this promise and replied, "We'll see, we'll see. I don't even think that far ahead. I try to live the present moment fully, seeing, experiencing and learning what I can in the now."

Uta Christensen

At that moment the train started moving, its monstrously heavy steam engine belching clouds of black smoke. Juan and Michael were thrilled to be on the way to their final destination in China. Juan was seated right next to him. He hugged her tightly and said, "It's wonderful that we're moving again. The farther we leave Beijing behind, the better I feel. It appears safer now that we are heading toward Chengdu in Sichuan and to Guilin after that. Who could possibly still be after us? We are so far out of reach now. It's a good feeling not being pursued anymore."

Instead of replying, Juan just nodded, smiling sphinx-like at him with a somewhat veiled look. She didn't respond directly to his reminder that they had been pursued or his assumption that they were now safe. Instead she told him that they would soon leave the province that's often called the 'cradle' of Chinese history. Even the name China may have been derived from the Qin (pronounced 'chin') Dynasty with its imperial seat in close proximity to Xi'an. "Today it's certainly not the center of China anymore," she said, "But in much earlier times the Wei River valley was a perfect location. Its fertile land could feed a large population. There were always threats of invaders from the north that required a strong military preparedness. It was also the crossroads of major trade routes and ancient China's important link to new knowledge from the outside world."

She paused for a couple of moments, then went on to say, "By the way, darling, our people were always receptive to new knowledge from outside, and they in turn transmitted to the outside world the wisdom of the sages. You and I have never talked about the ancient sages who lived on Hua Shan Mountain north-east of Xi'an. Hua Shan is one of Taoism's five sacred mountains where ancient hermits became one with the universe and where Lao-tzu, the most famous of the reclusive sages, was taken to transmit his wisdom. He gave us his cryptic and mysterious *Tao Te Ching* you may already know about."

Michael interrupted her. "Yes, I know of the *Tao Te Ching* and I even started reading it some time ago. But then I put it down and never picked it up again. It's quite esoteric," he said almost apologetically.

156

But Juan responded, "Don't worry about that. I know you'll pick it up again in the future. It's one of those spiritual books that are hard to get into, but once you become acquainted with it, you'll return to it again and again."

"So you have read it from cover to cover? And, what is it telling you? Do you think it's enlightening?"

"Yes it is, to answer your last question. It's so different from everything I'd read before. I was magically drawn into it without fully understanding it. I understand Buddhism. Its path to enlightenment is clear to me, though sadly I'm not really walking that path. I'm a child of the new China, the China that values material success, money, consumerism and sensual, sexual and some intellectual freedom. But mind you, like everyone else, I have to accept the fact that we're not allowed to value political freedom, of which we have none. You might want to call that a tradeoff. We have a degree of intellectual freedom. We can engage in philosophical discourse but not question the political philosophy of our rulers. With regard to philosophy, I'm always vacillating between Buddhism and Taoism because the first is practical as well as spiritual with a clearly laid-out path; and the second is esoteric and spiritual and is forever calling one to explore its mysteries."

Attentive to her every word, Michael interjected, "What does the word *tao* exactly mean in connection with Daoism? Do you know? If I knew its meaning I would most likely find a way to work through the *Tao Te Ching*."

Juan responded, "I have read that Lao-tzu conceived of *tao* to mean the unconditional and unknowable source and guiding principle of all reality."

"Wow that's a big concept—'the unconditional and unknowable source and guiding principle' of everything?" Michael repeated her words slowly, perfectly enunciating each as if he wanted to inscribe them permanently in his mind.

"It's very interesting to hear you repeat these words so clearly as if you were extracting their full meaning. I'm hoping that in the future we can follow these spiritual paths together. I can imagine how gratifying it could be to read the Buddha's

Heart Sutra and Lao Tzu's *Tao Te Ching* together. What do you think?"

"That would be my goal," he agreed eagerly. "We'll go at those scriptures from two different spiritual-religious traditions. How interesting that will be."

By now the train had left central Xi'an as well as its outskirts. All that thickly layered ancient history was behind them. It almost felt as though they were throwing those heavy historical burdens off their shoulders. They were sitting close together watching the green landscape flying past—the verdant fields that Juan had talked about earlier and that ages ago had supported a rich imperial tradition and civilization. They crossed over wide lazy rivers that Juan knew the names of. Every plot of land, as far as the eye could see, was cultivated. Farmers and their field hands were working in them, bent over. Much of the agricultural work still seemed to be done by manual labor, although there was also some mechanized farm machinery to be seen. As always, Michael noticed the absence of forests. There were none in this landscape. Even single trees were few and far between. It seemed that every bit of arable land was dedicated to agriculture.

Suddenly, after absorbing the landscape, Juan piped up as if a brand new thought had entered her mind. "Darling, I hope you don't think that Shaanxi Province's history stopped in the ancient world. No, it didn't. In 1935 the Chinese Communist Party, known as the CCP, found a safe haven in the Loess Caves of Yan'an quite some distance north of Xi'an. For the next decade this hideaway in the caves became the Communist Party's broadcast center for revolutionary thought and propaganda."

"Oh, wow, that's mighty interesting. I've not heard of this communist hideout before. So this relatively remote province helped shape modern China's history. I suppose one could travel to Yan'an and explore the Loess Caves' area. But what would one get to see? I also want to ask you, was Mao Zedong in any way involved in the CCP broadcast center at Yan'an?"

"To answer your first question: I don't really know. I've never had a chance to explore the area. And I don't know whether anything has been preserved connected with this Communist Party broadcast center. To answer your second question: I'm quite sure Mao was involved at the time of his Long March that took him and his People's Liberation Army one year to complete. I think the march was about 6,000 miles long."

"You're kidding, aren't you, sweetheart?" Michael responded in amazement. "That must have been a hell-of-a-march. Six thousand miles is very, very long. No one would survive that."

"No, darling, I believe I'm right. It was that long, and many of the marchers—I've read one in 10—didn't make it, but Mao did. He was a tough and driven man. After that year-long foot journey from a south-eastern province to the north-western province of Shaanxi, he emerged as the foremost Communist leader in China. The march ended in Yan'an, the city I mentioned earlier in connection with the Communist broadcast center."

Michael wanted to know more. "And why did Mao undertake the Long March in the first place? What drove him to do it?" He asked.

"Oh, it was Chiang Kai-shek, the Nationalist leader, who had, at the time, assumed nominal control of China. He was determined to eliminate the Communists. Mao must have felt the heat then. I think he wasn't ready, at that time, to confront Chiang and his massive Kuomintang forces. It took another 14 years, in 1948, for Mao's People's Liberation Army, the PLA, to defeat Chiang's forces, after starving them out in the city of Changchun, where about 160,000 civilians also perished during the siege. I'm not sure how many troops Chiang lost at the time. A PLA officer who documented the siege in his book *White Snow, Red Blood* compared the massive casualties to those of Hiroshima. He wrote: *The casualties were about the same. Hiroshima took nine seconds; Changchun took five months.*"

"It's unbelievable that many people were starved to death. Didn't Chiang Kai-shek flee after that to Taiwan, which was then called Formosa?" Michael wanted to know.

"You're right, quite soon thereafter. It was early in 1949 when Mao's army laid another siege, this time to Chengdu in Sichuan, the city we'll come to soon and where we'll have our two-hour layover. It was then the last Kuomintang-occupied city in mainland China. After suffering massive losses during that siege, Chiang evacuated from the mainland to Taiwan."

"I know Mao was a great leader, but didn't he also mess up badly in later years? I think he came out with some unsuccessful and outlandish schemes and eventually fell from grace?"

You're right again, darling. Mao is a controversial figure—especially nowadays. On the one hand, he is officially held in high esteem in China as a great revolutionary, a great political strategist, supposedly a military strategist, and even savior of the nation. Many Chinese also believe that through his policies, he laid the foundation for a modern China by transforming the country from an agrarian society to an industrial one with the potential of becoming a world power. On the other hand, his social-political programs like the Great Leap Forward and the Cultural Revolution cost millions of lives by causing severe famine and damage to the culture, society and the economy. He conducted political purges from 1949 to 1976 that caused the deaths of millions of people through executions and suicides. If you're really interested in that part of our history, you should do more reading about it because Mao's trajectory toward becoming one of the modern world's most influential revolutionaries and leaders is an amazing one, especially because of his peasant background. His family were farming peasants living in the south-western province of Hunan where Mao was born. The peasants of China were the segment of society that helped Mao achieve his power. But I don't think I want to talk about Mao any further. He is not one of my favorite greats in a long line of Chinese leaders."

"Thanks, sweetheart, for giving me all that information and answering all of my questions. I know there is a lot more to learn, and sometime in the future, I'll do as you suggest, make it a point to study Mao's life."

* * *

They still sat, as throughout their conversation, opposite each other. And now, as if needing a rest, they looked again out the train's window. Even though not much had changed in the land-scape, it was exciting for Michael and Juan, for they knew that they would soon cross into Sichuan. At that point the conductor came by to check their tickets. They asked him when they would cross from one province to the next. He said it was happening at this moment. He also pointed out that they would stop 45 min-utes in the city of Guangyuan. If they needed lunch, he advised them to get it there in the train station.

Juan and Michael thanked him for the information and looked forward to getting off the train for awhile. They asked whether Chengdu would be the next stop after Guangyuan and how long it would take to get there. He replied that it would be the next major stop and that it was still 250 km to Chengdu. He estimated that it would take about four hours of traveling time because the train would stop a short while in several minor cities to let off passengers and to take on new ones before having a long layover of two hours in Chengdu. For their information he had added that Chengdu is huge, the fifth most populous city in China.

Juan and Michael decided to find a simple lunch meal in Guangyuan and have dinner in Chengdu. They knew now that they would have enough time in Chengdu to leave the train sta-tion and find a restaurant nearby. Michael was looking forward to one of those famous Sichuan 'flamethrower' dinners.

After their informative encounter with the conductor, they lay down on the lower seats of the compartment for a little snooze. Both went to sleep quite soundly. It was the slowing down of the train and the jerks caused by its massive brakes that caused them to wake up.

In retrospect, when they thought about their stop in Guangyuan, it was nothing special. They found some food stands in the train station, bought some heavy dark flat bread and goat cheese and found a place, just a hole in the wall, that sold lamb kebabs. There wasn't enough time to leave the train station. When they got back into their compartment, it was still empty as if it had been reserved just for them for the entire trip. While they were out, someone had come into the compartment and set down one of those famous Chinese thermos bottles with superheated sterile water in it on their little window table, and two lidded cups with a few green tea bags next to them. By that time they were ravenously hungry and looked forward to their simple but solid Sichuan lunch.

While they were devouring their midday meal, Michael asked, "What about the Sichuan agricultural region? Wasn't it, and perhaps still is, of importance to China as a whole? You mentioned previously the ancient weir system that harnessed one of the rivers and provided continuous irrigation and wealth. It also contributed in large part to feeding the nation, am I right? And wasn't it at one time considered to be China's 'breadbasket'?

Juan nodded as she replied, "Yes, you're quite right in all of that. But during Mao's Great Leap Forward, the economic transformation program of the late 1950s, a significant change from individual farms to enormous communes occurred and eventually ended in disaster. It was estimated that up to 30 million Chinese people died of starvation. During the implementation of the Great Leap Forward, money and all private properties were abolished and large numbers of people were drawn from the country and urban areas to work the fields. But despite glowing projections, a massive slump in grain output happened. There was little incentive for the people to work the fields, and bad weather in 1959, as well as the Soviet aid withdrawal in 1960 made things worse. There was also a cover-up of the disaster and no foreign food aid was sought. China plunged into an enormous famine. By the way, these failures caused Mao to resign as head of state, although he remained Chairman of the Communist Party."

Michael, having listened intently to Juan's interesting account, replied, "I have vaguely heard about the Great Leap Forward. I would say the overwhelming majority of Americans don't know what it meant and what it was supposed to do. I've also heard of the severe famines and consequent starvation. So do you know what was done to rectify the situation?" he asked with curiosity.

"Well, to tell you the truth," Juan answered, "I don't know that history thoroughly, though I think I should. I did hear of a famous governor of Sichuan Province, who, in the 1970s, restored the agricultural system to individual farms that were let out to families. But those farms had to sell a portion of their crops back to the government. That system was called the 'Responsible System.' It was very successful and became the national model. To answer one of your previous questions, I believe, as of today, the fertile earth of Sichuan still produces a significant portion of the nation's grains and soybeans and perhaps other agricultural crops. Incidentally, this governor, as well as other political figures, opposed the use of military force during the 1989 Tiananmen Square student demonstrations and was forced into lifelong house arrest. Naturally, at the same time, he fell from grace as the Communist Party's national general secretary as well."

"So what are your personal feelings about political freedom? Does it matter to you? You told me that you have none, but I'm curious how you feel about it."

Juan looked at Michael and answered a little reluctantly, choosing her words with care: "Most intellectuals and some politicians would like to see a sea change in Chinese politics toward moderation and democracy. Personally, I'm convinced that what the students and the intellectuals as well as ordinary citizens demanded in 1989 will one day be sought for again and be demanded. Personally, I'm not an activist, but I'd like to see a democratic government in China and freedom of the press instead of repression."

"Sweetheart, I'm happy that you lean toward democracy, and I, too, hope that it will come about here. And I also realize now that you know a lot more than just details of dynastic-imperial history, but you don't flaunt what you know or overwhelm me with your learning. Learning is like precious ornaments, like gold, diamonds or pearls. You wear yours with ease and grace. The glimpses you give me of what lies stored behind that lovely forehead tantalize me and make me want to know more."

Juan was amused by Michael's compliment and happy that he would view her like that. "It pleases me greatly to have impressed you," she said, "And it amuses me to think that you imagine that I know so much. Ornaments can be deceptive, you know. They're worn on the surface."

* * *

The train ride between Guangyuan and Chengdu was uneventful and painfully slow with four uneventful stops in simple uninteresting towns. They could hardly wait until they would reach Chengdu. By that time it would be early evening. When they arrived, they grabbed their little bags with their most important belongings in them and left the compartment as soon as they could. Racing each other out of the train station, they saw before them a broad, tree-lined boulevard leading off the train station entrance into town. They felt that they couldn't go wrong walking down that boulevard. There must be restaurants nearby, they assured each other. It was 7:10 in the evening then, and they had nearly two hours to spare for their walk and their dining adventure.

After covering a short distance, they spied some bright lights ahead on a façade along the sidewalk they were following. When they came close, they couldn't believe their luck. It was indeed a restaurant and it looked good to them. As they discovered when they went in and were seated, the restaurant's specialty was freshly made mapo doufu, soft fresh pockmarked tofu. They were delighted to find a vegetarian dish after their so-so lamb kebabs for lunch. The mapo doufu could also be had with an additional portion of minced meat, which Michael and Juan asked the waiter to leave out. But Michael was eager to have the fiery garlic sauce, the salted soybeans, the chili oil and the hot Sichuan pepper with his doufu. Juan asked the waiter to have her meal spiced as little as possible. She had experience with Sichuan food in Beijing and always opted since then to go light on the burning stuff. She didn't advise Michael on the hotness and pepperiness of the meal. She really wanted him to experience the local taste. She wanted to see if he would react by wincing, cringing and grimacing while eating his meal.

When the dinner arrived, Michael dug right in. He seemed very hungry. Juan watched him unobtrusively. The first two bites Michael seemed to tolerate quite well.

He said boastfully, "This isn't so bad. I can handle the heat and the fire."

But it wasn't long until he looked a bit agitated. He was also fanning his open mouth with his hand. After a few more bites, he let out a groan, "Oh my god, I'm burning up. I boasted too soon. This is incredible culinary fare. I don't know how much I can eat and yet I'm hungry," he moaned.

"Look, darling," Juan responded. "I didn't give you any advice when you ordered. I really wanted you to become acquainted with this food, so you will know how some people in a far-off province of China eat every day. But I suggest that you order another, less spicy dish like mine. It's heavenly, especially the super fresh bean curd. Let's just order another plate."

"No, I want to eat some more of this. I need to experience it. I should be able to handle it," he insisted.

He continued almost heroically, determined even if he punished himself. He suppressed his grimacing and tried to keep a straight face as he chewed the food. Juan waited. She knew it wouldn't take too much longer. Suddenly, she started laughing. It was funny to see Michael punishing himself like that unnecessarily. That's when Michael crumbled. "You're right," he gave in, "I shouldn't continue to eat this hot, burning stuff. But I'm still glad I tried it. I guess one needs to grow up with this kind of food to be able to take it. Maybe you could order me the same palatable dish you're having."

"I'll be delighted." And she waved the waiter over. "Please, one more dish like mine. We're very hungry," she said.

Their dining out was saved when the new dish came and Michael remarked several times how delicious the food was. He even ordered two glasses of red wine so that they could celebrate a little. After all, they were not so far away from their destination. One night on the train and they would arrive in Guilin in the early morning hours. If the train was on time, arrival would be 8 a.m.

Suddenly Michael said, "You've saved me. I'm grateful to you. Overall, it was an interesting experience. I've eaten Chinese Sichuan food in California, but it was nothing like this fiery stuff. It was more than a bit hot, but I could easily tolerate it and I liked it. I suppose the Chinese-Sichuanese would have to tone down their cuisine in other countries; otherwise they wouldn't have much business."

Juan nodded her head and said, "I can easily understand that because I can't tolerate the authentic peppery Sichuan food. It wasn't in my childhood diet."

* * *

They were happy after their dining experience and walked arm-in-arm back to the train station. By then it was nearly 9 in the evening. They used the primitive combined washroom and toilet on the train as soon as they were under way. By the time they were both back in the compartment, they decided to go to sleep early. But before retiring, Michael folded his arms around Juan's waist, lifted her slightly off the floor and swung himself with her clinging to him around in the narrow space between the compartment's lower bench seats and upper bunks. When the train jerked a bit, Michael became destabilized and fell with Juan onto one of the upholstered seats. They both laughed so loud that they were afraid passengers from the adjacent compartments would look in on them to see what is going on. So they both clamped a hand over their mouths to shut off the laughter and got up quickly. When they felt assured that no one would peer through the glass compartment door, they put on their sleep wear—Juan her short lacy nightie and Michael his pajama bottoms—and climbed up the little ladder to the bunk bed above their seats. Not wanting to sleep in separate bunks, they had agreed to give sleeping together in the narrow bunk a try. The only way they could get comfortable was to lie together in a tight spooning position with Michael's back against the compartment wall. He eagerly sniffed the sensual perfume on the back of Juan's neck and inhaled deeply both her lovely scent and her warmth. These olfactory delights immediately set him off and Juan felt his hardness coming on.

"Darling, I thought we would just go peacefully to sleep," she whispered. "Don't you think the passengers behind this wall might hear or feel us?"

"I thought we could risk having the quietest and most peaceful loving we've ever done and no one would know. I think we can pull it off. It'd be a fine ending to this hot spicy evening," Michael whispered back while his hot breath was fanning Juan's cheek.

"It's fine with me, darling. Just show me how quiet you can be." She almost let out her usual ringing laugh but stopped herself before it took off.

Juan, who was always ready for love-making, was secretly happy that Michael would dare do it. And he, as soon as he got the go-ahead, while maintaining their spooned position, placed his hands around her small hips. When he was inside her, he used just the slightest movement, probing sensitively. They felt deliciously subtle to her and went on for a long time. Because they were both so relaxed and concentrated solely on the active parts of their bodies, their eventual peaking was one of the most delightful and pleasurable they experienced together. It made Juan cry out, "Oh darling, this was a lovely experience." She caught herself right away and stopped. Feeling a bit out of time and space at that heightened moment, she had forgotten where they were. Later on, it was Juan, lying awake for some time while Michael was sleeping soundly, who climbed down from the upper bunk and converted the bunk seat below into a bed and fell asleep right away.

13

Guilin

M ichael woke up with a start. It was already light in the
train compartment. He feared he might have overslept.
At the same time, he remembered that Juan was with
him in the bunk when they settled down for the night the evening before. For a moment, he imagined that she might have fled
from him. That thought sent a cold shiver down his spine. He
was surprised that he would have such a thought. But there was
no reason for him to be fearful that this would happen, and he
chided himself for being paranoid. Presently, his fears vanished
as he realized that there was only sleeping space for one person.
He leaned over the edge of his bunk and was immediately reassured. She was still asleep there below him.

"Juan wake up," he whispered several times after looking at
his watch and seeing that it was high time to get up. In less than
an hour the train would be moving into the Guilin train station.
Whispering didn't accomplish anything. He then climbed down
the ladder and gently tapped Juan's shoulder. When she opened
her sleep-filled eyes and showed him an expression of not knowing where she was and who he was, he said gently, "Sweetheart,
we've almost reached our destination. Guilin is less than an hour
away. I'm your lover and traveling companion. Please come back
to earth." That did it. Juan suddenly sat up and looked alarmed
about something.

"Oh, I was so involved in a disturbing dream that seemed to
have gone on the entire night. It had me in its grip. I couldn't
get out of it. I was sitting in a movie house, and a film I didn't

168

want to see was shown to me. But I was held there, and I had to look at it, over and over again. It was just like I was being held hostage or in bondage, for I was tied to the chair I was sitting in. There were no other people in the theatre, and I don't know who was making me watch the movie. The film showed people betraying and harming other people. I don't know why I should have had such a disturbing dream." She seemed distraught when she told Michael what she had dreamt about. He tried to coax her out of her unpleasant reflections by kneeling down in front of her, taking hold of her hands and kissing both of her palms. "Sweetheart, don't worry." He spoke soothingly, "That was just a dream. Today we'll be floating down the Li River among the tall green limestone peaks you told me about, that rise dramatically from the river bank into the sky." Still holding her hands, he continued, "That's what you wanted to see more than anything else on our journey south. Remember, even yesterday you said it was a wish you had even when you were a child but your parents wouldn't take you there."

"Of course, I remember all of that, and I'm looking forward to seeing that most unusual and magical landscape with you." She then got up suddenly. "Let's get dressed and be ready to get off this train," she said. "I don't want to linger on it one minute longer. I want to get on with our journey. Just think the day after tomorrow, we'll be in Guangzhou." By then she was already putting on her clothes and Michael busied himself with getting dressed as well. Juan was obviously excited. When she was just half dressed, she turned to Michael, threw her arms around his neck and gave full vent to her feelings. "Darling, I love you. You are the most wonderful person I've ever been close to."

"Thanks, sweetheart. Same in here," he responded while pointing to his heart, and clasping her in his arms with his hot face pressed against hers.

* * *

They accomplished all they had to do within an hour after getting off at Guilin's rather unimposing train station. There they made reservations for the evening of the next day for the train that was going to carry them to Guangzhou, their final gateway to freedom from pursuit. Both were excited when Michael held the tickets in his hand. Next they signed in at the Guilin Flowers Youth Hostel on Zhongshan Nanlu Boulevard, only steps away from the train station. The staff was friendly, but as is typical of youth hostels, the rooms were rather plain. Michael and Juan didn't mind. After all, they would only spend one night there. They inquired at the reception desk about a boat ride down the Li River and were told that they could get tickets for group or private boat rides at the nearby information center. The reception clerk pushed a map toward them on which she quickly marked the hostel, the train station and the information center. "Ah, it's very close," Juan said right away. "Let's go there now, Michael."

Out in the sunshine of the tree-lined boulevard, they held hands until they reached the information center. There they had to make a decision about what tickets to buy. The group boat ride was considerably cheaper than the private ride. Michael thought for a moment what tickets to purchase. He was running low in funds and had paid for much of the trip with his credit card. He knew he wouldn't be able to pay off the accrued balance this time, as he usually did every month. But then he thought, *This is a once-in-a-lifetime experience. I'm going for the private ride.*

Turning to the ticket clerk, he said, "I think we would like to go private on a small boat, if you have tickets for that."

"I think I can help you with that, sir."

"But, darling, wait. Either one would be fine with me. You don't have to splurge. I would rather do something in Guangzhou that will be extraordinarily memorable and beautiful. I'll explain to you later today what I have in mind. For me the group boat would be just fine."

"OK, but I've already made up my mind about this boat ride." He ordered tickets for the private boat leaving at 1 p.m.

Juan understood and jumped up and down next to him, clapping her hands. After Michael had completed the transaction, she grabbed his hand and pulled him out onto the sidewalk. As soon as they stepped outside, she threw her arms around Michael's neck and covered his face with kisses, not caring how the pedestrians would respond to her uninhibited demonstration of affection. "Thank you, thank you for doing that," she whispered in his ear. "I'm so delighted to be going on this ride with you. I hope we'll get a good guide and all will be perfect. I'm sure our trip down the river will be slower, quieter, and more relaxed than in the group boat. It'll be a very special experience." Her enthusiasm seemed extraordinary, a bit over the top in Michael's eyes.

"Sweetheart, it's OK. We may be doing this only once. So I thought we should go for the best and most enjoyable. That's all. I'm thinking not only of you but also of myself—what I would like best."

"Yes, I realize that and that's how it should be. But I'm simply excited."

Since it was still quite early and hours until they would take the boat trip, Juan suggested that they take a bus to Guilin's Solitary Beauty Peak Park, one of the major attractions just north of the City. "The bus ride will be short along Zhongshan Zhonglu Boulevard," she said. "On that route, we'll cross over Rong Hu and Shan Hu lakes, which are quite large, and then pass by Guilin's Central City Square before we get to the Solitary Beauty Peak. It's a 152 meter pinnacle. The climb will be steep but worthwhile because of the beautiful vista that will open up to us from the top. Oh, and what you don't know is that the ruins of a 14th century palace are at the foot of this peak. It was built by the nephew of a Ming emperor. The restored wall and gates surround the foot of the peak. Otherwise there is nothing much to see." Juan stopped her animated description of the Solitary Beauty Peak and the palace ruins. She looked quizzically at Michael to gauge his interest. Since he smiled at her, she quickly resumed. "Oh, and before we climb the peak or after the climb, we could have lunch at the old palace wall. There are many food stands, I have heard, that serve delicious Guangxi food."

171

"Yes, let's do the Solitary Beauty Peak this morning and from there walk to the tourist wharf if it doesn't seem too far away. But if we feel tired after climbing the peak, we'll take a bus. But now I think we should go to our room, take showers and dress lightly because it's going to be a very warm day. And let's not forget our hats. The sun will be intense."

They raced each other back to the Guilin Flowers Hostel, and hurried up the stairs to their third floor room. Michael purposely held back so that Juan would be the first to reach their room. She seemed elated and called out to Michael, the straggler, "I was first and I'm the first in the bathroom."

"OK with me. Go right ahead."

Michael stepped into the bathroom as soon as Juan vacated it and shut the door. While she rummaged in her suitcase for something appropriate to wear, her phone rang. She dashed to her handbag and answered hastily. Someone on the other end began talking immediately, not even giving her time to answer the phone properly. She just stood there in her panties and bra, nodding her head without saying anything, and as the caller went on, she nodded again. Apparently, the caller wouldn't let her speak. Finally she said in a low voice, rather curtly, "I'll think about it," and pressed the 'off' button.

At that moment she heard Michael coming out of the bathroom. *"Oh shucks,"* she thought. Her back was turned to him, and she wasn't sure whether he heard the four words she had used to finish off the call. She quickly stowed the cell phone back in her handbag and turned around.

"An early morning call, sweetheart?" Michael said and looked at her questioningly. "Is someone 2,000 kilometers away from us trying to stay in touch?" Michael was very curious. He'd overheard her curt response to the caller. "So what are you supposed to be thinking about?" To him it was a strange way to end a call without saying goodbye.

Juan held her gaze steadily on Michael, but a faint rosy flush covered her cheeks. He noticed it. *Could she be embarrassed?* He wondered. *And why does it take her so long to answer me.*

Suddenly she burst out, "Darling, you know who is calling me. She realizes that I'm getting close to the place from where I intend to leave this country. She just wanted me to think about my next huge step. Please try to understand her. She'd rather have me close by. She thinks she is not only losing her daughter, but also her best friend. But I didn't want to get into a long conversation. I just tried to assure her that I will give my decision to leave the county serious thought even though I've already made my decision."

Michael nodded and tried to be understanding. "Oh I feel sorry for her. She's losing you and is afraid that once you take off from Guangzhou she'll never see you again. Of course she doesn't want to let you go, and it must be hard for you to leave her. I worry that your loyalty to your family may conflict with what you feel for me."

"Don't be silly, darling. My life is attached to yours. I'll go wherever you take me." Her tone was firm and her momentary confusion seemed to have vanished. Her cheeks were as clear, pale—alabaster-like—as always. Michael, feeling a bit embarrassed, stepped toward her and folded her into his arms. They stayed like that, firmly entwined, for quite awhile, during which time he secretly chided himself for his recurring suspicions and doubts. *Do I really not trust her? But I do. She's told me again and again how she feels about me, and she's shown it in our lovemaking. She's given herself completely and has opted to flee the country with me,* he thought as he kept holding Juan pressed to him.

Suddenly she whispered in his ear, "All is fine, believe me, but let's get ready for our outing. I'm not even dressed yet. I'm sorry for the delay."

"Yes, sweetheart, that's exactly what we should do." He released her then.

* * *

In a flurry of activity, they got ready for their outing. Equipped for a long day of walking, hiking and sightseeing, they headed for the door. Michael asked her, "Do you think you have everything you need? This is your last chance to bring along something you've forgotten, something like sunscreen, lip balm or whatnot. And what do you think about breakfast? Should we grab something light in the coffee shop downstairs— tea or coffee, a boiled egg, perhaps, and a piece of toast? What do you think?"

"To answer your first question, I believe I have everything. To respond to your second question, your breakfast suggestion suits me fine. I'd really like some coffee with milk."

And so they departed. Leaving their key at the reception desk, they dashed into the little café, ordered the breakfast items Michael had suggested, as well as Juan's café au lait and hurried off to the bus stop with their food and drinks securely lidded. Just as they reached the stop, their bus arrived. *What perfect timing*, Michael thought. *A good omen for the day, perhaps.* The bus was only partially full, and they grabbed the nearest available seats right behind the driver, which gave them a fine view out the left window next to them and also through the bus's huge windshield. After passing the main bus station, they crossed the narrow Taohua River, went over a wide bridge that spanned the two enormous lakes, Rong Hu and Shan Hu, Juan had talked about earlier, passed the city's central square and would soon arrive at the Solitary Beauty Peak. Michael and Juan had been sitting close together, slurping their coffees and devouring their egg and toast while still trying to catch the sights of the city. "Wow, I think there really is a lot to see here in Guilin. It's a beautifully kept city, at least the public part of it is. I think we could spend at least one week here," Michael observed enthusiastically and added, "I wish we had more time to see and enjoy it."

Juan responded, "Let's be relaxed and in the moment. Forget about what cannot be, and enjoy this wonderful sunny day and seeing these seemingly eternal natural sights."

Hearing Juan speaking so sensibly, he did as she suggested. In moments like these, when he felt the calming effect of her presence, he appreciated her especially. And he wondered why he let himself slip into dark thoughts about her. For awhile they were quiet, withdrawn into their own thoughts. Juan seemed to be meditating, while he reflected upon his strange groundless tendencies to doubt her. *How can I have these periodic feelings of suspicion and even of mistrust toward her? Maybe it reveals some unexamined paranoiac tendencies in me. It's a negative quality of mine I need to be watchful of. In the presence of Juan, I'm beginning to recognize it. It could ruin a cherished and irreplaceable relationship. Juan has been so giving, so sensitive to my needs, so loving, such a good sport throughout our journey, how in the world could I doubt her? Shame on me!*

By the time they reached their destination he had put away his doubts and suspicions. Even though he was distracted by his thoughts, he had watched for some time the green pinnacle of the Beauty Peak coming into full view, at first like a small, very pointed green cone in the distance and then in its full 152 meter massiveness in front of them. As the bus stopped, he gathered up their small backpacks with one hand and with the other he grabbed Juan's hand and literally pulled her out of the seat and out of the bus, while she admonished him, "Easy, Michael, easy. Let me get out by myself. I might get hung up on something." Michael wouldn't relinquish her hand, but he proceeded more slowly and carefully than before. Out on the sidewalk, dropping their backpacks and the plastic bag containing their paper coffee cups, he embraced an astonished Juan around her waist, lifted her up a little and whirled her around and around until he felt dizzy—while she squealed like a little girl. People standing around them laughed with them, beholding their youthful exuberance. When Michael came to a standstill and released Juan, they both ran to a bench close by and dizzily dropped themselves onto it, laughing until they felt steadied.

"You always surprise me," Juan said, still laughing in fits and spurts. "I never know what you're going to do. No one has ever whirled me around like that in public, not even as a child. It's strange, but I love it. And I love your physical strength, too. But you know that already."

"Oh, it's good that you like it because you'll get it being with me, a lot of it. But now let's get serious and tackle that big lonely Beauty Peak in front of us. I guess we'll have to go through one of the old palace gates to pay for our tickets. Nothing seems to be free these days, not even such a natural piece of rock."

* * *

They tackled the beautiful but monstrous cone with determination. The circular trail, hewn into the rock's surface was steep and dizzying. They could hardly imagine how they would manage if some descending climbers had to pass them. But somehow they would manage, they assured each other. Michael was climbing ahead of Juan and set the pace. She struggled behind him but managed, if only barely, to keep up with him. From time to time, Michael stopped to take a deep breath and look back to make sure Juan was behind him. Sometimes she begged him to rest a couple of minutes before taking off again. He noticed how out of breath she was, but thought that the climb was good for her and would toughen her up. He intended to take her on many hikes in the Sierra Nevadas once they had settled in California.

They didn't look much at the scenery while climbing the precipitous trail, focusing instead on their footing. Once they reached the top, they would survey all the surrounding natural beauty. And when they finally got to the very top of the giant cone, they looked down upon the lush green landscape through which the Li River flowed languidly. But a more arresting sight than the river were the very tall, perfectly cone-shaped and lushly green limestone peaks that crowded the river's flat banks as far as the eye could see. It was a breathtaking vista. They stood in awe of nature's timeless beauty. Michael couldn't imagine how these striking cones, like giant toys, had originally been shaped eons ago. They sat down on the narrow top of the Solitary Beauty Peak and decided to rest there for an hour and to keep on feasting their eyes and imagination on the almost otherworldly landscape.

They found their descent not as strenuous as the ascent, but a little scarier. They had to go down slowly to avoid any missteps. At the bottom, they hugged each other feeling very pleased and relieved that they had made it down safely to the old palace wall. Feeling hungry, they strolled along the food stands to buy their lunch.

"I'll let you order for me, sweetheart. When it comes to food, I have to depend on you. But please don't order anything fiery from the menu."

"OK, I'll try my best. And I don't think we have to worry about all the exotic fare you can find in expensive specialty restaurants like snake soup, armadillo steaks, short-tailed monkey filets, mini-turtle dishes or grilled breast of horned pheasant. I think by now you're aware that Chinese people eat just about anything that runs, walks, scuttles, crawls, swims, slithers or flies. But I can probably find here among these open stalls some simple beer fish that's deliciously wok-fried, sometimes at your table. Additionally, we could order a portion of noodles and the local Liqun Beer. All of these other strange items I talked about can be had in Beijing, too. Although I've never been to Guangxi Province, I'm familiar with their cuisine. Trust me, the beer fish is delicious."

"OK, sweetheart, you make me salivate. Your recommendation sounds good and I'm hungry."

Well satisfied with their lunch, they sat for awhile on a bench under the enormous canapé of an old tree before they set off on foot to the tourist wharf a couple of kilometers down Binjiang Lu Street along the Li River.

* * *

The Wharf turned out to be more confusing then they had thought, surrounded by water taxis, rowboats, little skiffs, as well as large and small tour boats either tied up to the docks or circling in the water. *How can we find our small boat?* They both wondered. Juan had the idea of going to the wharf master's office. There they showed their tickets and were quickly ushered out of the small but crowded office. A teenage boy asked them to follow him. He dashed off past the docks. Michael and Juan tried to keep up with him. At the far-down-river end of the long wharf, he stopped suddenly, "There is your tour boat, the one with the small Chinese flag flying." He pointed in the direction of a flag-flying little boat among a score of others.

"Ah, thank you. I see it," Michael responded while digging in his pocket and coming out with a bunch of coins in his hand.

The young boy bowed before Michael, who thanked him as he dropped several coins into his hand. Then the boy quickly turned and ran off. Juan and Michael descended a steel ladder leading from the main wharf to a narrow wood-planked walkway along the wharf's wall that served as a docking platform for small boats. They headed straight for the power boat that they expected to be theirs if the boy was a reliable official guide. They were lucky. The man sitting on the transom of the flag-carrying boat had been waiting for them, even though it wasn't one o'clock yet. He jumped right out of the boat onto the narrow gangway, took their tickets, bowed and introduced himself as Lü Zhun, a short diminutive man with graying hair, who bowed deferentially before Michael and Juan. "Welcome to this private boat tour," he said very formally in Chinese, and assisted Juan into the boat while Michael climbed in by himself. When they were seated on the low rattan-backed wooden bench in the middle of the open boat, Zhun lowered himself into a squatting position on the gangplank above and slightly in front of his passengers. "Today's outing will take about two to three hours on the river," he told them. "Downstream I will row the boat, and upstream we will motor. We'll be heading south toward the city of Yangshuo that is less than half the size of Guilin. But we will not reach that city on this tour. It's too far. It would be a full day's trip of 54 kilometers. But we'll see the breathtaking limestone peaks, also called tower karst, rising in extraordinary formations next to and above the river. The peaks were formed through the erosion of an ancient uplifted seabed. Their beauty casts a spell on everyone, Chinese and foreigners alike. These giant green cones lie like huge chunks of jade along the river in the sunshine. Sometimes when a low fog settles over the river landscape and blots out the river itself and the low-lying areas, especially in the morning, the green karst piercing through appear like the links of a giant jade necklace draped on top of the fog. It's a marvelous landscape, as you will see, through which is threaded a sometimes pale green, sometimes silvery ribbon of the Li River. It depends on the sunshine. Oh, and this landscape has inspired over the centuries much famous Chinese art and poetry. You can see some of it in the city's art galleries and the museum."

While their guide recited his interesting spiel about the landscape, Michael thought, *He still waxes poetic even after spending all his life in this landscape.* But then he thought, *Ah, those must be just routine tidbits he recites over and over again to his passengers, at least twice a day. He almost impressed me.* Juan didn't comment on their guide's introduction. Instead she settled herself comfortably into the rattan backing of the wooden bench while the guide jumped onto the boat's transom. Michael thought again, *Juan must have recognized what the descriptive tidbits about this unusual landscape were, something this simple man has picked up somewhere in a guidebook, and he repeats them every day.*

Their guide got them under way quickly, deftly rowing and navigating among the many other boats, large and small. As they left behind the busy wharf and all the shouting and motor noises and floated down the broad languidly flowing Li River in silence, a wonderful serenity settled over Michael and Juan. There was just this rhythmic and subtly splashing noise the oar made as it dipped in regular intervals into the water. But beyond that, nearly perfect stillness reigned as they floated down the wide river. Had they been able to see themselves from the far river bank or from the top of a high karst nearby, they would have appeared like a toy in a landscape created by giants. From their perspective, these immensely tall green cones or jagged giants' teeth, as they are sometimes called, stretched out before them far into the distance. As they sat reverently close together holding hands, a formerly un-experienced serenity came over them during the boat ride going southward even when they encountered a barge, a sampan or a tour boat once in awhile. It ended for them when their guide reached the furthest southward point he intended to go to, turned the boat around and started the engine.

"Can't we go on as before in peace and quiet?" Michael shouted back to Zhun.

He replied, "I'm sorry, but the current is too strong for rowing upstream. I wouldn't have the strength, and if I had, we wouldn't get back until nightfall or later."

"OK," Michael shouted back. "I understand. Do what you have to do to get us back. It's been a wonderful boat ride, this journey south. Thanks."

On their way back to Guilin, they came across a wondrous river sight—a fisherman on a long, narrow raft that was skimming back and forth across the river while driving the raft dexterously with a long oar from the transom. An unusual sight were the jet black, long-necked birds on the raft. Juan and Michael's guide shouted from the rear because he saw Michael pointing to the raft. "He is one of our cormorant fishermen. You see them rarely nowadays. But in earlier times it was a popular way of fishing. If you listen carefully, you can hear the cormorant fisherman curse his birds. His handlers splash them by smacking the water with poles to make the reluctant birds dive. Choke collars prevent these birds from swallowing their catch, so they still have it in their beaks when they surface. The bird handlers then quickly take the fish from them."

"How interesting," Michael shouted back. "I've seen cormorants diving in the Pacific along the coast of California, but they weren't serving fishermen. These birds here are exploited workers. Are they permitted to swallow the odd fish for compensation?" Zhun just laughed in reply.

* * *

Getting back to the wharf, they were thrilled with their boat ride. Michael dug deep into his pocket and brought out some paper money and coins. He glanced briefly at the sum and handed it with thanks to their guide, who bowed and smiled happily. They both bowed as well toward him and headed straight for the ladder that would take them back to the wharf. Since they felt quite rested, they threw on their backpacks and decided to walk to their hostel. According to the Guilin map they had brought along, the walk was only three to four kilometers long. Part of it would take them by the Li River along Binjiang Lu.

Back in their hostel room, they threw themselves onto the bed to rest and to digest the day's activities. "This was a wonderful outing," Juan said. "Thank you from my heart for giving me this experience."

"Well, I have to thank you, sweetheart. Without you we would have bypassed Guilin and wouldn't have gotten to see such a fantastic landscape. Nor would we have had such a delicious lunch."

"Oh that was nothing, Michael. You shouldn't even mention it. You paid for it after all. But I'm now wondering how we will proceed from here. We have the early evening train reservation to Guangzhou tomorrow, but where are we going to stay when we get there? I have one fervent wish, or better put, one fervent desire for Guangzhou. May I tell you what it is?"

"Sure. Go right ahead," Michael responded sleepily.

"Could we splurge a bit in Guangzhou? I would so much like to stay at the River Pearl Hotel. It's such a fabulous place. It has been a dream of mine to stay there some day. But it's not inexpensive because it's world renowned. What do you think, Michael? After all those train compartments and inexpensive hotels and hostels, could we afford it?"

Michael didn't answer right away. He was suddenly wide awake, sat up on the edge of the bed, then went over to sit in a chair close to it. He looked at Juan quizzically while his mind ran over his current situation. *Oh, she is a material girl after all,* he thought while he looked straight into her eyes. He was reluctant to balk at the expense, but he knew he couldn't afford that hotel. He had used his credit card heavily, near to the max. He had lost his car and would be out of a job because as soon as he got back to California he intended to give his present employer notice. He couldn't go back to Beijing. He had given up his apartment in California before he went to China and needed to find a replacement which might be expensive. He wanted to find a nice pleasant place for the two of them. These thoughts raced through his mind and forced him to confront a dire reality, which had been obscured until now by their hasty escape and love-filled journey. Now she was asking him if they could afford a big splurge. The answer was clearly 'No,' but he sensed that he had better be very tactful in his response without prevaricating. *I've got to be truthful,* he reminded himself, *totally truthful. From what I've seen so far, Juan should be able to hear the truth and accept it."*

"Sweetheart, I have to confess that I'm financially stressed at the moment. All of our expenses have been charged to my credit card. I'm quickly reaching the maximum I can charge. I'm also thinking ahead. I'll have to quit my current job when we get back to California because I can't and won't go back to China, not in the near future at least. I've no place to live in California. I gave up my apartment when I left for Beijing. And I have no car. Things will be very tight when we get there, but they should improve as soon as I get busy, get a job and have an income. I hope you understand my predicament. Can't we be a bit frugal during the rest of our escape? I still have to get our airline tickets back to the U.S."

He looked at her pleadingly.

Juan nodded and digested this for a moment, looking down and reflecting. Her eyes were still downcast as she replied, "Sure, darling, I can live with being frugal for awhile. But please, couldn't we just stay two nights at the River Pearl Hotel? I've brought enough money with me. I can pay for the room. It's just a dream of mine to stay there. I don't know whether I'll ever get back to it." Her eyes stayed downcast as she said this. But then she lifted them to his with such a pleading look that it weakened his resolve.

"Sweetheart, I don't want you to pay for anything. I think two nights is a good compromise. So let's do that and enjoy our stay there to the fullest. Let's go all out then—do the dining, the dress up even if we have to buy new clothing, do the spa thing and whatever else will be offered. It'll be a blowout and a farewell to China, at least for quite some time, I reckon." Michael became animated as he spoke and seemed to have put aside all of his anxiety about the future. *"What the hell,"* he thought. *"We can do everything. It's once in a lifetime perhaps."*

Juan had been eyeing him speculatively all the while he spoke. "That is sweet and generous of you, darling. I'll appreciate everything, and afterwards we'll get serious and down to earth. But may I ask you one more thing? When I first met you, I thought you would be, like all Americans, well off financially and with nothing to worry about. But I see it's different than I thought. Still, your parents must be wealthy, no? Aren't they in a position to help you out?"

Michael again looked at her curiously, wondering, *How rich did she think I was when we met? And why would she ask if my parents are wealthy?* But he answered confidently, "Sweetheart, please don't worry about any of this. I can tell you that I'm capable of making a good life for us. I'm well educated. I hold a Bachelor of Science degree in electronic engineering and a master's degree in information technology. Both degrees are from respected California universities, and I will get a good, well-paying job. But I wouldn't take anything from my parents, would never ask them for anything. I would be terribly embarrassed if I did or if I had to. They are well off but not rich."

Juan had gotten up out of her reclining position. "Oh, I see more clearly now. Thanks, darling, for telling me. It's good for me to know what our situation will be so I can adjust myself to it. I'm glad not to have to think about it anymore. I love you for your honesty." She sounded upbeat as she said it. Presently she jumped off the bed, came over to him where he was sitting in the chair. She knelt down in front of him, pushed his knees apart, wedged herself in, folded her arms around his waist and placed her head against his chest. "Darling, you're such an honest and straightforward man. I think I would be able to trust you always. There wouldn't be any covering up, any evasiveness on your part

You're a very precious man," Juan whispered wistfully into his
chest as if she were speaking directly to his heart. He was so
touched that he didn't even notice the conditional phrases she
had been using.

Suddenly, he pushed her off a little, looked into her eyes and
said, "I need to run down to the Information Center before they
close to get the hotel squared away. I sincerely hope they'll have
a room for us. I'm going to do this now, and I want you to get
ready for a fine dinner. You deserve it after this incredibly long
outing. So get ready. It won't take me long until I get back." He
got up and pulled Juan up to him at the same time. He planted
a soft kiss on her lips which she presently tried to change into a
passionate one. But Michael was determined to make her latest
wish come true and whispered in her ear, "I've got to go, sweetheart. I'll be ready for that later." He smiled at her and headed
for the door.

As soon as he was gone, she thought, *I've got to make a call
and I've got to make it quick.* She opened the door of their room
gingerly and peered out into the corridor. She listened for the
footsteps on the staircase. She heard them. It was unmistakably
Michael racing down the stairs instead of taking the elevator.
That's what he always did. She closed the door quietly, looked
for her handbag and when she found it, she took the cell phone
out hurriedly. Her fingers trembled slightly as she called the
number. It rang several times. Then a voice on the answering
machine came on that she recognized and, at the sound of the
prompting tone, she said quickly, "It's me, Juan. I'm sorry I'm
unable to reach you. I'll be at the River Pearl Hotel for two
nights from the day after tomorrow. I've seriously thought about
what you said and I like it. Thanks. Don't call me. Can't talk
anymore."

She quickly stuffed the cell phone back into her bag. Michael
didn't come back immediately. She was glad she wouldn't have
to explain anything to him. She went to the door, opened it again
and listened briefly. She heard no footsteps on the stairs. Back
inside the room, she rummaged through her suitcase and at the

184

bottom found her favorite dress. She had forgotten that she had packed it, obviously for a special occasion. *Thank goodness,* she thought as she disappeared into the bathroom. She wanted to look lovely for this evening. She also wanted it to be one of their finest evenings. This day should end happily.

Michael came back to their room before Juan was done with the bathroom. She heard the room door being shut forcefully.

"I'll be done and out in a minute," she called out.

"Don't worry. Take your time. I can wait until you appear soft and fragrant like a gorgeous, just-unfurled blossom," Michael shouted back.

He sounds upbeat, she thought. *He must have been able to make the room reservation. All will be well. All will work out beautifully.* And then she rushed to get done and have him start his bathroom routine. When she emerged a minute later, all naked, with only a white towel wound around her head, she saw his eyes light up. He headed straight toward her and embraced her heartily while whispering into her ear, "We got the room. We'll have a wonderful time, a real blowout."

Juan, feeling his passion and knowing how quickly they could be entangled on the bed, whispered back, "Not now, not yet darling, but later, not too much later, but when we get back," and she wriggled herself out of his arms. He let her go and said with a laugh, "I can wait, sweetheart. Right now, you're wearing my favorite outfit, nothing at all. But since we're going out for a fine dinner, I won't ruffle you up."

* * *

Without telling Michael, Juan chose the most popular club to start the evening with a drink before dinner. She wanted Michael to get a taste of Club 100% Baidu, a very hip and loud bar. The hostel's receptionist told her that this was the most popular club in town and a great place to observe the locals. For dining, the receptionist recommended Yiyuan Fandian, an outstanding Sichuan restaurant with a great atmosphere and friendly servers. She also recommended the restaurant's specialty of fried eel

Uta Christensen

Sichuan style. Juan thought, *I'll make sure that we'll get the mild version. I don't want to play any more tricks on my darling.* Since they would be finished by 7:30, she figured, she could still take him to the Lijiang Theatre for a show of local acrobats, ethnic music and dance. She had read about it on a flier lying on the reception desk. While he was in the bathroom whistling to his heart's content, she slipped into her gorgeous lilac silk cocktail dress and her high heeled shoes and rushed downstairs in the elevator and made the dinner and theatre reservations. She was very excited and pleased with herself, and she would insist that she pay for all of it. That was her plan and she was intent on convincing Michael that it was her evening out and a gift to him, just as he had made so many gifts to her. She came back to the room before Michael was finished in the bathroom. She heard the whirring of his shaver. *Oh, great*, she thought and seated herself seductively in one of the room's not so glamorous chairs, knowing that he would be dazzled by her looks. He had seen her on this entire trip only in her blue jeans and T-shirts.

When Michael came out of the bathroom with a towel wrapped around his loins, he stopped in his tracks, with eyes wide and a surprised look. "Oh my, are you beautiful!" he exclaimed. "Too beautiful for me and for just going out to dinner. Do you know where we're going?"

"I know for sure. I have arranged it through the reception desk. It's all fine and perfect and a surprise for you. Leave it to me," she commanded.

* * *

When they finally returned to their semi-dark room around eleven o'clock, or a bit later in the evening, in high spirits, Michael gushed, "What a lovely evening you created for us. Drinks in that crazy, colorful, noisy and very local bar, an excellent and truly delicious dinner, and then that superb traditionally ethnic show. And all of that as a gift for me. Thanks from my heart, my sweetheart." He embraced her passionately.

"I'm so happy it pleased you," she whispered in his ear.

186

Then Michael released her, turned her body around and started unzipping her dress. She felt his hot breath on her neck and shoulders. She found it amusing when her zipper got hung up midway, and he tried frantically to make it go down all the way. *He started off so sure of himself,* she thought. But now she sensed his irritation and nervousness. She guessed that he had wanted to demonstrate how suave and adroit he could be. *Maybe this little hang-up will make him nervous and ruin his otherwise perfect confidence in his control of our lovemaking,* she thought. Before she could think about this any further, he got the zipper working again, ran it down all the way, pushed the straps over her shoulders—she wasn't wearing a bra—so that the dress began gliding slowly to the floor. She stepped out of the silken gown, tossed off her shoes and removed her panties. Then, in a quick movement, Michael picked up her slender body and carried her to the bed. Juan let it all happen, feeling a titillating pleasure and cooing coyly in his ear, "Darling, what are you up to?"

"Nothing."

He set her down on the bed very gently, took off his clothes and placed himself alongside her on the bed in full nakedness. "I just have to lie here for awhile and think about our fabulous evening," he said quietly. He grabbed her right hand and pressed it gently to let her know how appreciative he felt. Juan was willing to let him indulge in romantic fantasies for a little while, but she intended to bring him down to earth when she was ready. She waited for a change in his mood, and when he released her hand, she knew her moment had come.

In a quick movement, she swung herself onto Michael's relaxed and stretched out body. *I wonder how quickly I can make him respond,* she thought. She brushed her lips lightly across his forehead, cheeks and nose, but when she reached his lips she kissed him hungrily, devouring and penetrating. Michael didn't respond immediately, as though challenging her to make him come to life. She met the challenge with pelvic motions he couldn't resist. It happened all so dizzyingly fast that he barely knew what was happening. He had been so determined, playfully,

187

to resist her tempting motions. But now he was inside her while her upper body gyrated on top of him, mysteriously erect in the dimness of the room, her arms stretched up and swaying, her body moving in a slow circular motion, with the sinuous grace of a belly dancer. But her face, her lovely face, he couldn't see and didn't know what she felt because it was turned upward. Michael then let himself become one with that turning and grinding motion, letting his mind relax and surrendering his body to the rhythmic motions until they transported him into ecstasy. Juan, feeling him on the point of exploding, gently lowered her body onto his. She remained very still, her face resting on his shoulder.

"Oh, how wonderful!" he finally cried out. That's when she raised her torso up and released a volley of her trilling laughter, a sign of her own heightened experience, while Michael folded his arms around her.

* * *

Their next experience was awakening simultaneously to the new day, the day they would start tackling the last leg of their journey through China. But neither of them felt like getting up. They had no sense of what time it was. Nothing mattered on this day—whether what they might accomplish or what sights they would see. The only thing that mattered was to be on time and catch the evening train to Guangzhou.

But there was no point in wasting the day. They decided to spend it visiting southwestern China's original tourist attraction, that was and still is Guilin's Seven Star Park, also called Qixing Park, situated on the eastern side of the Li River. It covers an area of 137 hectares and contains seven prominent cone-shaped peaks, lime-stone karst, that due to their arrangement in the park, are sometimes likened to the Big Dipper constellation. The park, first opened to sightseers during the Sui dynasty that reigned from 581-628 A.D., also features the huge Seven Star Cave filled with bizarre floodlight colored stalactites and stalagmites and the Dark Dragon Cave with its massive inscribed stele dating back more than 1,500 years.

Their day in the park was enjoyable and relaxing. They walked for hours on the winding paths, sat on its extensive lawns, admired the immutable karst, and explored both caves, after which they lunched on a bench under the canopy of a giant tree and napped on the grass of a nearby meadow. At five in the afternoon, they returned to their room excitedly because the time had come when they would leave Guilin behind.

14

Guangzhou

Michael and Juan saw right away, when they arrived at the platform, that the train would be crowded. "Darling," said Juan, "there doesn't seem to be any hope that we'll have the pleasure of an empty compartment. Too bad! We'll have to share and lose our privacy." She was clearly disappointed after surveying the crowd. "I think you're dead right," Michael agreed.

And so it turned out after boarding the train, they encountered an older, very reserved gray-haired couple already primly seated on one side of the compartment. They looked at Juan and Michael curiously, who were dressed casually in jeans and T-shirts but bowed their heads to them. *Oh, no, not even people we can talk to*, Michael thought. *What a shame*. A similar thought went through Juan's mind.

It was already nine in the evening by the time they had stowed away their hand luggage and sat down. They were holding hands, and Juan whispered, "What bad luck. Couldn't it have been like on our recent legs of the journey? Then we could have enjoyed this night ride to our hearts' content."

"Uh, never mind," he responded, "We've to adjust to the situation. Such is life. It seldom plays straight or consistently," was his response. Then he added, "Just keep in mind what a wonderful evening we'll have tomorrow night. If I understood you correctly, it'll be luxurious," and he suddenly laughed out loud, but caught himself as he noticed how curiously the couple in the opposite seats were regarding them.

"We have to be more restrained," Juan whispered.

"Don't worry. We'll be making up our beds soon. And we'll sleep soundly tonight after our long day outside. Too bad we couldn't rest anymore in our hostel and had to give up our room in the afternoon. But if the train isn't delayed, we'll get into Guangzhou at nine in the morning. Maybe we should go to the washroom now and dress in T-shirts and shorts for the night instead of wearing a nightie and pajamas."

"Good idea." Juan responded. "Let's go now. I'll wait outside the washroom until you're done. And then you can wait for me. We'll come back here together."

"Or better yet," Michael uttered under his breath jokingly and half laughingly, "we can use the washroom together. Wouldn't that be exciting?"

"Oh stop it. You're making me blush. I wouldn't do that. Why in that awful train washroom? We could have done it every time in our hotel bathrooms. Why didn't we?" Juan spoke in such a low tone that Michael hardly understood her. But he caught the gist of it.

"I was only joking, sweetheart. It's a crazy idea, I know. I wouldn't embarrass you by doing it, but it's fun to imagine."

Having accomplished their evening routine, they returned to the compartment and set about making up the lower seat as a bed that Michael was going to sleep on. Juan's upper bunk was already made up. In no time they were tucked away for the night, went right to sleep, and so provided some privacy for the old couple.

* * *

Michael woke up at the first signs of faint morning light showing through the center split in the curtain. At first he didn't know where he was. But then he heard the rhythmic clatter of the train's wheels on the tracks. It sounded much smoother than the clunky noise of some of the trains they had been on recently. *Oh, since I'm seeing some light coming in through the curtains, we must be nearing Guangzhou,* he thought. *It's time to get up.* He looked over at the still soundly sleeping old man in the lower bunk opposite him. There was no stirring in the upper bunks as far as he could tell. He got up quietly, climbed the ladder to Juan's bunk half way up and looked at her peaceful sleeping face. As always, he was aware of her flawless beauty, and having come to know her as a person in the course of this journey, he was continually amazed that he could have such a tender, loving, good natured sweetheart. He tapped her shoulder lightly, and she immediately opened her dark mysterious eyes. "Sweetheart, we're getting close to Guangzhou. It's already faintly light outside. I want to see the countryside. I'll go to the washroom now before everyone else wants to use it and then watch the landscape fly by from a corridor window outside the compartment. I don't want to open the compartment curtains. Both of our companions are still sleeping soundly over there. What about you? Do you want to sleep some more? Or do you feel like getting up?"

"Oh, I'm not sure. I would like to sleep a little longer, but then I would also like to be with you and take in the landscape because we're now in Guangdong, one of the southernmost provinces of China, and it's foreign to me. I've read that it's mountainous but also has tropical forests. Close to Guangzhou, the train will run along the Pearl River, I'm sure. Let me know when you're done with your routine. I'll get up then and get myself ready," she said while yawning.

"OK, I'm looking forward to seeing you." He kissed her softly on the cheek, climbed down the ladder, grabbed his toiletry bag and slipped quietly out of the compartment.

A short time later, they both stood in front of the corridor window closely side by side with Michael's left arm around Juan' slender waist. "I've read that Guangdong Province was actually quite isolated for many centuries from the rest of China, mainly because of its mountains," Juan said. She paused a moment, then went on. "Fairly high mountains slope down from the north, along the border with Hunan Province; and beyond that high hills, created by the deeply cut river valleys of the Pearl River system, tumble down to the flat, fertile coastal lands in the very south. Guangdong's topography forced the Cantonese, as they were called through most of history, to rely on their own ingenuity and their innovative talents for survival. They were lucky because much of the population lived in the fertile Pearl River Delta with its rich agricultural land. Agriculture has always been extremely productive there and varied in its produce. Of course, the main crop is rice, which can be harvested twice a year because of the climate, and sweet potatoes are cultivated where rice cannot be grown. But there also exists a variety of other produce and products like tobacco, jute and sugar cane as well as tropical fruits, mainly bananas."

"You're utterly amazing. There's no doubt now, you're *the* walking encyclopedia. You've told me that you have never seen southern China and don't know it and yet you can tell me heaps about it. You must have always been exceptionally curious about your country," Michael said, dazzled again by her knowledge.

"Oh, you're making too much of my knowledge. I just know some things about China in general. It just sounds to you like a wealth of knowledge. I bet when we get to America, you'll be able to tell me something about every state in your country."

"Yes, something, but not much."

"What I haven't told you about," Juan continued her previous account of Guangdong eagerly," is that this southernmost province has always looked outward to the sea because part of the people's livelihood was earned through trade. It has a coastline more than 1,000 kilometers long where foreign merchants first made contact with China. Just as there was an overland Silk Road in the north of China, the sea trading route along Guangdong's coast had its beginning as the ancient Maritime Silk Road. But in modern times Guangdong was an economic backwater, so to speak, until Premier Deng Xiaoping opened up the province to economic development through his 'open door policy.' At that time three Special Economic Zones with trading links to Hong Kong were established. The economic activity in the Guangdong Province spread like wildfire and hasn't slowed down since. That much I can tell you," Juan said to end her discourse, then added, "Enough said for awhile."

"What you've told me clarifies what I'd vaguely heard about when Deng Xiaoping started loosening the economic restraints

on China. Those moves were positively thought of in the West. I
can assure you that. We all knew that something very important
was taking place in your country, but we weren't able to say
what was happening because it was for a long time very much
a closed society."

Juan just nodded but wasn't inclined to add anything to what
she'd already said.

"Sweetheart, let's now just watch the landscape fly by and
observe the activities as we near the big southern metropolis."

"Of course, darling, let's do that."

They were silent until they passed the first outlying sub-
urbs of Guangzhou and the first hint of the smog covering the
metropolis. They stood by the window with their arms about
each other, absorbed in the passing scenery. It was a beautiful
sunny morning. The broad Pearl River below them glimmered
silvery in the early sunshine. Filled with barges and sampans, it
teemed with activity. Along the banks a whole array of house-
boats were anchored with colorful washing hanging flaccidly in
the still air; and in certain other areas what seemed to be well-
established fish farms. And beyond the river as far as the eye
could see emerald green fields of rice and sugar cane. In the far
distance they spied the formidable mountains that had separated
the province from the rest of the country for many centuries.

Suddenly Juan piped up as she pointed toward the lower hills
and high mountains in the distance, "You won't believe what
I'm going to tell you now. I once read that Guangdong in early
times was thought of in the north as a land inhabited by barbar-
ians. It was where disgraced officials from the north were sent
into exile." She looked at Michael while she threw this historical
tidbit out to him. And he didn't disappoint her with his response.

"My, how interesting!" he replied. "I always thought the bar-
barians were the Mongols way up in the north. Aren't the Han
Chinese the majority of the population in the South?"

"Yes, that's true and that's a good point. But there were quite
a number of minorities at that time and there still are minorities
today. They may have at some point in the past been in the majority. I don't really know. They are the Miao, She, Li, Zhuang,

Teochew and the Hakka people. Who knows what the make-up of the majority and minority inhabitants were in the past." Juan sounded almost disappointed with herself for not knowing.

"That's all very interesting and much to think about and also hopefully to read about. What do you say, should we go back into the compartment now? We'll soon arrive in the center of the city."

"Yes, let's do that," Juan quickly agreed.

As they settled into their seats, the old gentleman across from them startled Juan and Michael by addressing them. "Excuse me," he began very formally, "I don't wish to intrude, but I'd like to introduce myself and my wife. My name is Chen Hangyu, and this is my wife Chen Zhi." He paused then and looked at them expectantly, perhaps wondering if they were offended by his presuming to strike up a conversation.

"Excuse me, for interrupting you," the old gentleman began very formally. "If you haven't been to Guangzhou before, and I think you may not have been, I want to let you know something very special about it. We've always lived in Guangzhou and are happy to return to it after visiting Guilin, which is beautiful. Oh, very beautiful," and he nodded his head vigorously. "But we're old now and can't be transplanted anywhere else. Do you want to hear something about an island in the Pearl River, a very special one?" he asked somewhat embarrassed for imposing himself on the young couple.

At first, Juan and Michael were speechless and quite surprised that the old man had something to tell them. Throughout the evening, he and his wife hadn't said a word. Recovering from the surprise more quickly than Michael, Juan responded graciously. "Sure, Mister Chen. My name is Li Juan," and, pointing to Michael, "this is my fiancé Michael Sorensen." With the palms of her hands pressed together and bowing slightly toward the old couple, she added, "Anything you can tell us about this marvelous city and the Pearl River Delta, we would appreciate hearing very much. We're newcomers here as you have guessed and are just passing through. But we're interested in learning about this area."

195

Mr. Chen smiled, obviously happy that he finally made contact with the young couple whose generation, no doubt, viewed the world much differently than his own. "So let me tell you about Shamian Island. If you spend some time here, you should go to that island. It's very different from the city itself. Its being special goes way back to the 19th century. In that century Guangzhou, Canton as it was called then, was plagued with diseases. So the foreigners who were living here took refuge on Shamian Island, which originally was just a sandbank in the Pearl River. It then became part of the colonial history of Guangdong. Mainly the British and the French settled there at separate ends of the island. Protected by guards and barbed wire, they built hotels, parks, stately homes, public buildings and tennis courts. The island was connected to the mainland by several bridges with great iron gates. Before 1949, the gates were guarded by Chinese police. They prevented the Chinese from crossing over. Also Indians were employed as guards by the foreigners. Today the island still has some of its former aloofness and relaxed atmosphere from Guangzhou proper with its choking traffic and its general hustle and bustle. In this modern era, major renovations have restored some of the old colonial buildings on the island. They are nowadays transformed into fine restaurants, cafés and hotels. Traffic, by the way, is restricted on Shamian. It's a wonderful place for walking and exploring. It's a peaceful respite from the big city. The old banyan trees still stand in rows and some crumbling mansions still retain a certain decayed splendor. And sometimes you can see some old, but still playable, red clay tennis court. Shamian's main boulevard is a lovely stretch of parklike gardens and trees and old Chinese men playing Chinese checkers." Hangyu finished his glowing account of the island he obviously loved and most likely visited a lot. He became very animated as he talked about Shamian and seemed indeed to become more youthful, while his wife sat quietly next to him just nodding her head in approval of what her husband said.

"My goodness, what an interesting place!" Michael exclaimed. "And what a history!" Juan added and went on, "As it happens, we'll be staying on Shamian Island, at the River Pearl Hotel.

We're very excited about that. We very much appreciate your telling us some of the history of Shamian. Thank you, thank you," she said once more and bowed toward Hangyu and Zhi. The old gentleman replied, "You'll love the River Pearl. You're a lucky couple."

That was all the communication Michael and Juan had with the old couple, because after Hangyu's rather vivid account and Zhi's approving nods, they both retired into their previous non-communicative shells.

Soon the inner city's density of streets, houses, shops, traffic and hordes of pedestrians was visible through the compartment window. *The eastern train station can't be far away now*, Michael guessed. He then got up and lifted down their hand luggage from the upper bunk. They would later claim their suitcases from the train's main luggage station. Now they were both excited to have reached the end point of their China escape. Juan kept nudging Michael lightly with her elbow in a playful sort of way. He finally acknowledged her efforts to make contact with him by bending his head toward her. She whispered in his ear, "We're almost there, at our jumping off spot." Instead of responding with words, Michael grabbed her hand and pressed it firmly. At that moment the train rolled into Guangzhou's vast and teeming station. Seeing the droves of travelers on the platform, Juan whispered again, "Please let's wait until most of the passengers have gotten off the train. There is no hurry. We're here."

"It's fine with me if that's what you'd like. There will be a major crush as the passengers get off onto the platform. And then they'll all have to fight their way through the waiting crowd." This time Juan grabbed Michael's hand and pressed it firmly while she whispered "Thank you," into his ear.

When they finally emerged from the Eastern Train Station, which mainly serves far-flung destinations, Juan and Michael were surprised at how easily the crowds flowed through the immense train station hall. They had no problem finding a taxi that quickly whisked them off toward their fine hotel overlooking the Pearl River. They sat in the taxi holding hands. Michael felt excited, more than he had felt arriving at any of the other

197

destinations, even those he had been most eager to visit. More subdued, Juan sat quietly next to him. She was contemplating the next steps beyond this taxi ride. When Michael glanced at her sideways, he was surprised at how subdued she appeared to be. *She must be tired,* he thought. *She is so different from her normal vivacious self. Or perhaps she has second thoughts now that we'll be departing China soon. But once we've made the jump to Hong Kong, she'll be OK,* he told himself. He understood that it wouldn't be easy for her to leave her country of birth, the only country she had ever known. Out of his feelings for her and his concern, he moved closer to her, folded his arm around her shoulders and leaned his face against hers. Juan grabbed his hand and suddenly said, "I'm OK, Michael. Don't worry about me. I'll do fine." For the rest of the taxi ride, they traveled in silence with Michael's arm still firmly around Juan's shoulders.

He was happy to see her come alive once they spied the grand 34-storey façade of the River Pearl. The taxi rolled up the wide circular driveway and came to a halt under the huge portico of the hotel's grand entrance. The taxi driver jumped out and opened Juan's door first. She scrambled out and stood for awhile looking at the massive doors and magnificent entrance. As Michael joined her, he saw how impressed and, perhaps, even overwhelmed she was by the elegance this fine hotel promised. He paid the taxi driver, helped him take out their luggage and let the hotel's porter stow it on a golden trolley that he wheeled away toward the grand entrance hall. When he came back to where Juan was standing, she was still looking up at the entrance beyond the broad flight of stairs. He was going to let her admire the hotel as long as she wanted because he knew it was her long-held wish coming true. He slipped his arm through hers and waited. "It's more than grand. I bet the rooms are opulent," she said excitedly. "Thanks for letting us stay here, darling."

"It's for you and me to enjoy," he responded.

Even though it was just 10 o'clock in the morning, the reception clerk said they were lucky that a room was already available for them on the 13th floor. Juan and Michael were elated. Now they could go to their room, admire the view of the Pearl River and beyond and relax for a couple of hours. Later on, after lunch, they would explore the city.

Leaving the reception desk, they crossed the exquisite, high-ceilinged atrium lobby. They set down their luggage temporarily and walked over to view the remarkable splashing waterfall and the fish pond at its foot surrounded by a miniature landscape of Southern China and topped with an elegant Chinese pavilion.

"How fanciful and unusual to find such a water display inside a hotel lobby. It appears like an oasis of tranquility," Juan cried out, clapping her hands as if she were applauding the architects who designed it. Equally impressed, Michael observed, "I could have imagined the waterfall and pond outside in a rich and gorgeously designed parklike garden, but not in here."

"I've never seen the like anywhere else. The grand hotels in Beijing are fancy, as you know, but not nearly like this one," Juan added.

They stood a little while longer watching the big colorful carps gliding languidly through the pond, sometimes disappearing through the spray and splatter into the waterfall and then popping out again into the pond's slightly rippled water.

Hand in hand, Michael and Juan tore themselves away from the impressive veil-like water display in front of an intricate rockery. They picked up their suitcases and headed for the elevator. But the biggest surprise awaited them when they entered their room.

"How elegant!" Juan exclaimed, and clapped her hands the moment she saw the room and all its furnishings.

Michael inhaled deeply as if he had to gather in some courage to say what he wanted to say. "How can we ever be content staying in a simple hotel after all this luxury? Tell me, Juan. That enormous bed, the fine linen, the mass of pillows, the antique furniture, the plush carpet and silk drapes, and we haven't even seen the bathroom yet." He appeared stunned and even somewhat intimidated.

"To go back to our normal accommodations will be easy. I don't think we'll expect any more than what we've had? But we should enjoy this while we have it. We'll fondly remember this luxury. Who knows when or even if we'll enjoy anything like it again? So let's enjoy," she responded a bit cryptically.

"Yes we will, sweetheart. I also agree with you that this will be something to remember. But to tell you the truth, I'm more comfortable in less sumptuous surroundings. I'm not the kind of man who would make staying here a habit. I can do without all of this luxury."

"Oh, so can I," she replied, but went on to reiterate, "Let's enjoy the short time we'll be here together, for it may not repeat itself."

"What are you saying? Do you mean to say that we'll never experience anything like this again? But, sweetheart, we've a whole lifetime ahead of us and we'll surely have a vast number of fine experiences. I agree with you, let's enjoy this moment, enjoy this day and this coming night for what they are and what they'll offer us." He stepped over to her and embraced her gently. He was a bit puzzled by her sudden oddly somber mood, as if the experience of being together in this fine hotel was already a thing of the past.

"Go in and take a long shower or a long bath, whatever you prefer," he urged her. "Freshen yourself up. Then let's lie down for half an hour before we go down to lunch. Wouldn't that all be wonderfully relaxing?"

Juan folded her arms around him now and squeezed him. "You're right. I will do exactly as you suggest. I hope you won't mind waiting for awhile. I'll take a bath, but if you just want to take a shower, you can come into the bathroom with me and do that. Don't mind me," she said coyly. "I'd like to have you with me in the bathroom."

* * *

They had a wonderful day, starting with lunch, which consisted of a scrumptious dish at the seafood bar in the hotel. In the early afternoon they took a lengthy sightseeing tour of Guangzhou and took in some of the revolutionary sights. Among them was the Sun Yatsen Memorial Hall that commemorates the man whom the Kuomintang and the Communist Party consider the father of modern China. The Hall is modeled after Beijing's Temple of Heaven. Then they stopped briefly at the Peasant Movement Institute, a school where Mao Zedong and Zhou Enlai taught before it was closed in 1926. Last, they moved on to the nearby Memorial Garden to the Martyrs. It is dedicated to the 5000 workers who were killed there while demonstrating in the neighborhood at the instigation of the Communist Party. Chiang Kaishek gave orders to have them killed, and they were gunned down by his Kuomintang forces.

Michael had studied the special sightseeing brochure he picked up at the reception desk because he wanted to see the revolutionary sights first. He was most interested in them. But he decided that they would do the other sights the following day—sights Juan wanted to see—the temples, gardens, mosques and cathedrals, as well as the Chen Clan Ancestral Hall and whatever else they could fit in. But in the morning they would have to spend some time at the city hall to get a passport ordered for Juan. Juan rather passively agreed to everything Michael proposed. She contributed so little that Michael asked her with some concern, "Are you not feeling well, sweetheart? You seem so quiet, so subdued. This is not the normal you."

"Oh, I'm fine, Michael. I enjoy just listening to you and your enthusiasm for seeing all the sights you've read about. I want to see them, too, and I'm glad you're taking the initiative. Don't worry about me. I just feel a little tired, maybe from the long train ride. I'll be OK," she reassured him.

* * *

They were both lying on the bed, still in their clothes, while Michael went over the day's excursions. After he finished, Juan said suddenly, "Darling, I want to run down to the reception desk to find a brochure about Guangzhou's Museum of Art. It was opened just recently, and it contains Chinese art from ancient to modern times. I read about it in the Beijing paper recently, and I would really love to see it with you, perhaps more than anything else. Will you excuse me for a little while?"

"Of course. Just come back as quickly as possible. I'll be waiting for you." He laughed and poked her in the ribs with his index finger. He felt elated when she let out her rippling, high-pitched laugh he hadn't heard for quite a while.

Juan jumped off the bed and slipped into her shoes. She turned around just before she disappeared through the door, smiled sweetly and waved at Michael. Then she was gone. He thought, *I'm just going to lie here and relax until she comes back.*

In the lobby, Juan went straight to the reception desk, where a clerk was busy entering information into the computer. "Excuse me," Juan said in an urgent tone, "a friend of ours may stop by for a short visit tonight. He doesn't know what room we're staying in. When he comes to ask would you please tell him our room number? Our room is reserved under Michael Sorensen," she said in her most efficient, business-like manner.

"Certainly, madam, I'll do that. Do you expect him soon?"

"I'm not sure. I know he won't come late. It's a business friend of my fiancé."

"It doesn't matter, madam. I'll tell him to go to room 1317. I'll be here till midnight." She rushed off toward the elevator, but then remembered that she was going to get the museum brochure.

"I'm sorry to have to disturb you once more." The reception clerk looked up questioningly. "Do you have a brochure about the Guangzhou Museum of Art? We would like to visit it tomorrow?"

"It's over there in the display case at the end of the counter," he said pointing in that direction.

"Thanks," Juan replied and hurried over to get the brochure.

* * *

When she arrived back in their room, Michael called out, "That was a fast trip. You must have found it right away," and he pointed to the brochure in her hand. "Let me see it. I'll be interested in it, too. I'm sure you'll be able to tell me volumes about the dynasties' artworks when we get there tomorrow," he prompted her. It surprised Juan a little that he was so interested.

"Stop it. You're flattering me again," she responded with a little laugh.

"Come here now, sweetheart, he beckoned her. It seems to me we haven't lain next to each other for quite some time." Warmly receptive, she tossed off her shoes and jumped onto the bed next to him.

"We could be very passionate now and I feel like it, but I want to reserve that pleasure for tonight. Let's just lie here and contemplate our good fortune. Let's ask the gods for a propitious jump-off into a new future together. All will be well once you get your passport from the Guangzhou passport office and your visitor's visa from the American Consulate. The latter shouldn't be a problem at all."

"Yes, you're right in everything you say and everything you imagine for us. But right now let's be in the moment. It's a fine time. Let's meditate together. A more appropriate moment may not come for us in quite awhile."

"I agree with you. Let's close our eyes." He took her right hand in his and held it firmly.

But the two of them drifted off to sleep, and Michael woke up around six in the evening. He squinted at his watch but couldn't quite make out the time. The room was rather dark because they had drawn the curtains before they had agreed to meditate together. He jumped up and rushed to the window. He thought they had missed their dinner reservation he had arranged for seven o'clock. As he parted the drapes and looked at his watch again, he saw that it was six. He went back to the bed and gently nudged Juan. "Sweetheart, wake up. It's time to get ready for our fine dinner to celebrate being in the River Pearl. We'll have to hurry. I hope you'll wear that beautiful dress again. I want you to shine tonight."

Juan opened her eyes just a tiny bit and squinted at him. "I can't believe we both went to sleep. We must have slept soundly for about an hour and a half." She suddenly sat up but then bent her torso so her head almost rested on her legs. She sighed, "Gosh, am I groggy. It'll take a while until I can get moving," she mumbled. Michael tried to prod her gently. "But we need to be in the dining room at seven; otherwise we may not get a table. It'll most likely be crowded."

Juan listened to him and responded, "Yes, I know we'd better hurry. Just give me a moment." She presently rose from the bed. "Thanks for waking me, darling, and I'm sorry for being so slow. I'll take a quick shower and wash my hair. As soon as I'm done showering, you can come in and take yours. I'll do my makeup and dry my hair while you're in the shower."

"OK, that sounds like an efficient plan of action. Take your time," he said, but he was hoping that she would hurry a little.

* * *

They didn't enter the dining room until 7:20. Michael and Juan looked around the vast, sumptuously decorated room. They noticed two banquets in full swing at two long tables with much talk and laughter. The plush dining room was packed. In the middle of the back wall was a podium. Two colorfully dressed young women in traditional slim-cut silk gowns were providing the background music, one playing the grand piano and the other the cello. The music they created was soft and sweet and seemed to enhance the festive and congenial atmosphere, a fine backdrop for the murmuring of many private conversations.

"Good evening, sir and madam," the maître d', outfitted in a black evening suit, greeted them formally and bowed deeply as he stood next to his little podium. As he straightened up, he flashed a friendly smile at his guests and then quickly glanced at his reservation list. "You are Mr. and Mrs. Sorensen, I believe," he said, and Michael nodded. "We are very busy tonight, sir. I don't have any more tables for two. I'm sorry. You're a little late. But I can seat you at a round table for four. You'll be seated with Mr. and Mrs. Jin. They are regular patrons of our hotel. A fine couple, very cosmopolitan. You'll enjoy them, sir and madam." Michael didn't know what to say right away. He let his eyes sweep across the vast room and spied a small table in the far right hand corner. "Oh, I see a small empty table over there. Could we have it, please?" he said, as he pointed to the table.

"That's already taken, sir, by a couple who will be arriving in a few minutes. I can't take it away from them. They'll be on time, I assure you. I'm sorry, sir."

"Oh, never mind, give us what you have," Michael responded in a pleasant manner while thinking, *How disappointing. Just the one evening I wanted to be alone with Juan. It was supposed to be a very special evening.*

Upon Michael's acceptance of the seating arrangement, Juan affirmed, "Yes, that will be fine for us. Thank you."

The maître d' nodded and picked up two menus. Having accepted the seating arrangement, Michael and Juan, with the maître d' trailing them, went over to the table where Mr. and Mrs. Jin were sitting. Mr. Jin got up and introduced himself and his wife. He was a man in the prime of his life, a little on the chubby side with a round, rather jovial face and magnified Chinese eyes behind thick-lensed glasses. He was smartly over-dressed in a black tuxedo with shiny satin lapels. "It's nice to have your company. We just got here about five minutes ago," he said in perfect English, as Michael and Juan sat down. The maître d' stepped forward, bowed deeply, placed the menus on the table and said, "The beverage waiter and your assigned dinner server will be here shortly." He then turned and went back to his receiving station.

While Michael and Juan still adjusted themselves to this unexpected situation, Mr. Jin smiled and said, "My wife and I love to meet new people. It's so interesting to talk to them. I want you to know we're from Hong Kong. We love to come to Guangzhou, mostly on business, on the high speed ferry. Such a fast and pleasant ride it gives you. Our business is mainly in Hong Kong, but we're also doing some business here, off and on." His wife was neither beautiful nor plain but definitely a quiet type, with her black hair pulled out of her face and knotted at the back of her head. She sat smiling and nodding at everything her husband said.

"It's nice for us to meet you, too. But you can speak in Chinese to us. I'm a fluent Mandarin speaker. By the way, I'm Michael Sorensen and this is my fiancée Li Juan. We don't know anyone in this city. We're just passing through. Actually, we are on our way to Hong Kong. But we won't be staying there, not this time. We'll be taking off for the USA very shortly. We'll only be in Guangzhou a few days until Juan can get a passport issued."

Mr. Jin nodded thoughtfully, then replied, "Oh, that could be a bit difficult, and it could be a lengthy process. But let me help you, if I may." Mr. Jin seemed eager to please. "I know an official at the passport office here. He can help you out and speed things up. I'll call him tomorrow morning if you want me to."

"Of course, that would be wonderful and we would appreciate your help very much," Michael responded, thinking, *How lucky can we get? I can't believe we happen to meet a man with a connection to the passport office, just like that.* Had Michael known who this man really was, he would have responded very differently. But at this moment he was aware of nothing besides the man's kindness and apparent concern. Feeling grateful and ready to trust this man he'd just met, Michael responded warmly, "I'll give you our information after dinner. We feel already thoroughly indebted to you. Isn't that right, Juan?"

"Yes, yes I can hardly believe this is happening—that you should be here at the same table, Mr. Jin, at this moment in our time of need. Thanks from our hearts." Indeed it appeared to be a remarkable good fortune that they would be seated with this couple, but for some reason Juan felt uneasy. It was almost as though they had been planted there. But why should they be planted here? Unable to think of any reason, she put away her suspicions.

"It's a pleasure for me to help you," Mr. Jin replied. "Where will you be off to after Hong Kong?"

"To California. We'll be flying into San Francisco," said Michael quickly.

"Ah, beautiful San Francisco. We have spent some very pleasant times there, haven't we, Zhi? Very memorable." Mr. Jin was effusive, while Mrs. Jin just nodded slightly. Juan and

Michael looked at each other, and Michael thought, *Mm, this woman is strangely reticent and passive as if she's not really attached to Mr. Joviality. Well, she may be just a woman for the night. For all I know, he could be a pimp, and she could be one of the girls in his stable.* After that he didn't give the couple's situation any more thought. Juan had similar thoughts but also decided not to speculate about this woman.

Mr. Jin insisted on ordering drinks for the four of them; he simply wouldn't accept Michael's "No, thank you." Michael felt rather uncomfortable but then accepted the kind offer. When it was time to order the appetizers, the main dishes and the desserts, Mr. Jin again insisted on ordering and paying for the appetizers because that would be easier, he claimed. This time Michael responded very firmly but still didn't get anywhere. Again he accepted the offer with profuse "Thanks." Mr. Jin even suggested a main course for Juan and Michael, Prawns à la Provençal. He said it was one of his absolute favorite dishes in this restaurant. Juan and Michael looked at each other, thanked Mr. Jin for his suggestion and ordered his recommended dish.

A round of schnapps came first, and Mr. Jin announced immediately, "We must drink to this special evening and our meeting here," and raised his little glass up high with a loud, "gan bei!" and, "To your next journey and your life together." Mrs. Jin lifted her glass as well and so did Michael and Juan. Michael felt compelled to reciprocate, stood up and bowed slightly toward the Jins and proposed "A toast to your well-being, wealth and long life and to our luck of meeting you." Mr. and Mrs. Jin laughed and clapped their hands after Michael's performance. No sooner had they drunk "bottoms up," than a tray of colorful Singapore Slings arrived.

"No, no. That's too much, especially for me. I drink very little alcohol," Juan protested.

"But lovely young lady, this is a very special evening, and we need to celebrate it. I'm sure you can make an exception just for tonight." Juan couldn't possibly say no to his jovially smiling face. And so the evening progressed. They ate and drank and talked about world and local events and about traveling.

And Mr. Jin wanted to know how Michael learned to speak Mandarin Chinese so well. So Michael felt he had to talk about his education in the States, the Chinese tutor he had hired in Beijing and the work he did for his Beijing company. The more he drank, the more he revealed—how he met Juan and how they fell in love, but he thought clearly enough not to talk about the car crash and about his and Juan's flight from Beijing.

At the end of their meal, Mr. Jin proposed going to the lounge situated next to the dining room for a nightcap. "We need to end our meeting here tonight and the enjoyment I have experienced in the proper manner," he enticed them cordially and continued before Michael could protest, "Please don't say 'No.' The lounge in the next room is very cozy and the music is stimulating in the old-fashioned way. Believe me, it's a swinging place at this time of the evening. I've been in there many times. We can even dance a little. Come on and join us," Mr. Jin pleaded.

Michael laughed and said, "Only if the rounds are on us. You've already hosted us all during dinner."

"OK, it's a deal, but only the first round. If there are any others, they'll be on me. Is it a deal?"

"Sure, it's a deal," and Michael stretched out his hand which Mr. Jin shook, while he thought, *There won't be any other rounds. No way, one will be enough.*

With the dinner bill settled, the two couples moved into the lounge. It was indeed a cozy place with plush chairs and couches, dim indirect lighting, an impressively long richly carved bar of the finest rosewood. Against the far wall, on a podium with a square parquet dance floor in front of it, a four-piece band was playing old time dance tunes of the pre- and post-Sinatra era. The place was fairly crowded, but there were still a couple of tables that could seat four.

After the first round of gin and tonic drinks arrived, Mr. Jin initiated a round of clinking glasses and more best wishes, first for Juan and then for Michael. So Michael felt compelled to get up to propose a toast to Mr. and Mrs. Jin. After that the band started playing an old-fashioned foxtrot, a dance Michael was hardly familiar with except that his mother had sometimes played foxtrots and tangos for him and told him how she and his father danced them in their early years and loved them. It surprised Michael that Mr. Jin would ask him if he could take Ms. Li for a little spin on the dance floor.

"Sure, go right ahead and enjoy yourselves, Michael responded pleasantly, but thought, *Why is he doing that? Juan and I should be dancing up a storm.* Meanwhile Juan had gotten up because Mr. Jin had extended his hand to her. As they went out on the dance floor, Michael observed them carefully. He wasn't in the mood to dance with Mrs. Jin. He smiled at her and excused himself, telling her that he didn't know this dance. Mrs. Jin laughed and said, "Oh, that's fine. I don't know it very well myself. Don't worry." Michael nodded, but this latest move of Mr. Jin prompted him to make the stay in the lounge as short as possible. He just sat at the table and watched them dancing. He noticed how animatedly Mr. Jin was talking to Juan while she nodded her head. He held her tightly and led her expertly across the dance floor. Michael found it amazing how Juan adapted herself to Mr. Jin's lead, just as he had observed her at the Blue Moon. *How could she know, being brought up in China, the moves and steps of the foxtrot so well? She must have taken lessons in all the Western dances while working at the Blue Moon to please the expatriate customers in the club,* he was thinking. Then he thought further, *Juan had hardly talked to Mr. Jin during dinner. The conversation took place almost exclusively between Mr. Jin and me. I must ask her what in the world was he talking about.* It looked to Michael as if Mr. Jin was trying to persuade or convince her of something, but of course he couldn't be certain.

The dance seemed to go on forever. Michael was determined to have the next dance with Juan, even if he had to butt in and take her away from Mr. Jin. But that wasn't necessary because Mr. Jin brought her right back after the music stopped. Before Juan could even sit down, Michael stood up and said, "Now it's my turn, sweetheart. This dance is mine." Unfortunately, it was a waltz, which wasn't one of his favorite dances, but he still led her out onto the floor. As they danced slowly, swaying lightly back and forth, and Michael holding Juan tightly, he asked her what Mr. Jin had talked so animatedly about.

"Oh, it was nothing but gobbledygook to me. He is pretty full of himself—about all the sights he has seen, the experiences he has had, and the places he had been to and others he still wants to see. He is merely a bullshitter, letting me know that he is well-to-do and a man of the world. I just listened and didn't reply. I'm glad I don't have to dance with him anymore. Please, darling, after this dance let's call it quits for tonight. I'm rather tired. I had too much to drink. And I want to go to bed," she pleaded.

"I promise you, sweetheart. I'm going to call it an evening as soon as we get back to the table. We simply have to excuse ourselves. I'll be very polite, though, and I'll give him our information. I do want him to help us with getting the passport as soon as possible."

"Thank you, darling."

They danced until the waltz came to an end, while Mr. and Mrs. Jin sat quietly at the table until Juan and Michael came back.

"Oh, Mr. Jin," Michael said right away as he sat down, "Before I forget I want to give you our room information. We're in room 1317, and we'll be there tonight and tomorrow night. Juan and I would be very grateful to receive help from you regarding the passport. It was so kind of you to offer."

Michael wanted to say more, but Mr. Jin butted in, "Don't worry, here is my card. I'll call the passport office first thing in the morning. After that I'll leave a message for you at the reception desk regarding the passport and the name of the official you should see."

"That all sounds great, Mr. Jin. Thank you so much. It was wonderful meeting you and your wife. I hope we'll see you again and good luck with your business here in Guangzhou. As for now, Juan and I would like to excuse ourselves. We're very tired because we were on the train all night and could hardly sleep."

"Oh sure, Mr. Sorensen. Mrs. Jin and I understand. We'll have to leave, too, and get some rest. Good night then to both of you. I'll leave a note at the reception desk tomorrow morning."

Juan and Michael responded simultaneously, "Thank you, thank you very much for a lovely evening."

The two couples shook hands and Juan and Michael were the first to leave the lounge. They didn't look back and wave. Having left the lounge, they were relieved once the elevator took them to the 13th floor.

15

Betrayal

As soon as they entered the room and locked the door behind them, feeling secure and relieved to be free of the Jins' company, Michael embraced Juan tightly and kissed her passionately. She didn't respond in kind and even tried to wriggle free, but he was reluctant to let her go. "Sweetheart, I love you," he whispered in her ear. "You looked wonderful tonight, so desirable. I'm so proud of you. I'll always cherish you, and I'll make your life as pleasant and satisfying as possible. I just hope we can get out of here in a couple of days with Mr. Jin's help. How fortuitous that we met him tonight, don't you think? I hope he wasn't just full of air."

All the while Michael was speaking softly and lovingly to her, Juan was trying to free herself. And once his strong arms released her, she said apologetically, "Darling, I'm sorry, I feel quite tipsy, a bit dizzy and even a little faint from all those drinks I was made to drink. I don't know what was in them, definitely too much alcohol. Can we please sit over there at the little table, talk some and drink a few glasses of water. It'll help flushing our systems out before we go to bed. Please, darling."

"Sure, let's do that. We'll have all night and can sleep in a little tomorrow morning." They didn't undress yet, just kicked off their shoes and Michael removed his jacket. Their luggage was still packed sitting in front of the closet.

They weren't seated very long at the little table across from the bed in front of the window, the drapes of which had been drawn earlier in the evening, when Michael got up while Juan

212

stayed seated. He filled two glasses of spring water from the little fridge across the room. He had just come back to join Juan and to sit down when they heard a knock on the door. Michael looked at Juan quizzically as if he wanted to say, *Was that really a knock, and if it was, who could it be? It's already 10 o'clock.* They sat very still and waited to see if someone would knock again. Michael whispered, "Perhaps it's Mr. Jin. He knows our room number. Maybe we left something in the lounge, and he's bringing it to us." Juan, sitting very upright and alert on her chair and appearing tense, didn't respond to him.

They heard the knock again, this time more forceful. "You stay right here, sweetheart, while I check who is at the door. Please don't move from your chair. Let me handle it. It could be someone from the reception desk to bring us a message. Sit tight, please, and let me handle it," Michael repeated himself. He seemed confident, but she could see that he was anxious and perturbed. He got up and walked rather hesitantly to the door. Later on, he reflected that he'd had some premonition at the moment before opening the door, and his inner voice tried to prompt him to call the reception desk instead. But to his regret he ignored the voice that cautioned him and kept right on heading for the door.

As soon as he had turned the lock and before he even pressed down the handle, the door was pushed open so forcefully against him, hitting his body and head so hard that he was instantly knocked onto his back on the floor. Three rather tall and husky men he had never seen before, dressed quite formally in black suits and well groomed hair, rushed into the room. The last one secured the door. In his stunned state, Michael observed what was happening in slow motion as if it were a movie he was watching that had suddenly been slowed down. One of the men immediately pounced upon Michael, straddling his abdomen and clamping his wrists to the floor. Another man knelt next to his head. Before Michael knew it, he had a double strip of duct tape over his mouth. At that moment, he moved his head to the side and glanced over to where Juan had been sitting just a minute ago. She was standing now, slipping her feet into her shoes,

213

while the third man stood behind her and gripped her elbows. She seemed strangely serene to Michael. She didn't fight the man; she didn't scream. She just did what he commanded her to do and let him guide her across the room.

This must be a dream, Michael thought, *This can't be reality. I must wake up,* and he tried to move his head enough to see Juan. He saw her being led straight to the door by the man gripping her arm. As she passed by him still lying supine on the floor, she said, "Don't worry about me, Michael. Everything is fine. I'm OK," and she let herself be led out the door. He knew then that he had been set up and that Juan had betrayed him. All the suspicion and doubts he had kept at bay came rushing back; and in a moment of blinding illumination, he saw clearly that she had been lying to him about the telephone calls and probably much else besides. But he had been so completely infatuated that he wouldn't permit himself to suspect or doubt. Yes, she had turned out to be a black swan after all. He thought of Mr. Jin at that moment. *What a talkative fool I've been this evening. He was an impostor. I now bet that those two scoundrels are not husband and wife and are not even staying at this hotel. And what had Mr. Jin been telling Juan on the dance floor? And who else was involved with her? Who were these goons who had burst into our room? They must all be working for someone, but whom?*

When the door closed behind Juan, Michael realized that she would be gone forever. The pain of discovering her betrayal was great, but greater still was the pain of realizing that he had lost her. For all her lying and treachery, he still loved her. *Where will they take her? Will she wind up back in Beijing?* he wondered. His feeling of loss was unbearable.

At that moment Michael felt the man who had taped his mouth tying up his legs with a rope. Then he and the man who had been sitting on Michael's chest managed to turn Michael face down to the floor and tied his hands behind his back. He tried to struggle, but it was hopeless against two strong men, who quickly tied him up. They were professionals and he was helpless in their power. They had succeeded with their surprise intrusion. Michael couldn't guess in those moments, and with his mind still in a fog from all those alcoholic drinks he consumed, what all of this might mean for him. Suddenly, he wasn't even so sure that Juan was lost to him forever. He thought of how wonderful she had been on their journey and that she would find a way back to him. He even thought of waiting some time for her in Guangzhou. And so he tried to delude himself even as they tied him up securely on the floor and then flung him onto the bed. They even secured him more by tying him to the bed.

The men never said a word to Michael. Since he was obviously a foreigner, they thought he wouldn't understand them. They just did their dirty work without words as fast and as efficiently as possible and left. In his tied up condition, there was no way Michael could alert anyone in the hotel. He couldn't move, he couldn't scream. He would be lucky if the room service employee let herself in midmorning the next day to tidy up the room. Only then would the hotel know what happened; only then could he be freed. Before that deliverance, he would spend a miserable night. How could he sleep with his tied up hands behind his back? The night would seem like eternity. He would suffer from thirst and maybe hunger before they would find him, and he would have soiled himself in his immobile position. It made him sick even thinking about what he would have to go through before he would be released. He felt a sickening response rising from the center of his stomach and was now worried that he would choke on his own vomit. That thought unnerved him. *If I could only meditate myself into a relaxed state, as Juan taught me,* he thought. But the truth was that meditating in his desperate situation, no matter how hard he tried, did not work for him. Sometimes he tried lying there very still and other times he would wriggle and thrash his body back and forth. Unbelievably, in the end he just went to sleep out of pure exhaustion.

He woke up when the door was being unlocked. That's how light he had been sleeping. Panic immediately set in. He thought the men were coming back to check on him and would maybe do something more horrible to him, like castrate him. His heart suddenly beat so hard in his chest that he thought it would explode any second. Thinking about how vulnerable and helpless he was, he stared at the door in terror. But the door wasn't thrown open. It opened slowly and a woman's face peeked into the room. She saw the man on the bed without a cover and almost backed right out of the room. But then she noticed that his head was raised and that something wasn't right with his body. It appeared stiff as if tied down and he still had his shirt and suit pants on. She left the door, turned on the overhead light and came into the room. Then she realized that something was very wrong. This man was tied securely to the bed, his arms and legs were also tied and his mouth taped. She looked at him aghast and frightened.

Michael meanwhile made some grunting noises, "Mm, mm, mm," while moving his head from side to side, signaling that he needed to speak to her. But she immediately lifted both hands and waved them in a negative motion, while Michael experienced the agony of frustration. *Someone is here to help me but isn't doing a thing. I can't take it any more.*

"I'm sorry I can't touch you," the woman suddenly found her speech and managed to say as she moved toward the telephone. "I have to ring security and management. They'll be here in less than half a minute. They'll deal with everything and will get the story from you." She dialed a one-digit number. Presently she said. "There has been a break-in in 1317. The guest, a man, is tied to the bed. Come at once." And she hung up. Turning to Michael, she said, "I'll stay here until our people enter this room. I'm sorry, I'm not allowed to deal with any of this," and she moved back to the slightly open door.

Shortly thereafter the door was thrown open as three men, two in uniform and one in a black suit, burst into the room. "We're hotel security and management," the man in the black suit said to Michael. "We're here to help you."

They rushed to his bedside, all three of them, untying the rope that bound him to the bed frame and undoing his tied up legs, while one of them tried to remove the masking tape ever so slowly. Internally Michael was crying for joy and hugely relieved. He was being released from his ordeal. But he was embarrassed that he was lying on a soaking wet blanket.

"You're Mr. Sorensen, correct?" Michael just nodded. "Don't think of anything right now. Just keep calm," the man in the black suit said soothingly. "Don't worry; we'll get you out of here quickly. We're sorry that this happened to you. I don't think anything like this ever happened before in our fine hotel. Don't speak yet. We'll roll you over now to untie your hands."

When his hands were free, they felt numb and he kneaded his wrists right away. "I'm totally exhausted," Michael said in Chinese. "Thanks for rescuing me."

Looking surprised at hearing Michael speak Mandarin, one of the security guards replied, "That's our job. It's good that you speak our language. You can take a shower now and get dressed while we keep this room secure. When you're ready, we'll take you down to the office of our hotel manager, Mr. Zhong Zuguang, for questioning," he said, and pointed to the man in the black suit, who now bowed to Michael.

"OK, whatever you say," Michael replied.

"I'll see you in my office later. Don't worry. We'll also secure your luggage. The talk will just be between you, me and my assistant manager. Can I see you in half an hour or do you need more time?" the manager questioned Michael politely.

"No, half an hour will be fine. It won't take me long. I'm glad to get out of this torture chamber," Michael replied sluggishly.

The manager left, but the two security men stayed, while Michael stumbled into the bathroom. The two men waited patiently and said little. They listened to the water running behind the shut bathroom door. They knew when it was turned off. Then the electric shaver came on, and they hoped the man would soon be done. They hated standing around like this. They would rather be engaged in action. They wished they could have been there when Mr. Sorensen really needed them, and they wondered how he had wound up in such a dreadful condition. They weren't in a position to question him but they were curious nonetheless. He didn't seem to be loitering in the bathroom, he hadn't broken down. After all he had gone through, he still seemed to have it together, so it would seem.

Michael came out of the bathroom, the lower half of his body wrapped in a towel. "Excuse me," he said, addressing the guards while they nodded. He went to his suitcase and took out fresh clothes then gathered up his shoes from the floor. He again disappeared into the bathroom but was out in a couple of minutes, fully dressed in a white shirt, gray slacks and black shoes. His light brown hair was still wet and slicked back. "I'm ready for you to take me to the manager's office. I want to get this over with," he told them.

"Do you have all your personal items together?" the tallest of the two asked him. "Is everything out of the bathroom and closet? If not, gather it up and put it in your suitcase, which we'll hold and take care of until you leave the hotel. You won't be coming back to this room."

"All is already in my suitcase," Michael replied. But he thought, *That's interesting. I can't come back to this room but I've already paid for it. I assume they'll take care of that through the manager's office.* He didn't even take a last glance at the room and didn't dare think of Juan for fear his heart might start aching. He needed to keep his wits together and needed to leave Guangzhou as soon as possible. No longer able to delude himself, he knew this morning that she wouldn't be coming back.

The guards took him to the elevator. They had his suitcase and kept it when they dropped him off at the manager's office. Then they left him. Mr. Zhong received Michael in a friendly manner. He first asked him whether he was hungry or thirsty. When Michael said that he was both, Mr. Zhong suggested that he and his assistant take him to the hotel café. "We can talk some there perhaps and resume talking when we get back to my office. Are you ready to go?"

"Yes, thank you," Michael responded curtly. He was eager to get the interrogation over with, but he was indeed both hungry and thirsty, so he was ready for the café. They went in and sat down together, and Michael was invited to go to the buffet and take whatever he would like to eat and drink. "We'll just have a cup of tea," Mr. Zhong told him. He seemed very friendly and relaxed now and continued, "I think I want to wait with the questioning until we get to my office. I don't want anything to be overheard by the café staff."

"I understand. I'll eat my breakfast quickly. I want all of this to be over as fast as possible, as you can imagine.

"Yes, I can," Mr. Zhong replied.

When Michael came back in a minute with his breakfast food, orange juice and coffee, he saw the two men sipping their tea. They gave Michael ample quiet time to eat his breakfast and refrained from talking. Fifteen minutes later they were on the way back to Mr. Zhong's office.

As Michael sat down in front of Mr. Zhong's desk, in a large rather lavishly decorated room, he said, "Thanks for the fine breakfast. I really needed that. Very much appreciate it."

"That's the least we can do, Mr. Sorensen," Mr. Zhong replied, smiling and bowing toward Michael. "I have all the paperwork you filled out yesterday at the reception desk here in front of me. I'm impressed with your Chinese language skills, and I'm glad I can continue in my language. Yesterday was your first time ever in our hotel, I assume? And I see from the paperwork that your final destination is San Francisco."

"You're correct."

"What brought you here?"

"My fiancée, Miss Li Juan, and I were on our way to Hong Kong and from there to California."

"Why did you stay at the River Pearl? There are many other fine hotels in Guangzhou."

"Every visitor to China, especially to Southern China, knows of the fabulous River Pearl. Also, my fiancée, who is from Beijing and had never been to Guangzhou, wished very much to stay in your hotel. With everything she had heard about it, she was fascinated with it. So I thought this would be my gift to her."

Mr. Zhong nodded and said, "This was a fine gift to her. But tell me why do you think these men came uninvited to your room, gagged you, tied you up and led Miss Li away? Does she have anything in her past that might give us a clue?"

Before he answered, Michael thought, *He uses very careful language. He didn't say 'abducted,' but 'led away.'* But he replied, "I don't know, Mr. Zhong. I haven't known Miss Li very long. She is a lovely lady, and my heart is broken. Someone obviously tried to prevent her from leaving this country. But I have no clue who that could be. I'm just glad that the three men who barged into our room didn't do anything to me but tie me up. You might say that that was an assault but they didn't physically abuse or hurt me. They just tied me up. I'm anxious to leave Guangzhou as quickly as I can," Michael said in a determined way.

"I understand, Mr. Sorensen," Mr. Zhong replied, and bowed again before continuing. "We will help you with that. We will pay for the high speed ferry to Hong Kong and we'll make the reservation for you. We'll also pay for your flight from Hong Kong to San Francisco to make amends. We're very sorry for what happened to you, even though it wasn't our fault. We will also refund you the two nights' hotel reservation because you won't be staying here today and you hardly slept last night. We do not want to get a bad reputation for our hotel. It has first class, five star rating and stringent security. How these men could have come in and headed straight for your room is a puzzle to all of us, the security personnel and my office. Did you have a good look at the men? Did you recognize any of them? We understand that you were seated in our restaurant with a Mr. and Mrs. Jin. We don't know who they are. Did you know them?"

"No, I swear, I didn't know Mr. and Mrs. Jin. Neither did I know the three men who tied me up," Michael replied curtly, but he was puzzled that Mr. Zhong said that "we," presumably including the maître d', didn't know who the Jins were. He thought, *No doubt if I had the means to pursue this matter and could track down Mr. Jin, I could get some answers. But would I be able to bring Juan back? If I can't do that, then I'm ready to leave this country.* He noticed that Mr. Zhong's assistant manager was writing everything that was said into a computer. His fingers clicked the keyboard fast and furiously.

"Mr. Sorensen," and Mr. Zhong now sounded very serious, "to tell you the truth, there is nothing much we can do to solve

220

this riddle unless we involve the provincial and central government police. How would you feel if we helped you, as already mentioned, to leave the country as soon as possible so that no further harm can come to you?"

"I would feel good about that, Mr. Zhong. You're very gracious and helpful but I can take care of the airline ticket from Hong Kong to San Francisco. You needn't burden yourself with that."

"Oh, no, no!" Mr. Zhong came back somewhat excitedly. "We insist that we take care of your travel to San Francisco, that most beautiful city. I assume that California is your home state. This is our gift to you, and I hope that it will mitigate your emotional woes a little. Please, Mr. Sorensen, accept our gift," he pleaded.

"OK, Mr. Zhong. I will accept with gratitude. Thank you," Michael smiled at Mr. Zhong and bowed slightly adding, "Is there anything else we need to talk about?"

"Not as far as we're concerned. There is a ferry to Hong Kong leaving at noon. We made a reservation, just in case you want to take it. You'll also get a coupon for a free lunch on the ferry. By the way, there is an early afternoon flight to San Francisco tomorrow at 2 p.m. Would you want to take that? We'll also throw in an overnight hotel accommodation in Hong Kong."

"Yes, that all sounds fine to me. I can't believe how generous you are. Thanks from my heart," Michael replied, ready to go along with the itinerary Mr. Zhong had outlined for him. While he still had reason to suspect that Mr. Zhong was an accomplice in the plot to have Juan spirited away, he saw that there was nothing to be gained by resisting. In a state of weary acceptance, he persuaded himself that it really might be, as Mr. Zhong indicated, a matter of the owners and management being concerned about the hotel's reputation. *They would want to prevent any of last night's happening getting into the news,* he thought. *The hotel's reputation of being the best and finest needs to remain unflawed, especially with all the new hotel construction going on in this city. That could be a real threat to the River Pearl's number one position.* He then rose from his seat and Mr. Zhong rose with him. The men shook hands and Mr. Zhong smiled brightly. "Let's go to the reception desk and find out what the office staff has arranged for you," Mr. Zhong said pleasantly.

Within the hour, Michael was on the high speed ferry to Hong Kong. He stayed in a fine hotel that Mr. Zhong had booked for him; and he boarded China Air to San Francisco the next afternoon.

16

Closure

After returning to California, Michael stayed at his parents' home in San Jose. Their house was large and there was no problem for him to stay for a short time, while he attended to several urgent matters. He had to resign from his position in Beijing and find a new job. *Since I haven't given my company timely notice or kept them informed as to my injuries, they may not be inclined to give me a recommendation,* he thought, *But I must find a job soon.* Having put all the expenses of his journey with Juan on his credit card, he would have to pay it off or face bankruptcy. He hoped that his insurance company would cover at least a portion of the loss of his car. If credit card debt drove him into bankruptcy, he wouldn't be able to obtain credit to purchase another car.

Dealing with these matters was stressful, but what made him depressed was his terrible sense of loss whenever he thought of Juan. And she was seldom out of his thoughts. He tortured himself with memories of their wonderful happy moments together and remembering the waking dream he had of a life with her. He was honest with himself in realizing that he was emotionally unstable. Sometimes he felt depressed and seemed to be adrift in a stormy sea without a stable hold on anything. Late at night, in total privacy, when his parents were asleep, he could not contain himself and cried into his pillow. While it broke his heart to accept his loss, there was no denying that his beloved had chosen to leave him and disappear. He was devastated but not angry with her, even though she apparently was a party to what had happened. Trying to make sense of what had happened and why could drive him crazy. *If only I could find some closure,* he thought, *some certainty about what had really been going on behind the scenes while the two of us went on our love journey and our grand, miscarried escape.* He knew only for sure that that's what it was for him. But beyond that he was certain that he was truly in love with Juan. As soon as he and Juan were going to arrive in California, he had a plan ready. He wanted to make their relationship legal, at first at the city hall and later through a fine reception involving his family and friends. He had it all laid out in his mind. He had been serious about making Juan his life's companion. In retrospect, he thought of how naïve he had been in making such plans for himself and Juan whom he had known only a few months before they went on their escape.

Michael was afraid to let his mother know how he was feeling. She would worry too much. She had always worried about him. For her he painfully maintained a façade that revealed nothing of his emotional misery. He had written to his parents about his car accident but didn't mention what it involved. He had also written to his mother that he had met a young woman in Beijing and that he had a good time. He would never confide in his father anything about his personal concerns. His father would have laughed at him for pining for a fickle woman. If he had known of his son's tears, he would have let Michael know how unmanly he thought his behavior was. He would have said, "How can you let this short, gone-awry affair bother you so much? Don't be a wimp. Be a man. It's not as if you were a teenager, and it wasn't your first love affair either. You dropped Annie. Now you've been dropped. That's life."

So Michael, in the supposedly comforting circle of his family, felt utterly alone. But persistently, he kept on looking for a job and tried to solve other problems related to his Beijing interlude. He felt destined to be more lucky and successful in reassembling his life in California than he had been during his sojourn in China. And one day he came home and was able to tell his parents that he had found a suitable job with a high tech company in Cupertino, a town near San Jose, and that he would be moving soon. It was his mother who heard the good news first. She felt elated that day and hugged and congratulated Michael profusely. He didn't understand her emotional outburst. But when she slipped an envelope into his hand that she had kept hidden behind her back, Michael realized that she had sensed his emotional stress since his return and that the young woman he'd mentioned must have been more than a friend. Michael also realized that nothing had changed from his growing up years. His mother, as if by telepathy or by her being sensitive to vibes from his psyche, must have known that her son was suffering.

After glancing at the envelope's sender, Michael felt an electrical current running through his body from his head down along the spine to his genitals. For just seeing her handwriting and her name to bring about this strong mental-physical reaction made him aware of how he was still possessed by Juan.

Suddenly he realized how closely his mother was observing him while he stood looking at the envelope. It gave him a strange sensation. Startled, he said, "Mom, why are you looking at me like that? It's just a letter from a dear friend. Have you shown it to Dad yet?"

"No, Michael, I haven't. It's your private business. But I suspect that it's serious business. So go and read the letter. I hope it will lift your spirits," she said and walked away.

Michael dashed after her. He embraced her. "Thanks, mom, for being discreet and sensitive. I know you understand more than Dad does. I love you and always have." He stood for awhile with his arms around her neck. It was she who freed herself from him. "Michael, darling, go and read the letter," she said firmly, and went into the kitchen. Michael went upstairs into his room.

* * *

He closed the door behind him and even locked it. He sat down on his bed and held the letter in front of him, staring at it as if he wanted to learn what it said without reading it. Once he even sniffed it. Maybe he could still discern a whiff of her sweet perfume. After a while he got up, went to his desk and with a pair of scissors carefully cut the envelope. He didn't want to tear it. He wanted to preserve it as he was already certain he wanted to keep the letter for as long as he lived.

He unfolded the fine white paper. Instead of her personal handwriting, he only saw the typed English script. Now he wondered who had written this letter. It seemed unlike Juan to be this impersonal. But then he put his thoughts about this aside and began reading the letter:

Dearest Michael,

I'm trembling as I write this letter to you because I know in your mind I have done great harm to you. I believe you were sincere in your love for me and I was, too, but to be truthful I was torn between you and your life and the life I could make for myself. If this computer-composed letter looks cold and mechanical to you, look at the hand-written insert. I did compose the letter in my writing, but I had it translated so that you could understand it fully.

I'm doing fine, and I hope you have been able to pick up where you left off. Though I know you're very capable and sure of yourself, the experience with me in my homeland must have shaken your confidence a little and your sense of direction. I know I'm the cause and I'm truly sorry for that. I wanted to give myself to you but in the end I couldn't. There were indications during our time together that made me realize how dependent I would be on you in your country, financially and in other ways. Since my childhood I have been striving for self-fulfillment and independence, not because I innately started off that way but because I was forced into self-reliance and independence. I know you remember what I told you about myself and my family.

While I'm writing about independence, I have to admit that I was contacted by phone by my former employer. I didn't tell you the truth. And for that again I'm very sorry. I hope you'll have it in you to forgive me. I was annoyed at first by being contacted, but when I learned what kind of offer he made, I started wavering. The more I resisted, the better the offer became. It was in the end a 25 percent ownership in the business. I was going to turn it down, but when you told me about your financial situation, I thought I would be a burden to you for years until I had full command of your language and could contribute to our life. I then thought it would be best that we go our separate ways since love, and that was all we had, is not reliable. Love can be true at one point and fickle at another, and it can waste away. I could not let that happen. I chose the safer route to travel. I know I may end up without love, but I will have success. I'm back at the Blue Moon and I feel quite equal to my former employers now. I'm still giving my customers an entertaining time, but it's somewhat curtailed now because I'm also partially engaged in running the business. I'm feeling freer and in control now in my conversations with my business partners and my clients. And I'm more freely gracious and giving because I feel secure in myself and in my status. My customers feel that, I know, but they still love dancing and conversing with me.

Oh, the most wonderful opportunity coming my way is a part-time teaching position in the Social Science department at Beijing University. Through connections of my partners—they know of my educational background—I'll be teaching a Chinese history course on a standby basis, as needed. I will also pick up my own studies and will work toward a higher degree in my field. I will always remember how you encouraged me to teach because you enjoyed my telling you the historical background of the wonderful sights we saw. I am so grateful to you, my beloved Michael. You made me understand that I have a gift to teach what I know and love about my country and its history.

As for our last evening at the River Pearl, I feel dreadful. I will never get over it until the end of my life. They came because I allowed them to come. I was false, and I put you through agony. What I learned afterward is that Mr. and Mrs. Jin were placed in the dining room to let me know what was going to hap- pen that evening. They weren't even husband and wife. It was all a ploy. Mr. Jin was simply a go-between. He clued me in. I know you will always remember the dance I had with him, that you did not willingly grant him, and which gave him the opportunity to talk to me during this dance.

Uta Christensen

Michael, the longer I think of you and me, the more I realize that I have to thank you for everything I can now attain. You saved my life at the Great Wall, and you took me on a wonderful journey that opened the minds of potential benefactors and will get me into a profession which will mean everything to me. Without knowing, you brought it all about. I will always, above all, be grateful to you and will always cherish the love you gave me. Nothing can surpass that. I hope you can forgive me.

Still in my mind, my heart and my body,
Juan

CPSIA information can be obtained at www.ICGtesting.com
Printed in the USA
LVOW042049100412

277019LV00001B/77/P